Two

'I've been setting _____ the next few days and nights,' said Khalil, 'and you'll need to be completely rested before the action starts. You do realise what's being set up, don't you? You'll be tested to your sexual limit. What I've got set up for you is little short of an orgy, but with you taking the brunt of the men alone.'

Melinda's eyes sparkled. It was an exciting and dangerous prospect.

'So, how many?'

'Difficult to say for sure,' answered Khalil. 'I've been preparing for about a dozen.'

Melinda swallowed hard. 'So many!'

'If the number is brought down any lower than that, then I fear you will not be tested fully. I know them all, so there's nothing for you to be worried about. I know their sexual proclivities. Some like it rough, some gentle. But all of them prefer to be dominant.'

Melinda realised this was to be a holiday like no other.

To
The Ladies Who Lunch

Two Weeks in Tangier

ANNABEL LEE

Black Lace novels contain sexual fantasies.
In real life, make sure you practise safe sex.

First published in 2001 by
Black Lace
Thames Wharf Studios,
Rainville Road, London W6 9HA

Typeset by SetSystems Ltd, Saffron Walden, Essex
Printed and bound by Mackays of Chatham PLC

ISBN 0 352 33599 8

Chapter One

Saturday

Tangier! Exciting, dangerous Tangier! Melinda peered out of the porthole as the Royal Air Maroc plane gradually lost height preparatory to landing. She hadn't expected Morocco to look like this. The small, flat-roofed, whitewashed houses were what she'd expected but, when her inheritance had included two properties in Tangier, she had vaguely visualised ... well, not the Sahara, exactly, but certainly not this lush, green landscape.

But then, she had also expected her fellowtravellers to be a bit different. No one remotely resembling a desert sheikh – not even one in mufti – had she seen in the departure lounge. Whatever had happened to the mysterious Tangier of legend? And why had Great-Aunt Laura's connection with the city turned her into the black sheep of the family? A 95-year-old lady who, until her death, was rarely mentioned and then never in front of the children?

Tongues began to wag a bit once her will had been read. Melinda had inherited everything because, according to Great-Aunt Laura, she was the only member of the family 'never to have come creeping round licking my arse.' Melinda smiled at the fast-approaching runway. She wondered how hard Great-Aunt Laura's solicitor had tried to have that bit more respectably phrased. It suggested that other family members, while overtly tut-tutting about the old lady's character, had been covertly sucking up to her – and, given the size of the inheritance, that really wasn't very surprising. There had been just one condition: Melinda had to add her great-aunt's surname – Carr – to her own. Her parents had been furious that she had been perfectly happy to do so.

'How *dare* you take that old harridan's name?' her mother had said.

'You might at least consider the family's position,' her father had added more mildly.

'What position?' Melinda had demanded. 'You're a retired GP and Mummy's a very minor pillar of a small local golf club. And besides, what did Great-Aunt Laura ever do that was so awful? Taking her name seems a small price to pay for financial independence.'

But her parents gave no explanations and when she tried to discuss it with other members of the family, the older ones slid away from the subject and the younger ones took refuge in knowing nudges but nothing else. Maybe they didn't know either, but wanted to unnerve the heiress by giving the impression they knew something she didn't – a sort of safety-valve for their envy.

At any rate, Melinda was no wiser now than she had been then – except, she thought as the plane bumped gently down and the runway rushed past at the terrifying speed they always chose, that it had something to do with Morocco, and Tangier in particular. It must do. Why else would her parents have been so opposed to her coming to take a look at this part of her inheritance?

'It's not safe,' her mother protested. 'Not on your own. Anything could happen! Be sensible. Take someone with you. Why not take one of your old boyfriends?

You always parted on good terms with them and you've been seeing a bit of Clive again lately. I'm sure he'd go with you.'

I'm sure he would, too, Melinda thought. They'd enjoyed each other's company for a couple of years without ever quite getting round to actually living together. Clive wasn't a bad lover, though not a particularly inventive one, and she'd have liked to have love-making – or even good old-fashioned shagging – on tap, but it hadn't worked out like that and they drifted apart once she began travelling to look at bronzes for Delamere's, the rather grand auction-house into whose hands she had placed her career hopes. Then suddenly, out of the blue, Clive had phoned and, with a frisson of anticipatory pleasure, Melinda had been happy to have dinner with him.

She gave a little smile of remembered pleasure. It had been a good evening; absence might not have made the heart grow any fonder but it had certainly honed up the hormones and she'd happily agreed to spend the next day with him. The spell had been broken when he mentioned her great-aunt's legacy. Most people mentioned it because it intrigued them that the old biddy had been worth so much. The spell-breaker was Clive's throwaway and exaggeratedly hypothetical assumption that when she married, she'd obviously put everything into joint names. It was the first time he'd ever mentioned marriage, even hypothetically.

Clive had been very miffed at her reaction.

'Not bloody likely!' she'd said. 'You have to be joking!'

'I was only speaking hypothetically,' he had protested.

'Pull the other one,' Melinda had replied, but the kiss with which he had sought to convince her had lacked something of the enthusiasm of their reunion up to that

3

point and Melinda had known that if he sought her out again, she wouldn't be available.

All the same, she wouldn't have been averse to a companion on this trip, preferably male and, even more preferably, virile. After all, a holiday was a holiday, and a celibate one wasn't something she'd ever knowingly signed up for before. Still, there was a first time for everything – including a visit to North Africa. One of the older women at Delamere's had laughed at her hesitancy.

'Don't worry about it, Mel. Just cover your head and your arms and carry a hat-pin and you'll be safe enough.'

Well, she was modestly dressed and she had a head-scarf just in case; she didn't own a hat-pin and she wasn't entirely sure she wanted to be 'safe'. It was a matter of degree. She didn't want to be raped and she certainly didn't want to be murdered, but neither did she want to discourage absolutely any form of approach.

But she did want to discover what she could about Great-Aunt Laura, and Tangier was going to be the place to do it. Since no one in the family seemed willing to tell her, she'd do her detective work here. It would give a purpose to her visit. Not a purpose that need press heavily on pleasures that might arise but certainly one which could usefully fill in otherwise unoccupied time.

The plane drew to a stop and the click of released seat belts prefaced the louder click of overhead hatches being opened. Melinda tried to feel the nonchalance of the regular traveller she was, but she couldn't. She felt the excitement, even an unexpected stimulation, at the thought that when she stepped off this plane, she would be stepping into the unknown.

* * *

4

She followed the other passengers across the tarmac and joined the queues for passport control, more than a little relieved to see that notices were printed in French as well as Arabic. She couldn't help noticing what seemed to her a disproportionate number of men in uniform. Young men, all dark, all slim, all handsome. Were all Moroccan men like this, she wondered, or was it just the effect of those very well-cut, well-fitted uniforms? Uniforms did have a habit of enhancing the wearer. Then she remembered that the better the uniforms, the tighter the population was controlled. It shouldn't affect a tourist but it was something she'd be wise to bear in mind.

A little man, well overdue for a shave and in workmanlike blue coveralls, leant across the barrier as the queue moved slowly forward.

'Miss Carr?' he said, pronouncing the title 'Mees'. 'Melinda Carr?'

Melinda looked at him, surprised. 'Yes?'

'I help you. Benani, he wait. I get your baggage.'

For the first time she noticed that beyond the passport desks were a dozen or so similarly dressed men, each with a baggage trolley. Porters, she supposed. She smiled, reassured. Benani was the agent who had managed Great-Aunt Laura's Tangier properties. Benani Khalil, according to his letterhead, though she wasn't sure which of the names was his Christian name. No, she corrected herself as she put her passport on the desk, that can't be right. His given name, perhaps. I'll have to be careful. It would be so easy unwittingly to give offence.

The porter was quick and efficient and although the Customs seemed to be holding up all the other English travellers and going through their bags, her porter said something that seemed to include her surname and she was waved through, but since it seemed unlikely her name could have had that effect, she must have misheard.

As soon as she was through the barrier, a man approached. He was taller than most of the others who were waiting to greet passengers but not all that tall by British standards. Perhaps it was because these men all seemed so slim that they appeared taller than they were. He was extremely handsome but the thing that first struck Melinda was the quality of both the fabric and the cut of his obviously bespoke suit. Managing properties must be a very lucrative business.

'Miss Carr?' he said, 'Miss Melinda Carr? I'm Benani. Khalil Benani.' And he held his hand out to her.

Melinda took it, smiling. 'You've solved one of my problems already,' she said, noticing the contrast between his dark hair and olive skin on the one hand and his grey eyes on the other. 'I had wondered which was your surname.'

He bowed. 'I hope you won't have any problems more serious than that,' he said, 'but if you do, remember I'm here to solve them, too.'

'I hope you won't be kept too busy,' she said, though as she looked at him she couldn't help hoping that wouldn't be the case.

'I, on the other hand, find myself on the horns of a dilemma,' he replied. 'I don't wish problems for you, but if they're the only excuse I can have to see something of you then a few minor ones that only a Moroccan can solve won't be entirely unwelcome.'

Melinda blushed and lowered her gaze, to glance up at him from beneath her long blonde lashes. 'Very gallant, m'sieur,' she murmured.

'But also very true.' He nodded towards the bureau de change. 'I suggest you change some sterling,' he said. 'You won't need much to tide you over until the banks open, but it's never a good idea to be penniless. Twenty pounds will be ample, I suggest.'

6

The money changed, they followed the porter out of the concourse and Melinda's spine involuntarily tingled as her escort's hand on her waist guided her through the glass door. It was an entirely normal, chivalrous gesture which she must have encountered a hundred times before – but never with quite that electrifying effect. Except that, by some accident of their being on the move, his hand had not actually been on her waist but very slightly below it so that she was conscious that her buttocks had tensed out as if in response. She hoped he hadn't been aware of it.

In a car park populated by aged Renaults and the occasional Peugeot, the sleek, black Mercedes with its black-tinted windows stood out both in style and well-polished condition. Melinda's hazel eyes widened involuntarily and she had to remind herself that the car simply fitted the same image as the suit.

Her luggage safely stowed in the boot and the porter tipped, Khalil Benani opened the passenger door. 'Or would you prefer to ride in the back?' he asked.

'The front will be fine,' Melinda told him. 'I can see more from there. Besides, you're not exactly a chauffeur, are you?'

He laughed. 'If a chauffeur is what you want, a chauffeur is what I can be, but I'd rather be beside you.' He turned his head and his eyes didn't seem to miss much. 'It's easier to talk that way,' he added.

They slowed down for a cursory police check before he continued. 'Tell me, Miss Carr, do you resemble your great-aunt?'

'I don't know,' Melinda replied, taken aback by a question which was about the last one she expected. 'I only ever met her once, when she was in her eighties and I was only a teenager, so there can't have been much resemblance at that time, and I've never seen pictures of her when she was my age so I don't know.'

'Only once? Yet she left you her Tangier property?' He seemed surprised.

'More than that,' Melinda told him. 'She left me everything. Said it was because I was the only member of the family never to have licked her arse.'

He shouted with laughter. 'That sounds like your great aunt,' he said.

'You knew her?'

He shook his head. 'No. She left Tangier before I was of an age to be interested in meeting her but I've heard a lot about her from my father, who represented her as perhaps I shall represent you. They got on very well.' He glanced across at her again. 'From what my father told me about her, I'd guess you share her colouring. She, too, had those strange-coloured eyes and an abundance of thick, fair hair. I think hers must have been longer than yours, though. My father said it reached . . . she could sit on it if she let it down.'

'Then hers was longer,' Melinda agreed. 'I've always rather fancied hair that long. Mine only reaches my waist and, believe me, that can be quite inconvenient, especially when it comes to washing it.'

By this time they had reached the city itself. The brief dusk had turned rapidly into night and the streets were bustling with people, many of them dressed much as Melinda would have seen on an English street, but many more were in the *djellabahs* she was soon to recognise as the usual outer garments. She was intrigued to notice that, while many of the women wore scarves, many also wore nothing on their hair.

'Scarves aren't obligatory, then?' she remarked.

'Married women usually wear them and some of the older ones will also be veiled. The younger ones choose. You'll soon learn to recognise those who wear the scarf – *hijab* is the correct word – to indicate the strength of their religious conviction. The method of wearing it is

8

distinctive. Once we're round this roundabout,' he went on, 'we shall be in the street with your apartment.'

He turned off the roundabout as he spoke and Melinda looked around her with increased interest. It wasn't quite what she'd expected, not given Great-Aunt Laura's fortune. It was a street of modern flats, but the ground-floor of each block was taken up with shops or motor-repair garages and the whole impression was of something that, in a few years, might look as if it were in serious disrepair.

Khalil Benani double-parked outside an entrance that was no more inspiring at first glance than anything else in the street. Once through the doors, however, it was a different scene. The strict lines of the marble floor were softened by terracotta pots of small palms and rubber plants and everywhere was scrupulously clean. The lift carried them to Melinda's seventh-floor flat. The dark landing was more than somewhat daunting but Khalil knew exactly where the light switch was and Melinda felt immediately more comfortable even in the dim light it cast, just sufficient for her companion to find the keyhole.

The flat was certainly secure: it took three turns of the key before the door opened. Khalil preceded her through the door and switched on the lights. Melinda gasped. This was not what she had expected. No one, having seen the outside of the block, could have anticipated this. She couldn't help wondering if this was Great-Aunt Laura's real taste. It was a far cry from the tiny cottage she had lived in when Melinda had visited her that one time.

The place was bathed in the brilliant, glittering light of two huge crystal chandeliers and the room she was looking at could never have been seen in any English home. The entrance was separated from the *salon* beyond by a waist-high partition topped with black marble in contrast to the white carrara marble of the

9

entire floor. A round dining-table, just large enough to seat four, stood in one corner of this foyer and beyond it the walls were lined in their entirety with divans upholstered in one of the most luxurious green and gold brocades Melinda had ever seen. A densely woven, ornate, but predominantly green carpet, which she recognised as being of the best Rabati manufacture, filled the centre of this area and supported a large, low, glass-topped table. The walls, like the floors, were white; they were sparsely decorated with gilt-framed embroideries and on one wall a huge gilt-framed mirror was entirely at home, though it might have been equally at ease in a French château. It would, Melinda thought, have looked decidedly out of place in Neasden.

'This is magnificent,' she said. 'Is this how my great-aunt furnished it?'

'Some things have been renewed over the years,' the agent told her, 'but the style is unchanged. It's a very popular holiday letting. Americans, in particular, go for it in a big way.'

'I imagine they do.' Melinda laughed. 'What about the rest?'

The kitchen was best described as rudimentary but the bathroom left nothing to be desired and neither did the two bedrooms.

'I told the maid to make up the double bed for you,' Khalil told her as he demonstrated how to raise and lower the outside shutters. 'This room's at the back, so it's quieter, but if you prefer the other, that can soon be arranged.'

Melinda looked at the subtle lines of the *bâteau-lit* and decided it would do admirably.

'You'll want some dinner,' Khalil told her. 'All there is in the fridge is some milk and a bottle of water. I'll get you a baguette, so you've something to eat, but I'll

10

leave you to unpack and then I'll come back and take you out for a meal.'

'There's really no need. I ate on the plane,' Melinda told him.

He shrugged. 'Most people would not regard that as a meal,' he said. 'All the same, I'll come back and introduce you to a good place for breakfast. I'm sure you'll be able to eat a little something.'

True to his word, he took her to the *salon de thé* that embraced the corner of the street and boasted the improbable name of Havana. Inside, he ordered her mint tea, telling her that she certainly wouldn't be able to sleep if she had coffee, and he also ordered her something called *erghaif* – a sort of large, square and very thin crumpet, which was served warm and rolled up after having been spread with honey. Melinda found it utterly delicious.

'You read French?' Khalil asked. 'Good. They only serve this sort of thing – toast, croissants and so on – but if you come here for breakfast, you'll find something you like. The menu will be in French. They always are. Don't forget to tip, though. Do that and they'll move heaven and earth for you if you need it.'

Melinda laughed. 'Thank you. Have you any suggestions for tomorrow? I'd like to see the other property if it's possible.'

'Tomorrow,' he replied, as he guided her out of the *salon de thé*, 'is a day I propose to devote to you.'

Melinda's laugh was more self-conscious than she would have chosen. 'Why, thank you, kind sir,' she said, hoping it sounded suitably light. 'Then tomorrow is something I shall look forward to.'

He smiled but made no immediate reply. When they reached her apartment, he insisted that she use the key because locking and unlocking the door required a knack, and he told her he had no wish to see her locked

11

out. He followed her in and immediately lowered the outside shutter to the huge room. 'Keep the shutters down when the lights are on,' he told her. 'It's safer that way. We often don't fit curtains to pull right across. With shutters you don't need them but it's easy for English people to forget.'

'Thank you,' she said. It seemed inadequate and Melinda was suddenly conscious that he was standing very close to her. Their relationship was a strictly business one. It had to be. But there was a magnetism about the man that she hadn't expected.

'So you don't know whether you're like your great-aunt or not?' he asked suddenly.

'No. Not to look at, anyway,' she replied.

'Ah. Not to look at, maybe. And in character?'

She turned and looked up at him. 'I don't know that, either. How can I when I know nothing about her?'

His hand briefly touched her thick French pleat and she wondered if he was going to release the pins that held it. She knew she shouldn't want him to, but she did. She was disappointed. His hand flickered instead softly against her cheek and gently stroked down the line of her neck to the cleft above her collarbone. Melinda shivered with anticipation. I think he wants to seduce me, she thought. And why not? Just so long as we can keep business separate.

As if he had picked up her vibes, the hand that had rested just below her waist returned there and, though the pressure it exerted was minimal, she found herself responding, arching her bottom in a way that brought the rest of her body closer to his. His arm encircled her and he kissed her, his tongue forcing her willing lips apart. He lightly touched the contours of her ear, her neck, before lingering briefly over her tightening nipples. Then he moved his other hand gently downwards, seeking the skin beneath her jeans so that she luxuriated in the feel of his cool fingers on the hot cheeks of

12

her buttocks. She could also feel his stiff erection through the fabric of his suit and through the hard denim of her own flies. She fumbled for his zip but he pushed her hand away.

'No,' he murmured. 'Not now. Not yet. It'll keep.' He kissed her. 'Expect me about ten,' he said. 'Oh, and might I suggest you wear a skirt of some sort?' He grinned. 'I'd hazard a guess you've no need to hide your legs.'

It wasn't easy to disguise her disappointment at this abrupt brush-off but Melinda forced herself to smile. 'I thought short skirts weren't appreciated in places like this,' she said, 'so I only brought long ones.'

He grinned and she had the uncomfortable feeling he knew exactly what was going through her mind. 'Who said anything about short?' he asked. 'When will you Westerners learn that the most obvious isn't always the most satisfying? From what my father always told me, your great-aunt knew that very well.'

'I'll do my best to meet with your approval,' Melinda said stiffly.

His finger brushed her cheek. 'Oh, I'm sure you will. That's something I have no doubts about whatsoever. Make sure you lock the door behind me. Don't rely on just the initial lock.' And with that he was gone.

Alone in the flat, Melinda felt unexpectedly restless. She just hadn't been prepared for a property agent to be quite so ... so disturbing. For disturbing he most certainly was. He was handsome but she knew that had nothing to do with it. It helped, as did the outward signs that he was a successful man, but there was more to it than that.

She ran a bath. Nothing quite like a warm bath to make you feel sleepy, she thought. She certainly needed some sort of aid because Khalil Benani had left her feeling very wide awake. She put her fingers under the running tap and wondered what he would look like

13

without the natty gents' suiting. She didn't think he'd be in any way diminished.

Dropping her clothes on the floor, she stepped into the bath and found she was now perfectly placed to see herself from head to toe in the mirror opposite. She turned from side to side, watching her reflection, and then ran her hands sensuously over her body. Not bad, she thought. Not at all bad. Not fashionably starvation-thin but one heard of many more men who liked a nice armful than who craved stick-insects. She slid down into the water until only her head and the tips of her darkening nipples pierced the surface and she recalled the feel of Khalil's stiffening cock against her clothed body. Had he been playing with her emotions when he had so abruptly brought that little interlude to an end? It seemed so. It had certainly been one of the most tantalising encounters she could remember. Or was he just teasing? Did he really intend to pursue it any further? He certainly had some will-power but no, somehow she didn't think he would be satisfied with mere teasing.

The very thought of what, exactly, might satisfy him brought an ache to her loins. She closed her eyes to enjoy the feel of her fingers tracing lightly round her taut nipples and over her diaphragm and then on, down to the forest of fair curls and the inner side of her thighs, until her legs parted of their own volition and the gentle movements ceased as she rammed her long-est finger into herself as far in as it would reach. A man was better. Even a man's fingers were better, she thought, but she knew to perfection how to reach the right spot; not too soon – pleasure was most pleasur-able when it was extended. She writhed in the warm water against the hardness of her fingers, rubbing them alternately against her clit and then moving them back deep inside, back and forth. When she came it was with a sob of pure delight. She bore down on her finger and

14

wished it could be longer and thicker because then the pleasure would be tinged with just enough pain to enhance it. But this would do. For now. Perhaps tomorrow Khalil would leave her without the need to find her own release. She moved once more to re-invigorate the fading orgasm. I want it, she thought. Suddenly I don't want this to be just an ordinary holiday. Business, yes, but I want something over and above that. The trouble is, I'm not sure – beyond the immediate – exactly what. I just have a hunch there's something more out there. And I want it.

Chapter Two
Sunday

Melinda awoke, confused. Her eyes told her it was still dark but her ears detected the sound of people moving about somewhere outside the apartment. She reached out for the travel-alarm beside the bed. Ten past eight. Plenty of time to doze off again.

No there wasn't. Not if Khalil was coming for her at ten, and particularly not if she wanted to prove to him that she was perfectly capable of looking both modest and desirable. She didn't think he was a man to be impressed by an overabundance of casualness in a woman's dress. She'd been dressed casually enough yesterday and she knew he'd been interested, but she hadn't been wearing anything that wasn't to be expected from someone on a long journey. She had a hunch it wouldn't do for today.

When she rolled up the shutters, she was taken aback by the sunlight that streamed in, and it wasn't even high summer. She soon realised that one effect of the brilliant sunlight was to kill stone-dead any thoughts of dozing off for a bit longer.

Regretting that she hadn't had the forethought to bring some tea bags or some coffee with her, she poured herself a glass of ice-cold water and was rewarded by the feeling that her brain was really awake now and ready to cope with whatever the day offered.

First, a bath. Then the right clothes. While she ran the former, she studied the limited wardrobe she'd brought with her. Why was she never entirely satisfied with what she had brought on holiday? She wondered just how hot the sunshine was and a brief trip to the balcony outside the second bedroom soon told her that a stiff wind destroyed any warmth there might otherwise have been. A skirt, he'd said – and not short. Pity. She liked showing off her legs but she knew it was not to be in this country. With some regrets, she settled on a fashionably long, blue-grey skirt and waistcoat and added a vivid blouse. No way did she intend to become a discrete part of the scenery.

The bath brought back memories of last night's enjoyment and she was tempted to indulge herself with a little delicate exploration again, but then she remembered Khalil. No, she thought. Don't spoil it. Leave it. Let it build up so that the relief when it comes is all the greater. She had no doubt that come it would, and just thinking about it made her clench her pussy muscles in anticipation. She had a lot of control over those muscles and wondered whether it was a control her property agent would appreciate – always assuming, of course, that he wasn't just a teaser. Now that was a depressing thought. Perhaps a little teasing on her part wouldn't come amiss.

When, an hour later, she emerged into the sunlight outside the apartment block, she had the satisfaction of knowing she looked stunning. The pale blue-grey might enhance her fair colouring but it was the vivid lime and carmine of the blouse that drew the eyes of passers-by. Her only ornament was a pair of plain, white ear-rings which, she knew, would look even more stunning once her skin had tanned – and she recognised her good fortune in having the sort of blonde colouring that took a tan quickly and well. She had twisted her long, thick hair into a loose knot, taking care not to scrag it back from her face with too much severity and to make sure it was wide enough to give width behind her neck. A quick spray of Cinnabar completed the picture. Many people had told her it was too heavy, too obvious to be elegant. Melinda had never agreed with them and now, in a city where palm trees lined the streets and hibiscus tumbled over walls, it seemed entirely appropriate.

As she entered the marble-lined ambience of Havana, the admiring expressions of the heads that turned from their newspapers was reward enough. She had made the right decision. She looked good.

The *salon de thé* wasn't crowded and she was aware, self-consciously at first, that she was the only woman there. Maybe that was the real reason heads had turned. Then she remembered the clear admiration on the faces concerned. Her very presence might have been enough to attract attention in the first place, but if there was nothing critical in the men's expressions, she didn't have much to worry about.

She took her time selecting a table, choosing one at the side where it was well lit by the window and where she could quietly watch the comings and goings outside as well as her fellow customers. Common sense told her it might not be a very good idea to study these too obviously: such scrutiny by an unescorted woman might well be misconstrued. She smiled to herself. How was that for inconsistency? Here she was, not at all averse to a bit of nookie, yet anxious about being misconstrued when such misconstruction would, in fact, have been absolutely spot-on. Except that too-obviously casual pick-ups were dangerous in a sense that was a long way from being a turn-on. She saw no good reason for being seen to be too easy a lay and,

18

above all, there was Khalil Benani to look forward to – she hoped.

Was he humouring her, simply wanting to keep a client happy? Was he only interested in teasing her as he had done last evening? Or was he really attracted to her? Only time would tell. For her part, she found him immensely attractive. Compelling, even. Yet she knew nothing at all about him except what he did for a living. She didn't even know if he was married. Did it matter?

Melinda had to think about that one. She'd never seen marriage as the ultimate career move anyway: the evidence was all too clear that nowadays marriages were as likely to be disastrous as to be successful. Mothers seemed to jump – mentally, at any rate – from first date to church wedding to motherhood and living happily ever after where their daughters were concerned. Maybe girls used to think the same way, but not any more. Not the girls she knew, anyway. Men's ideas didn't seem to progress much beyond first date followed – if the first date included dinner – by bed. Why should women be any different? Melinda had no great objection to this except that it seemed a bit crude, a bit obvious – and very much a case of singing for one's supper, and that had a tendency to kill any thoughts of 'romance' stone-dead. Sometimes one simply had to make up one's mind whether just to enjoy the sex and to hell with the romance. She sighed. Was it possible to have the two things – lust *and* romance – in the same package in real life? And without any complications of jealousy? Probably not, she decided, and sighed again.

'As bad as that, is it?' a voice said, and Melinda looked up to see Khalil Benani standing there. She glanced at her watch and realised, guiltily, that it was already ten o'clock and she still hadn't finished her coffee. She opened her mouth to apologise but Khalil raised his hand as if to ward off any apology.

'May I join you?' He sat down opposite her without waiting for the formality of an assent. 'The concierge told me where you were.'

'The concierge?' Melinda supposed there must be one but she couldn't recollect having seen her either last night or this morning. 'I didn't see her. Where was she?'

'Not "her" but "him",' Khalil corrected her. 'In Morocco a concierge is always a man. Usually his wife does the cleaning. It's their job to know who comes and goes even when they're not in evidence themselves.'

Melinda wrinkled her nose. 'I'm not sure I'm very happy about the idea of being spied on,' she said.

'Why? What are you intending to get up to?' he asked, smiling ironically.

Melinda flushed. 'It isn't a case of what I'm *intending* to do,' she said. 'It's just the thought of being watched when I don't know it's going on.'

'So you wouldn't mind being watched if you did know?'

Melinda had the disconcerting feeling that the question wasn't entirely hypothetical but, before she could press him on any underlying meaning, he smoothed over the slight uncertainty he had raised.

'Just remember, the concierge is there for your own security. If a flat is robbed, he can tell the police who came and went.'

'If he knows who they were,' Melinda pointed out.

'This is Tangier,' he replied. 'He'll know – and if it's a foreigner, he'll be able to give a good description. This is a city – and a big one – but it's still a village in many ways. Everyone knows everyone else and if they don't know them personally, they know their relatives by blood or by marriage and they certainly know all their business. If you're going to spend much time here, it's as well to remember that.'

She looked at him curiously. 'So they'll have known about my great-aunt?'

'Of course. Well, their fathers will have. It's a long time since she was here.'

'Did she spend much time here?'

'About four months a year, I understand: two in spring and two in autumn, though at one time she was here right the way through your cold season. My father said she never visited in the heat of summer – and never during Ramadan.'

'Why not? During Ramadan, I mean.'

He shrugged. 'You need to know us better and then you won't need to ask the question,' he said, leaving Melinda with the distinct impression that he had slid out of an answer he didn't want to give. She decided this might be a good time to change the subject. She could always return to it another day.

'Where's the nearest bank?' she asked. 'I need to change some travellers' cheques. Twenty pounds isn't going to go far.'

'The Boulevard Pasteur is full of them. I'll show you, but they don't open on a Sunday, anyway. They open at half past eight most mornings, close again at about eleven – sometimes earlier – and stay closed until late afternoon. None of that need bother you, though,' and he took a bundle of notes out of his pocket and put them on the table in front of her.

'Only a couple of hundred pounds' worth,' he said. 'I took it from your great-aunt's account via the machine this morning.' He looked at her astonished expression. 'You did know she had money here as well as property?'

Melinda shook her head. 'It wasn't specified in the will. Just that I had everything. It was her solicitor who told me there were two properties in Tangier and he didn't think she'd ever sold them. He'd written to the Moroccan authorities to find out if there was anything

21

else but didn't receive a reply. I don't think he had any idea there was a bank account as well.'

'Then how did he imagine her property was managed? Rents paid in dirhams can't be exported, taxes have to be paid; so do caretakers and maids, not to mention electricity bills and so forth. There had to be a bank account.'

'Is there much in it?'

He shrugged. 'A fair bit. These things are relative. I've told the bank you're her sole heir. They've had a copy of the will, which your lawyer sent my firm, but you can't draw on the account until they've seen a copy of the death certificate.'

Melinda nodded. That was fair enough, she supposed. 'But you can draw on it?'

'We have a limited power of attorney. Miss Carr appointed an independent accountant to check the business side of things and an independent lawyer to keep an eye on everyone else, and the remuneration was generous enough to remove the risk of misappropriation: only a fool kills the goose that lays the golden eggs.'

'And am I the next goose?'

He laughed. 'Quite possibly, but only in the nicest and most alluring possible way, I assure you. Shall we go?'

The Mercedes was double-parked again and Melinda wondered how easy it was to do that with impunity. She didn't fancy trying to get away with it in Knightsbridge. As he opened the car door for her again and she slid into the passenger seat, she remembered the old saying that if you see a man opening the car door for a woman, either the one or the other is a new acquisition. She smiled to herself. She rather thought that in this case it was more a matter of good manners and gallantry. She hoped so because it was a small attention that was really rather nice.

22

Khalil watched her long, slim legs as she drew them elegantly in and smiled in appreciation. When he got in beside her, he said as he concentrated on pulling away from the other cars, 'I'm glad you took my advice. You look very well. Very elegant. Very English.'

Melinda chuckled. 'Thank you,' she said. 'I didn't know the English were associated with elegance.'

'A certain kind of elegance,' he clarified. 'Clean lines. Understated. The sexiness of restraint.'

'Restraint is sexy?'

'Very. Especially when you suspect it's solely on the surface. It encourages the desire to uncover the truth. And now,' he went on with a complete change of subject and tone, 'now we do the touristy thing.'

As he spoke, he changed gear and his hand brushed briefly against Melinda's thigh. It might have been by chance. She didn't think so. The man was a tease. The question was, how likely was he to go beyond teasing? Melinda felt herself tighten again. She hoped she'd find out before long. Just sitting beside him was disturbing enough.

The car headed downhill into streets ever more bustling until they were in a large open space where cars, taxis and buses competed with motorised tricycles in the road that encircled an open area that was a cross between a very large roundabout and an ornamental park which was apparently expected to flourish without the care of gardeners.

'The Gran Socco,' Khalil informed her as he parked the car – singly, this time – outside a small pension. 'Behind that wall is the medina, the old town. The word "medina" just means "town" but tourists use it only to refer to the old parts. It gets very confusing. It's a pity it's Sunday because the goldsmiths will be closed and I think you'd enjoy them.'

He guided her across the road. 'Not all the shops will

23

be open, anyway,' he told her, 'but some of the better ones will and you'll get a feel of the place.'

'Don't forget I also want to see Great-Aunt Laura's other house,' Melinda reminded him.

'I haven't forgotten. It's in the medina, up near the kasbah. We'll make our way up to it.' He glanced at her curiously. 'You do know there are more than two properties, don't you?' he asked.

'No,' Melinda said, startled. 'Two was what I was told.'

'There's a third. Maybe your lawyer didn't know about it, or maybe he thought she'd sold it years ago. It isn't one she ever lived in but I'll arrange for you to see it. It won't be immediately, though.'

'Why not?'

He shrugged. It was a gesture with which Melinda was becoming very familiar. 'It isn't all that close by and the caretaker needs advance warning. These things take time.'

'Is it in a state of disrepair, then?'

He seemed surprised. 'Disrepair? No, not at all. It does still get used from time to time and your aunt's estate – *your* estate, I should say – benefits. I'll sort it out. You'll see it in a day or two. Probably.'

The look he then gave her left Melinda puzzled. It could almost have been described as calculating, as if he was assessing something. And why 'probably'? If it was her house, 'probably' shouldn't enter into it.

Even with about half the little shops closed, the medina was a fascinating place and Melinda heeded Khalil's advice not to buy on this, her first visit there. 'Are you any good at bargaining?' he asked her.

'No. I feel awkward doing it,' she confessed.

'Like most of your countrymen. It's an inhibition you must learn to discard. The first of many, perhaps. Who knows? Bargaining's a game. You need to learn to play

24

it – and in your particular circumstances, you need to become very expert very early.'

'Why? What's so particular about my circumstances?'

'You are who you are,' he replied, 'and that means you're known to be rich.' It was a plausible answer but Melinda didn't think it was necessarily the whole answer. 'In any case,' he went on, 'to start with you have me as your agent. I shall try to teach you. It's all a game, you see. You have to learn to enjoy it.'

He was probably right, Melinda thought, but she couldn't help wondering if there were some sort of hidden meaning in his words.

A very few goldsmiths' shops were open and Melinda was intrigued by the display on the topmost shelves of wide and ornate gold belts. 'Eighteen-carat gold,' Khalil told her, 'and they can weigh as much as two kilos. They're marriage belts. They represent the bride's wealth. At one time, when she was divorced, she'd sell the belt and live on the proceeds. A sort of alimony. Nowadays they're more of a status symbol.'

'Are they ever actually worn?' Melinda asked, fascinated.

'Certainly. If you ever attend wedding celebrations, all the married women present will be wearing their belts.'

'Two kilos is an awful lot,' Melinda said thoughtfully.

'But worth having, I think. Wasn't there one in your great-aunt's effects?'

Melinda turned a surprised face towards him. 'No. Why? Should there have been? Did she marry a Moroccan?'

'Marry? No, not so far as I know. I had heard . . . but it was probably unfounded gossip. And now, down this little lane are the shops selling slippers. You must have some embroidered *babouches*. Gold ones, I think, and your first lesson in bargaining.'

The selection of glittering, gold-embroidered slippers

was enchanting and Khalil's insistence on guiding her foot into each one she pointed to inclined her to pro-longing the experience. His hand on her ankle was firm and, if it sometimes strayed just the merest smidgen higher, it was tantalisingly enjoyable. She was barely aware of the lesson in bargaining she was supposed to be receiving.

The tenant of 'her' house had been advised of her visit and was waiting to show it off to her, together with his family. Up beyond the old palace that had so recently been converted from a very unpleasant jail to a fasci-nating museum, its upper floors looked directly over the old city walls to the Straits of Gibraltar. It had been kept in excellent repair, far better than most properties in the old city seemed to have been, and the abundance of wood was painted with gold motifs on coloured grounds of green and red and black. Some of the motifs were in the highly decorative Arabic calligraphy; others were geometric or occasionally floral.

'Great-Aunt Laura lived in this house?' Melinda asked as she sipped at the sweet, refreshing mint tea they were given.

'This was her home. Much of the existing furniture is hers, too. When we were told to let it, she was perfectly happy for that to be included.'

'It's beautiful. The views over the straits are breathtaking.'

'I believe Miss Carr insisted on having her *salon* on the floor that gave the best view,' he told her. He hesitated. 'This may not be the best time to mention it, but the present tenant – who has been here for the last five years – is naturally very anxious as to whether you will want the place back to live in yourself.'

Melinda shook her head. 'I don't have any immediate plans. It's far too soon, for one thing. After all, I've been here for what? Less than twenty-four hours. You can tell him I live in London because I work in London and I can't imagine doing anything else in the foreseeable future. Mind you,' she went on, looking around, 'I wouldn't rule out changing my mind and if I did that, I can't think of a lovelier place to live.'

Khalil smiled. 'I'll assure him he's safe for another year or so. And now we'll go. There's something else I want to show you.'

He took her into the nearby museum but bypassed all the exhibits to reach an upper floor. 'This is what I wanted you to see,' he said, leading her to a rail which overlooked a Roman mosaic. It showed a number of naked women in a boat. True, there were a few pieces of gauzy drapery floating around but they were cleverly placed to accentuate the basic sexuality of the scene as a whole.

Melinda chuckled. 'I thought things like this were only found at Pompeii,' she said, aware that Khalil's hand was resting on her belt, his fingers sliding beneath the top of her skirt, not far enough to reach bare skin but sufficient to reawaken her desire for more.

'It's the sort of thing kings and rich men have always enjoyed, I think,' he said. 'Poor men would, too, only they can't afford it.'

'Are you talking about the picture or the women?' Melinda asked.

'Both, of course. Let's go. Everything else you can enjoy best on your own sometime, I think.'

He led her out of the museum and out of the immediate kasbah area to a small *salon de thé* situated up several flights of stairs. The main room, like Melinda's house, looked out over the straits, taking in the harbour as well. Khalil ordered coffee and petits fours but led her out of the main area to a smaller one, traditionally furnished with carpets, divans and soft cushions, and much more dimly lit.

27

'Only tourists seek the glare of the sun,' he said by way of explanation. 'Try this. I think you'll like it.'

He handed her a crescent of pastry filled with marzipan. It was delicious. 'Mmm,' she murmured as she swallowed it. 'Mmm,' she murmured again with rather more pleasure as his hand slipped beneath her skirt and his fingers trod their subtle way towards her rapidly moistening sex.

'I think this is something you will enjoy,' he said softly.

'I think it's something you can make very enjoyable,' she replied, squirming with delight as his fingers teased at her panties.

'Lace,' he commented, smiling. 'Not what a woman wears and doesn't want seen.'

Melinda leant towards him and kissed his face gently. 'Are you *very* good?' she whispered.

He kissed her. Now his fingers had found what they sought and he played with her until she felt the fire burning between her legs for greater, deeper gratification. 'You'll get a chance to judge for yourself,' he replied and allowed his fingers to stray just far enough inside her to increase her longing to an almost unbearable pitch.

'If I looked elsewhere than your face,' he said softly, 'I'd find you wet and flushed with desire. I can feel how much you want it already but this is neither the time nor the place.'

'The time is perfect,' Melinda told him. 'And if the time is right, what's wrong with the place?'

'We need more privacy. I don't want a quick fuck and forget it. Do you?'

'No,' she whispered. 'No, I don't.'

He withdrew his hand. 'Then we go now and I take you home. And no, I'm not going to make love to you when we get there. I'm going to leave you alone until dinner-time and then I'm going to take you to the best

28

Moroccan restaurant in town and we'll see what happens then. OK?'

It was far from OK but Melinda knew she definitely wouldn't really enjoy anything as brief as the present situation would necessitate. She nodded. 'I can wait,' she said.

It seemed a long walk back to the Gran Socco even though, being downhill, it must have been much quicker, and when they returned to the flat, Khalil made it clear he meant what he said. He didn't even get out of the car to open the door for her. Melinda was disappointed.

As if he sensed this, he caught at her fingers. 'I do have other work to attend to, you know,' he said gently. 'I'll pick you up at eight.' His gaze wandered over her body. 'Wear that again. I like it.'

She laughed noncommittally. She would, of course, but she wasn't going to agree to any of his requests that easily. She forced herself not to look back as she crossed the road and entered the apartment block.

He didn't come up to the flat when he returned that evening, just announced his arrival on the intercom. 'I'll be with you in a moment,' she told him, determined not to appear too eager.

The afternoon had passed more easily than she'd expected because she had quite simply fallen asleep on one of the divans. Maybe such fatigue was the result of the previous day's travelling; perhaps it was a reaction to the suppressed and frustrated excitements of the morning. Her bath had been leisurely and although she had toyed with the idea of wearing something else, something in her opinion more appropriate to dinner in the city's leading restaurant, she had finally decided to do as he had asked. There was plenty of time for the rest of her wardrobe.

Khalil smiled as she emerged from the lift. 'Good,' he said. 'I'm glad you decided to wear that. I like it.'

'I nearly didn't,' she told him. 'I've something else more appropriate.'

'There's always tomorrow,' he said and grinned. 'At least, I hope there is.'

Melinda smiled up at him. 'I'm certainly not ruling tomorrow out at this stage,' she said.

El Korsan – the Corsair, Khalil told her it meant – was a softly lit, discrete restaurant in a hotel that burgeoned behind a modest and insignificant façade. Melinda recognised immediately the signs of an establishment that must certainly carry the 'luxury' rating as opposed to the more ordinary five-star category. They crossed the patio with its plashing fountain and softly whispering palms and were greeted by a maître d' who very obviously knew Khalil well. He seemed to take a great interest in her after Khalil said something to him in Arabic.

'What did you say?' she demanded.

'I told him who you are. Miss Carr was well known here.'

The restaurant was decorated throughout in Moroccan style, or rather, in an adaptation of the traditional style that was likely to appeal to visitors. Khalil guided her choice of meal and Melinda was surprised that he didn't suggest one of the several varieties of couscous.

'You can get a good couscous anywhere,' he said. 'It's the Moroccan equivalent of . . . oh, of Irish stew, I imagine: it's tasty and filling and everyone eats it most of the time, but it isn't one of the great delights of Moroccan cuisine. B'stilla, on the other hand, is.'

Melinda didn't waste breath insisting that neither the Irish nor anyone else ate Irish stew all the time, since she suspected it had been a figure of speech anyway. The b'stilla was superb, a mixture of delicate spices, pigeon and almonds in a flaky filo-type pastry and

30

decorated with icing sugar criss-crossed with cinnamon. It was difficult to decide whether to concentrate on the food or the dancer.

Melinda had more than half expected there to be a belly-dancer. What she hadn't been prepared for was the fact that this one was covered from neck to ankle in a shimmering, slinky gown that seemed to consist entirely of row upon row of small square mirrors.

'I didn't think belly-dancers dressed like that,' she said.

Khalil shrugged. 'She's good. Not Moroccan, but very good. The clothes you're used to seeing aren't Moroccan, either. Modesty requires that dancers cover themselves – and don't normally dance for men who aren't members of their own family.'

'She is,' Melinda pointed out.

'Yes, she is, but she's leaving out some of the moves that would be misconstrued.' He cast a thoughtful eye over his companion. 'You ought to learn,' he said. 'You're the right shape for it. You have curves. It's a form of dance that can turn men on quite fast.'

'So I believe,' she said drily.

'Of course, other men don't necessarily need anything so obvious,' he went on as if she hadn't spoken and, his eyes still on the sinuous dancer, his hand beneath the tablecloth slid under her skirt and up her leg.

It was instinct that made Melinda part her legs, the better to enjoy his initially delicate and almost virginal brushing against her sex. She wanted to seek some additional satisfaction in returning the compliment but that was more difficult to do: her hand could brush his bulging crotch but she dared not do anything that would attract the attention of the neighbouring tables.

He glanced down at her, smiling. 'Don't worry,' he said, 'I can wait until later,' and his fingers became

31

more insistent, more probing until she longed to cry out with the mounting pleasure she was feeling.

The rest of the meal was a prolonged affair. Khalil ate in the Arab fashion, using only his right hand. This might occasion no comment in Tangier but it freed his left hand to play with Melinda's pussy and she contorted herself to enjoy the hot, juicy sensation of writhing against his touch while at the same time keeping entirely still above the waist so that no one watching them across the restaurant might have the least idea what was going on. It was fun but it wasn't easy. The food was delicious but Melinda was barely able to appreciate it in the greater enjoyment of the sensations Khalil was inducing. If we don't leave soon, she thought, I'll come here, in public. It might be fun but I'd rather be home and not under any restraint.

As if he read her mind, Khalil withdrew his hand and sent for the bill, even though the cabaret, which he had been so avidly watching, wasn't finished. When they got back to the apartment, he took the key from her and let them in. He switched on only the soft and subtle wall-lights of the *salon* and then, without comment, kissed her hard and long while his hands pushed her waistcoat off and unbuttoned her blouse, sliding his fingers beneath the lace of her bra to toy delicately and provocatively with her nipples. They needed little encouragement to harden.

Melinda's breathing shivered with pleasure. Her fingers played with his rapidly stiffening cock through the fabric of his trousers. Then they crept up to his jacket and removed it gently, synchronising the action with his removal of her blouse. As she turned to put it over the back of a chair, she felt his hand reach under her skirt and make its way into the top of her tiny thong. She turned to face him. 'Do we undress each other or do I undress for you?' she whispered.

'Undress for me. Then you undress me. I want to

32

watch the way your body moves as you do it. Not too fast. Not too fast with me, either: I like to watch it stiffen.'

Melinda wondered just how much more it could stiffen, but she obediently stepped out of her mules and unbuckled her belt, laying it across his lap as he lounged back on one of the divans and making sure as she did so that it brushed against his bulge. A quick release of the zip sent her skirt cascading to the floor, revealing the thong that was little more than a lacy G-string and which, she knew, made her legs look tantalisingly endless. She moved in front of him then in imitation of the evening's dancer. She heard the catch of his breath as her bra slid to the ground, and knew he was thoroughly hooked. She began to tease the top of the thong but Khalil put out a hand.

'Come here,' he breathed.

She stood before him as he fondled her breasts, watching the nipples harden and stand away from the darkening aureolae, and Melinda knew it was exciting him almost as much as it excited her. Then his hands slid down and slowly, tantalisingly, lowered the thong. Then he sank his mouth into the softly curled fur of her pussy, like an animal seizing its prey, his tongue moving back and forth.

'Yes,' she murmured. 'Oh, yes.'

He put her hands on his crotch and Melinda, still enjoying the sensation of his tongue playing with her, forced herself to take her time. The he stood up. She unzipped him gradually, undid his belt and eased his trousers down. His shirt was next to go. He pushed her into a kneeling position to make it easier for her to remove his underpants and she took good care to brush against his cock as she did so, guessing that a slight touch would be even more stimulating than a hard one.

It was, and she couldn't resist the temptation to draw her tongue gently along it. His gasp of pure pleasure was almost reward enough. Instead of seeking more, as she expected, he raised her to her feet and they stood together, skin against skin, the dark curls of his chest and those of his loins pressing against her.

He picked her up and carried her into the bedroom. He laid her on the bed before switching on the bedside lamp. 'You don't prefer the dark, I hope,' he said.

Melinda smiled and shook her head. No, she thought. I like to see it all.

His hands stroked her body and his kisses descended once more from her mouth to her neck and on to her breasts where he lingered to tease pleasure for her. Then they continued downwards. Melinda knew she should seek to return the enjoyment but she could only moan with the pleasure she was feeling herself as his mouth and his tongue reached the site of all pleasure.

This time his tongue entered her more electrifyingly than fingers ever could. It teased inside her and she found herself clenching on it, responding to the pleasure it had so quickly created. She thrust her pelvis up towards him and writhed, the better to enhance the excitement of that roving tongue. His tongue answered with movements that varied from gently flickering around the edge of her clit, teasing her into unprecedented ecstasy, to roughly plunging in and out. God, she thought, he can do things with his tongue I'd only ever dreamed about! She could only wish it were bigger so that her orgasm could explode with greater force.

When he finally stopped, all she felt was anticlimax. It had been good. She had come. But it had also been incomplete. There should be more. She wanted more. She could see his erection now and ran her fingers along it, feeling it twitch. 'Take me,' she murmured. 'I want to feel you inside me. I want to feel that blissful moment of penetration. The moment that proves I'm a woman.'

'Oh, you're a woman, all right,' he told her.

34

His fingers parted her sex. He knew she was moist enough. He knew, too, she had only just reached an orgasm of surprising power. Could he really bring her to another so soon? His fingers played with her, feeling the wet relaxation of her opening. He had already realised she was quite small. That would make her all the more exciting, but he must take care. He couldn't help feeling it would have been fun to have been the first one, to have had the immense satisfaction of introducing that tiny space to the joys that were available. Yes, she was ready. He pushed the swollen head of his cock into her and was rewarded by her squeal of ecstasy. With one hand still rubbing her, he moved his cock back and forth, gently at first, penetrating a little further each time until he could go no further in. At that moment, he sensed her orgasm rising in perfect harmony with his own. This woman was going to be something else, he thought. I wonder just how often she can be brought to a climax?

He hoped Melinda was conscious of perfect satisfaction. There was power thrusting into her, reaching her limits yet not hurting. Pain could be enjoyable, too, but not now, not this time. She raised herself to be closer to him, to give his penetration more scope and felt, as he did, the bliss of perfect unison.

With a feeling of exultation, he came, releasing himself into her as she moaned to receive it. She spread her legs still wider, the better to catch every drop. 'Yes,' she moaned. 'Oh, yes.'

He withdrew slowly, gently, guessing she wouldn't relish the feeling of emptiness that must follow. He was reluctant to withdraw. He had a feeling that if he'd stayed there, he might have come again. Another time, perhaps. He kissed her gently.

'Well,' he said. 'You asked the question. It's up to you to answer it. Am I good?'

Her smile was tired and satisfied. 'Oh, yes. You're good – but I think you already know that.'

He shrugged. 'I think a woman's assessment of a man's performance will depend on what she's looking for. I look forward to discovering together just how much pleasure we can extract from each other.'

'That sounds like a perfect way to spend a holiday. Why don't you come and lie with me for a while?'

'When I've washed,' he replied. He got up out of bed, wondering if she would hear the shower through her semi-sleeping consciousness.

When he returned, still naked, and climbed into bed beside her, he told her it was her turn to shower.

'I'd rather lie here, snug and warm,' she told him. 'I can do that later.'

'No. Now. If you want me to stay a while, that is.'

Melinda thought the shower would destroy the mood but, oddly enough, it didn't. It made the gentle lying together seem cosy, friendly, natural. Already she was anticipating more. She could feel herself stirring and found herself wondering just how many orgasms he would bring her to this night. She wriggled her hips at the delightful prospect of the rest of the night and wondered how close Khalil might be to wanting more. Her hand strayed towards his prick, flaccid now against his thigh. She stroked it gently, running her fingers down to the firm balls at its base, but he gently pushed her hand away.

'Not now,' he said. 'Not again – not tonight, at least.' He kissed the top of her head. 'Will you be all right on your own tomorrow?' he asked. 'Until the evening, that is. I've work to attend to, I'm afraid. Arrangements of one sort or another to make. Do you mind?'

'Of course I mind. You give me a stick of candy and then snatch it away. Of course I mind.'

He glanced down at his thighs and chuckled. 'A stick of candy,' he repeated. 'I've never heard it called that before. I like it. But you must understand, this may be your holiday but it isn't mine.'

'I know. I'm just being selfish. I'll be OK.' She paused. 'I don't suppose you'd like to stay here all night?'

He laughed. 'I'd love to but I can't. Tomorrow – who knows? No promises but we'll see.' He slid out of bed and Melinda studied him properly for the first time. He certainly was an attractive man, slim and dark with broad shoulders, narrow hips and the obligatory small, tight buttocks, but he was quite without any of the exaggerations of men who rate their physical development as of prime importance. She still thought he was in his thirties, though perhaps his self-assurance suggested he might be older.

He was standing close to the bed now, reaching for his shirt, and she couldn't resist the impulse to reach out herself and touch his smooth, tantalising skin.

He laughed and moved just out of her reach. 'I daren't risk you making me rise again,' he said. 'I really do have to go if I'm to be fit for work tomorrow. If I stay here, I've a hunch I shan't be.'

Melinda let him go then. She was tired and happy and only a shade disappointed that he wasn't staying. It would be interesting to see what tomorrow brought.

Chapter Three

Monday

Melinda awoke late, consumed by a disconcerting feeling of incompleteness. She lay in the darkened room, listening to the muffled sounds of the city drifting through the daunting combination of wooden shutters and glass windows and wondered why she felt like this. She cast her mind back over the previous day, taking her time to recall every sensual detail from beginning to end. It wasn't just the physical happenings she dwelt on, though those were exciting enough. What really stirred her was reliving her responses to the sensations Khalil had engendered, from the first delicate stroke of his fingers on her breasts and then down to stir life into her loins, through the glorious, powerful act of possession that the instant of penetration represented, to the final joy of feeling him come inside her.

Even the recollection of last night was enough to start her arousal, a stimulation by proxy, as it were. She couldn't deny that sex with Khalil had been just about perfect. It had progressed from gentle beginnings to a powerful and thrusting fulfilment that had been all she could have desired – yet she still had that odd feeling of incompleteness. It didn't make sense. Was it because he hadn't spent the night with her? Because she hadn't woken up with him beside her? It must have something to do with that but, now she came to think about it, she had always felt a bit like that, regardless of whether her current lover had stayed the night or not. Perhaps it was only the strength of last night's satisfaction – which was certainly greater than any she could remember ever having achieved in the past – that made the incompleteness, the sense of emptiness, seem all the greater.

Not that she had ever felt unsatisfied before. Not at the time, anyway. It was just that Khalil had been so expert that anything that had preceded him had been overshadowed and she knew he would be the yardstick by which she measured all future lovers.

So why did she feel so empty? Was it possible she had fallen in love with him? No, it wasn't that and it took her less than three seconds to acknowledge it. Love didn't enter into it. She liked him. She wouldn't have had sex with him in the first place if she hadn't. She freely admitted he was compellingly attractive and excellent company, but that didn't alter the fact that she knew equally well that love, real or imagined, had nothing whatever to do with it. So why did she feel as she did?

She would have preferred him to spend the night though, even if he had, he'd have had to leave by now to go to work, which would only have made a difference of a few hours. Of course, had he stayed, she imagined he'd have taken her again. Maybe more than once. She moved restlessly on the bed as she contemplated what might have been.

And then she knew the real reason she felt so incompletely fulfilled. It was the feeling that if ever there were a man who could make her come repeatedly during the night, it would be Khalil. A gut-feeling made her very much doubt he would be limited to twice a night with perhaps a third time in the morning if she was very lucky. That was what she had come to expect in the past. It dawned on her as she lay there that she had never yet been really satisfied. She had never been fucked until she could take no more. She wouldn't even need to orgasm every time. Just fucked and fucked and fucked again.

And that was how she wanted it to be. My God, how she wanted it like that! She let out a shaking breath as the realisation dawned, and with it another, now that she was throwing off the inhibitions of her conventional thoughts. Hadn't Khalil said something about losing her inhibitions? True, he'd been talking about bargaining but she had a feeling he'd meant something more. Perhaps he'd got her true measure straight away. It was almost as if he knew her better than she knew herself. He had certainly woken her up in a way she hadn't anticipated.

It wasn't just a matter of longing to be satiated, though that was there right enough. It was also a matter of variety. She wanted the path to satiety to be paved with as many conceivable variations as possible. Everyone fantasised, but those fantasies other people had mentioned to her had always seemed very limited. Why were so many apparently limited to black lace underwear and sucking his cock? And why had her lovers never been particularly interested in what hers might be? She had a hunch Khalil might be different.

The one thing that really brought her on was the desire to be taken, to be possessed, to be used. She had woken lovers up in the night and encouraged them to make love again and she knew they liked her to take the initiative. None had ever returned the compliment. Not once had a lover started to have sex with her while she was asleep. Why couldn't these things be mutual?

She'd always wanted a man not to withdraw when he had come, but to stay there until he stiffened again.

Now that would be exciting, but the couple of lovers to whom she'd suggested it had objected that it was impossible and had given her some very peculiar looks. Melinda didn't think it need be impossible. She found herself tightening her pussy muscles as the very thought of the possible multiplicity of orgasms heated and moistened her cunt in vicarious anticipation. If any man could do it, she suspected it would be Khalil. She sighed. Tonight would be interesting. She just hoped it would go further than its predecessor, no matter how immensely pleasurable that had been.

But there was a long time before tonight. A whole day to fill. Thank goodness she'd been so tired. A late awakening at least cut down the time she had to fill. A bath would fill some of it and a bath could be fun.

It was, but after the satisfaction of the night, the stimulus of her fingers, while it certainly roused her, was very much a poor relation. It was pleasurable enough to enjoy until the water got cold, but it was a poor substitute for Khalil. Mind you, she reflected, I always have preferred a cock to my own finger.

She climbed out and wrapped herself in a towel. She sensed the unwelcome beginnings of a headache. 'I can do without that,' she said aloud to the bathroom and padded barefoot to the bedroom. Aspirin was something she always brought with her but rarely needed to use and she thought she'd put the bottle in the drawer of the bedside table. She opened it and felt around. The little bottle had found its way to the back and, as she brought it back, her hand brushed something else. Something cylindrical and fairly cold. Melinda's fingers closed round it and she brought it out.

It was a candle. It seemed to be of pretty standard length but quite wide, certainly much too wide to fit into the empty candlestick she had seen in one of the kitchen cupboards.

A slow, appreciative smile curved her full lips. Now

41

there's manna from heaven, she thought. She released the towel and sat on the edge of the bed, stroking her inner thighs with the pointed end, then up to her pubic hair and lightly across the labia to descend the other side and then back, lingering a little longer this time at the halfway mark. As it passed gently, suggestively over her outer lips, she felt herself clench, as if by doing so she could snatch the makeshift dildo into herself. The moisture of sexual desire that had been washed away by the bath returned and, next time the candle reached the apex, Melinda spread her legs and suddenly, violently, rammed it hard inside. She liked to be taken as much as to be seduced. This would do for now.

She rolled over on to her stomach and spread her legs across the edge of the bed so that the mattress caught the candle-butt and kept it in place while she moved against it, pushing, writhing, feeling her juices lubricate the welcome intruder and the nub of her clit hardening to the stimulation. It didn't take long for her to come, after which she lay briefly, exhausted, on the bed. But when she stood up and the candle began to slip out, she pushed it back.

No, she thought. I don't want it out yet. I don't like a fast withdrawal. She had started to move against it again when she caught sight of the small pile of underwear she had put out to wear. She reached out for the panties – rather more practical ones than yesterday's thong, but then, she wasn't completely confident she'd have the chance to turn Khalil on again – and put them on. It wasn't something she'd ever tried before and she wasn't even sure it would work, but it did. Admirably.

The panties held the candle in place. If anything, Melinda decided, it was even better than the deliberate stimulation she'd just enjoyed. Every time she moved, she could feel the base of the candle pressing against her clit, moving deep inside her, and sometimes, when

42

it slipped down against the natural give and take of the fabric, it would seem to be withdrawing, only to push back in with the next move. The excitement lay in never quite knowing what it would do next. Melinda liked that. She liked the orgasms it provoked, too. Not huge ones, perhaps, but three in the time it took her to dress and do her hair.

She was tempted to keep it in while she went to Havana for her breakfast. It would be fun to come there, in front of all those people without them knowing a thing about it. Except that they would, of course, because Melinda knew if there was one thing she couldn't do, it was to suppress the outward signs of her enjoyment, and she had a feeling that a public *salon de thé* in Morocco wasn't the best place to make that evident. Still, she could save the candle for another time. She removed it and chuckled. Ideally, she thought, I shan't need artificial stimulation for much longer.

The fair-haired woman who stepped out of the apartment block into the sunlight looked every inch the restrained and stereotypical Englishwoman and Melinda was fairly sure, as she stepped into Havana's marble-clad shade, that none of the newspaper-reading men who glanced up at her thought there was anything more to her than that. It gave her an ironic satisfaction that they would be so very, very wrong.

She soon discovered that Khalil hadn't understated things when he had said there were plenty of banks along the Boulevard Pasteur. She took advantage of the first one she came to and changed some more money but then, as she walked along the ornately paved street, she began to wonder why she'd bothered. The majority of shops either catered exclusively for tourists of the less discriminating sort, or were boutiques selling clothes, some of which looked interesting but all of which lacked the sort of finish Melinda expected to find when she paid that sort of price. Even if she bargained, she thought, the price would be too high.

As for the tourist shops, well, there was a limit to her desire to own a brass camel or a gaudy, chemically dyed kilim rug, unevenly woven and of a colour that couldn't conceivably work in any English colour scheme she had ever come across. There was some very nice blue-and-white pottery which might be worth a second look some time and some shops selling leather handbags – blatant copies of designer bags right down to the prestigious logos, which were of a quality that would fool any but the specialist, with prices that in England one would pay for good quality plastic. Melinda decided she would certainly be going home with one of these. The biggest problem would be to decide between Chanel and Kenzo, but it wasn't a problem over which she was likely to waste much sleep.

She began to realise that the *salons de thé* were as numerous here as pubs had been in her parents' youth: virtually one on each corner. They all boasted exotic names: Paradise, Hawaii, Oslo, Miami, Mexico and, in the centre of the city, the one every guide book had mentioned, the Café de Paris. It was definitely a let-down, she decided. Its location was superb but any glamour the name evoked was strictly confined to the name. There were a couple of tourists, who looked unmistakably English, sitting outside, women who clutched their handbags to their inadequately supported bosoms, their pallid arms testimony to their recent arrival. Melinda was glad her own were covered. Perhaps this afternoon she'd sit out on that little balcony and remedy the situation. She certainly wasn't inclined to sit outside any *salon de thé*, no matter how salubrious it looked and, while she was sure it was advisable to be careful with one's handbag, such obvi-

44

ously wary body language must surely send out quite the wrong message.

No, the Café de Paris was eminently resistible. She turned up a side-street and was glad she had. Vienna was definitely her sort of watering-hole. Whoever had designed the interior had managed to evoke *fin de siècle* Vienna. The coffee supported this impression and the tray of pastries would have excelled even the coffee, had the pastry-cook only made use of real cream, but that, Melinda decided, was nit-picking.

The waiter, assuring her that he spoke French, was able to tell her how best to reach the beach. Since one of the city's attractions must undoubtedly be the four miles of sandy bay, it would be stupid not to see it.

'Are you going there now?' he asked her.

'Yes. Why?'

'Then, madame, keep hold of your handbag – and make sure your money is hidden inside it, not just in your purse.'

She thanked him, realising that when she had paid him, he must have seen how her purse bulged. She sat down again and rearranged the contents of her bag, making sure that the bulk of the money she had just changed was safely in a zipped-up compartment. Not much use if someone snatched the bag, of course, but at least she'd been warned. He deserved the additional tip she left him.

The walk to the bay was steeply downhill and it crossed her mind that coming back up wasn't going to be fun. If she was sensible, she wouldn't try walking the whole length of the bay and back.

When she reached what might best be called the promenade, she was surprised and disappointed. Not by the street itself, which was wide and divided into two carriageways by a wide central reservation lined with palm trees, nor by the side opposite the beach, which was, as she'd expected, lined with hotels, some of them quite nice, touristy-looking ones. The disappointment lay the other side. Instead of simply a paved promenade edging the sand, a railway line passed along, cutting off any view of the bay except from the upper floors of the hotels. It was odd to have to cross a railway line to get to the beach and even more disconcerting to realise that, having done so, the area immediately beyond the tracks was made up of one-storey 'beach clubs', each apparently belonging to one or other of the hotels. Having crossed the rails and found a small gate leading through the barrier to one of these 'clubs' – which was closed and shuttered – Melinda could see that the glories of the bay hadn't been exaggerated.

The sand stretched in a wide, slow curve. At one end she could see the medina scrambling, white-washed, up the steep cliffs, while below it the modern harbour was hosting the Algeciras ferry and what looked like a cruise ship, as well as private yachts and working fishing boats. At the far end of the scimitar-sweep of sand stood a lighthouse on the final headland of the bay. The coast between was a curve of six- and seven-storey buildings that might have been hotels and might have been blocks of flats. They must all have had magnificent views, especially since the railway seemed not to follow the line of the bay all the way round, but turned off after a mile or so.

Melinda had the sand almost to herself. There was a group of young men – no, not so much young men as adolescent boys, she decided – playing football close to the water's edge, and she also spotted a man with a couple of camels whom she guessed was hoping to catch a stray tourist and offer him a ride. Fine, but she wasn't interested in camel-rides, so she made sure she steered well clear of him and ignored his attempt to hail her in English, German and French, in that order, trying to guess her nationality from her appearance and getting it absolutely right. She didn't make the mistake of answering. She ignored his calls and increased her pace. She could do without being hassled by itinerants.

The sand was so soft that it was proving quite difficult to walk on, at least at any speed, and she determined to return along the promenade, clearly visible now that the railway had changed its route and the beach clubs had dwindled away. Meanwhile, it would probably be easier in her bare feet. She bent down and removed her sandals, vaguely aware that she could no longer hear the shouts of the young footballers. Perhaps she had walked further than she had thought.

But as she stood erect again, she realised that the reason she couldn't hear them was very different. They had been silent because they had been converging on this lone, vulnerable woman. As soon as she stood up, she found herself encircled by a menacing gang of a dozen or so well-muscled and athletic men, all of them grinning broadly, but none of them uttering a sound.

It was the silence that was so alarming. Melinda could feel her heart beating faster as she realised these were not young teenagers at all, as she had first thought, but more probably in their early twenties, though one or two might have been a bit younger. But before she had a chance to discover whether her alarm was justified, the menacing group suddenly scattered. Melinda glanced round and saw a tall man in a superbly cut uniform approach.

'Are you all right?' he asked in flawless French.

Melinda nodded but he seemed unconvinced.

'I'd like you to come with me and make a statement,' he said. 'Meanwhile my men will catch them.'

'But nothing happened,' Melinda pointed out.

'Only because I came along,' he said grimly. 'Tourism is important here. We must nip this sort of thing in the bud.' Melinda was ushered into his car and driven back to police headquarters.

Eyes opened wide as so senior an officer made his way to his office accompanied by an extremely desirable European woman. Opened and quickly averted once their superior's angry countenance was observed.

Coffee was quickly brought for Melinda and the officer pulled a pad of officially headed paper towards him. 'Which hotel are you staying at?' he asked, taking up a ballpoint as he spoke.

'I'm not. I have a flat here.'

He frowned. 'You mean you rent one, I take it?'

'No. I own it. I inherited it a few months ago.'

'Ah. That explains why I haven't seen you in Tangier before. May I ask the address?'

Melinda told him and he seemed taken aback.

'You inherited this apartment? Did you inherit anything else?'

'A house in the old city,' she told him, 'and I gather I also own another one, but I haven't seen that. My property agent is arranging it for me.'

'That will be Benani, I assume.'

'You know him?'

He smiled. 'That's my job.'

'I suppose it must be.' Melinda was feeling a little more relaxed now, relaxed enough to study the man on the other side of the desk. He was taller than most Moroccans she'd seen and she guessed him to be in his late forties, the greying hair at his temples lending an air of distinction to a handsome face above a frame which she suspected was hard muscled under the superbly well-cut uniform.

'And your name?' he went on.

Melinda told him.

He pressed keys on his computer console and nodded. 'Melinda Upton Carr. You arrived on Saturday

48

with the RAM flight and were met by Benani. Is that correct?'

Melinda nodded and recalled the comment about the implications of the quality of police uniforms. Not much slipped past this lot, that was for sure.

'So you inherited from Miss Carr?'

Melinda nodded. 'My great-aunt.'

'A fairly distant relationship, yet you share a name?'

She explained the situation and detected a quiet chuckle when she told him the reason for making her the sole heir.

'I can imagine Miss Carr putting it something like that,' he said.

'You knew her?'

'Personally? No. My father did, though. She was something of a legend in Tangier.'

'So I'm beginning to learn,' Melinda said. She was beginning to get a bit miffed at not having the slightest idea what it was that had made Great-Aunt Laura the legend she was. Everyone's father seemed to have known her. Put like that, it was something easily misconstrued.

'And do you intend to pick up the reins she dropped in the same way you've picked up her property?'

'Hardly,' Melinda told him tartly. 'I've no idea what those reins were, so how can I?'

If she'd hoped to be told, she was disappointed. He shrugged. 'True enough. Benani is arranging for you to see your other house, you say? That suggests he has things well in hand. Good.'

He stood up, the interview over. 'One of my men will drive you back to your apartment and see you safely inside,' he told her. 'I hope this incident hasn't given you a distaste for Morocco and its people. I look forward to the opportunity to meet you again, in a less stressful situation, perhaps.'

'That would be nice,' Melinda said politely, but

completely unable to imagine how such a situation might arise.

Because he had come for her the previous evening at eight, Melinda assumed that Khalil would arrive at the same time today so, when the bell sounded a good half-hour earlier, she was still in her jeans and T-shirt, and only just thinking about what to wear. When she saw who the caller was, she opened the door wide to let him in.

'You're earlier than I expected,' she said. 'I'm not suitably dressed for dinner.'

He looked her up and down. 'No, you're not.'

'Give me two minutes – well, ten,' she amended.

'Fine, but I'll choose what you wear.' He walked into the bedroom without waiting for an answer and Melinda, who decided her best tactic was to leave him to it, heard him slide back the door of the fitted wardrobe. When he emerged he was carrying precisely the dress she'd decided upon, the one she would have preferred to have worn the previous evening.

It was one of those dresses that looks depressingly and austerely conventional on the hanger, but put a body inside it and it metamorphoses into something rather different. The dark midnight-blue was a perfect foil for Melinda's honey-blonde hair and the straight line of the button-through style was only relieved by the transparent georgette of the sleeves. The lustrous silk jersey of the rest of the dress clung to every curve. It covered everything and hid nothing. She wasn't sure whether Khalil realised that or simply thought it was as modest as it looked on the hanger.

'Oh, yes,' she said noncommittally, 'I quite like that one. It'll do very well, I think.' With these words, she took the dress from him and whisked herself into her bedroom, closing the door firmly behind her.

Because it revealed everything beneath it, she usually

wore a legless, smooth leotard under it and she had naturally brought it with her. Now she hesitated. She certainly didn't want the line of the dress spoilt by her visible panty line and she'd often thought about wearing nothing underneath it but had so far lacked the nerve. But now, why not? They weren't going to be meeting anyone who knew her, after all.

She put it on and studied herself in the mirror. Her breasts weren't small but they were pert enough and didn't sag. Of course, the instant her nipples hardened – as they were at that moment – they were very visible, but if she seemed to be oblivious of the fact, they'd be a turn-on. Tonight, after all, she had decided she wanted more. Lots more.

She reached for the Cinnabar spray. Neck and wrists, of course. Then, after a moment's hesitation, she undid every button and sprayed between her breasts, then lightly down her body with a final burst into the curls of her pussy. Then she buttoned up her dress again and made a demure appearance in the *salon*, where Khalil was leaning back on one of the divans.

He stood up as she entered and his eyes widened with appreciation. 'Very nice,' he murmured. 'Very nice indeed.'

'I'm glad you like it,' Melinda replied, her eyes modestly downcast as if she were totally unaware that her nipples had already hardened in response to his admiring glance.

Khalil came across and kissed her on the cheek and his hand, which had rested lightly on her waist, slid down outside her dress. 'I thought so,' he commented.

'Are we in a hurry?' Melinda asked.

By way of reply, his hand found its way between two of the lower buttons and caressed what it found there. Melinda's pussy jumped as she rubbed herself against his touch like a cat on heat, telling him all he needed to know. 'No particular hurry,' he told her, 'but you shouldn't try to eat all your cake at once.'

Her hands and the feel of him against her belly told her that he was hardening fast. 'Not even a lick of sugar candy?' she suggested.

'Later. I plan to take you for a little drive first. Then dinner. Then – who knows?'

'A drive? To see the other house?'

'Not yet. A couple more days should see it ready for you, though how ready it will need to be, I haven't yet made up my mind.'

'What's that supposed to mean?' Melinda asked, annoyed. For God's sake, it was her house, dammit. Why all the delay?

'Oh, I'm just being enigmatic,' he said off-handedly, but Melinda knew he was being nothing of the kind. For some reason it didn't suit him to take her there or tell her anything about it, and that was beginning to annoy her. For the time being, she'd play it his way, but only for the time being.

He ushered her into the car and they drove down to the road along the bay and cruised at a leisurely speed in the direction Melinda had walked earlier. In the distance, the lighthouse beamed sporadically across the waters of the bay, the rapidly deepening night creating the illusion of increasing brightness in the lantern.

When they reached the lighthouse, Khalil pulled off the road and drove directly into what could only be the garden attached to the building. He ignored the notice that denied access to visitors and drew to a halt close to the edge of the pathway. He nodded to the lights across the water. 'Those are the lights of Spain and Gibraltar,' he said. 'Over there, to the left, is the old medina and below, quite unmistakable, the harbour.'

'Quite beautiful,' Melinda said. 'Just about as beautiful as it could be. What a pity the lighthouse isn't available for conversion.'

He chuckled. 'It probably would be if you approached the right people and made it worthwhile. Of course, you'd probably have to guarantee the light kept on working and you'd have to put up with the intrusion of tourists looking at the view. Apart from that, it would be ideal.'

His hand was resting on her thigh now, enjoying the touch of the silky jersey fabric. Melinda raised no objection.

'I hear you had an unpleasant experience earlier today,' he said.

Melinda turned to stare at him in the darkness. 'The police told you about it?'

'The Commissioner suggested I take better care of you.' He paused. 'Tell me something – and I want the truth. What were your feelings when you realised what those men were probably after?'

'I didn't have much time to think, but no one wants to be raped.'

'I'm sure that's so, but isn't it something a lot of women fantasise about?' His fingers had undone the lower buttons now and were softly stroking the satin flesh of her inner thighs. Melinda moved gently, the better to catch every butterfly-soft sensation. It was difficult to concentrate on his question.

She chuckled. 'I can't speak for anyone else,' she said, 'but I certainly think about it myself. Of course, I wouldn't want it for real,' but even as she spoke, she imagined an idealised scenario of being taken roughly by a gang of good-looking boys.

His fingers left her sex to explore her higher up, undoing buttons as they went.

'Don't,' Melinda protested softly. 'What if someone comes by?'

'They'll see nothing. The tinted glass takes care of that. How does the fantasy differ from the real thing?'

53

'I suppose the difference is that deep down you have a choice.'

'And it's gentler?'

Melinda thought about that, luxuriating in the warmth-inducing pleasure of his touch. His head was nuzzling her breasts now, leaving his fingers free to pursue the earlier quarry. 'No,' she decided. 'Definitely not. Gentle is for seduction. What we're talking about, fantasy or not, isn't. It's domination.'

'You've been deliciously generous with your perfume,' he said. 'I think it goes a long way down.'

Melinda chuckled. 'All the way down,' she told him and was rewarded by his determination to prove or disprove her claim.

'Do you like to be dominated?' he asked, pausing briefly in his research.

'Oh, yes. I'm fairly pushy professionally, you see, and I long not to have to take the initiative all the time when it comes to sex.'

She groaned as he reached the destination her perfume had been leading him to and, with no further preamble, he pushed his tongue inside her. Its suddenness was so unexpected that it caused her whole pelvis to thrust into the air, gyrating sensuously.

As it did so, Khalil slid a hand beneath her and with no prior indication of his intent, replaced his tongue with his hard, swollen cock and rammed it into her as powerfully as he could. Melinda, who had been so absorbed in what his tongue had been doing to her that she hadn't even realised it had been released from the captivity of his clothes, gave a startled cry. The force with which it had been done was alarming but this all added to the pleasure. He lifted her buttocks and forced her above the leather seat, to make penetration easier and deeper.

Her smallness made it hurt, but it was the most pleasurable hurt imaginable. 'I can feel every nerve you have tingling against mine,' she breathed. 'Don't leave. Please don't leave.'

By now she was so wet that his stiff and swollen cock seemed in danger of withdrawing completely every time it drew back. This is bliss, she thought. I wasn't asked. It was barely suggested and I don't want it to stop. Not now. Not ever. But already she knew he was close to coming and she wanted that, too, even if it meant the end.

For his part, Khalil was enjoying the sensation of thrusting into so tight an orifice. Melinda might be no virgin, but she was as tight as one. A small man would no longer feel inadequate; a big one – and Khalil knew there were many bigger then he – would experience sensations they could normally only dream of. As for him, he was happy to concentrate on bringing her out of her sexual straitjacket. She didn't seem to have been educated into the sexual experiences he guessed she was made for. He liked to be pleasured, too, but right now he wasn't complaining. He gave one final, shuddering thrust inside her, which provoked a squeal of delighted pain as he climaxed, pulsing his juices into her. As his erection faded, he went on pushing gently, knowing she wasn't yet ready for the shock of a sudden withdrawal.

'Is that what you had in mind?' he asked, bending his head to kiss her now empty pussy.

'Something like that,' she agreed. 'It's the surprise that's the turn-on.'

'I think we'd better go back to your apartment. I doubt if either of us is wearing clothes that will stand even the limited scrutiny of the most discretely lit restaurant.'

'I can live without dinner tonight, anyway,' she told him.

* * *

Melinda closed the apartment door carefully behind them both. She'd make them both some coffee. After all, there was no rush. They had the whole evening. Maybe even the whole night. She turned the key the requisite three times and was startled to find herself grabbed firmly from behind and forced, face-down, across the padded seat of a dining-chair that stood against the white wall of the small entrance hall.

Before she realised what was happening, she felt Khalil's cock against her still wet and swollen sex, and this time as he went in her cry was of real pain. Penetration from behind went deeper, and she knew Khalil was determined to find her deepest recesses. But it also increased her sense of helplessness, of being taken, of being possessed, and her joyous response to having been given no choice, no warning whatever, was to raise her buttocks as high as she could, the better to facilitate his actions. She was wet all over now and every thrust seemed to penetrate further and to contrast deliciously with its near withdrawal immediately after.

Then his hands let go of her hips, which they had been guiding on to him, and instead slipped between her legs, toying with her now ultra-sensitive clit. She caught her breath with delight, widening herself to enable more searching, teasing fingers to enhance the brutality of their fucking. He came before she did this time and knew that her groan was partly of disappointment. So he stayed there, stroking her gently until he felt himself harden once more.

Melinda felt it, too, and was immediately alert again, aroused by him getting hard again so quickly. Instinctively, she moved against his strengthening prick and felt it swell further. So it could be done! she thought. It really could! A fantasy realised, and she smiled to herself as his thrusting began again, not quite so forceful perhaps but seeming to reach every nerve in her body. No man who had taken her from behind had ever done more than penetrate and thrust, but this time Khalil's skill with his fingers was bringing her to a pinnacle of ecstasy that made her cry out as she climaxed against him and felt him pumping rhythmically into her small, warmly moist space. When he withdrew, she could feel the flow down her legs in a steady, warm trickle. It made the act of withdrawal seem less drastic.

As she enjoyed these sensations, he slapped her bottom playfully. 'I think you enjoyed that,' he said.

It was almost a pity to stand up. She laughed as she did so. 'You noticed?'

Khalil returned the laugh. 'It was hard not to.' He ran a finger down her cheek. 'Do you mind if I bathe first? Then I can leave you to take your time over it.'

Disappointment filled Melinda. 'You're not staying?' she asked, aghast. She had been so sure he would.

He shook his head. 'I had intended to when I came, but I hadn't bargained for such a –' he sought the right word, '– such an energetic evening.'

'Are you telling me I've worn you out?' Melinda demanded.

'Aren't you exhausted?' he countered.

'Tired, maybe, but certainly not exhausted. Oh, a brief respite will be welcome but then there's the rest of the night. Which,' she added, 'has only just begun.'

He smiled. 'Tomorrow I'll stay all night. I promise. But we'll start at a less demanding level, I think. I don't suppose you've ever considered entertaining more than one man at a time?'

Melinda looked surprised. 'It's another fantasy, yes, and I know plenty of people indulge it, but I never have.' She grinned wickedly. 'Why? Have you got a friend lined up?'

'Not for tomorrow, no. Nor the night after. After that – who knows? Perhaps it's something we can discuss.' He paused. 'You're a rewarding woman to educate,' he said.

57

'And you're a first-class teacher. Have you really got more delights up your sleeve?'

'Not my sleeve, exactly, but I think quite a few of your inhibitions will have dropped away by the time this holiday's over.'

'Now there's an intriguing thought,' Melinda remarked.

'I'm glad you find it so,' he said, smiling broadly. 'You'll have to enjoy yourself tomorrow until the evening. I'm sorry, I know you don't like doing that. I suggest you take yourself into the medina. You'll be safe enough provided you hang on to your bag and don't have too much in it. I've still one or two things to sort out on your behalf. Then I hope I'm going to be able to devote myself to your entertainment for the rest of your holiday.'

There was something in his tone that told Melinda a protest would be a waste of time. 'I'll hold you to that,' she warned him.

'Don't worry. You won't have to.' And with these words he disappeared into the bathroom.

His shower was brief and his parting kiss was quick and almost fraternal. It's a good job I don't imagine I'm falling for him, Melinda thought as she locked the door behind him. Because he's certainly not falling for me. Fun is the name of the game here, and I think that suits me just fine.

There was one reservation, though. Fun might indeed be the name of the game but Khalil was a businessman – and if his car and his clothes were anything to go by, he was a successful one. Melinda had a hunch that business was behind almost everything he did and if love played no part in their relationship, then business did. She was, of course, a rich woman now and he managed at least part of her affairs, but somehow she didn't think that was necessarily the entire answer. Ah, well, she thought as she ran a bath, time will tell.

Chapter Four
Tuesday

Melinda stretched her naked body sensuously against the sheets, much as a cat stretches when it first wakes up. Last night had been the most satisfying so far, she decided. Definitely the best. She listened, still drowsy with semi-sleep, to the muffled sounds of the city and the clatter of people in other apartments getting ready for another day's work, and wondered what had made it the best. After all, she wouldn't have thought the night before would have been easy to beat, yet now its gentle seduction had been well and truly eclipsed.

She went back over the previous day: experience had taught her that this was as good a way as any of extending the pleasure of any sexual interlude, and that was as important as any analysis of whys and wherefores. She didn't have much difficulty finding the reason, not even through the drowsiness which was fading now but still wrapping her in warmth and satisfaction.

It had been the surprise of Khalil's actions. Not surprise that he had wanted her and had taken her. There hadn't been any doubt from the very beginning that sexual pleasure was the object of the exercise for both of them. She was tempted to think of it as love-making, except that she knew it went beyond that or not as far, depending on one's way of looking at things. Melinda thought it went beyond that, though she suspected that most people would have been horrified if she'd openly admitted as much.

There had been the surprise of being brought to a climax in a car in a very public place with her breasts, her belly and her sex-curls open and apparently exposed to any casual passer-by. Khalil had said no one could see through the tinted glass but Melinda wasn't entirely convinced. There was an excitement in even contemplating the possibility that he was being unduly optimistic. She smiled. It was a long time since she'd had it in a car. She'd have said she'd outgrown that particular location. She'd have been wrong.

And then there was the sudden, totally unexpected way he had thrown her across the chair and taken her ferociously hard and without discussion or foreplay. That had been fun. Even thinking about it was arousing. She was wide awake now, revelling in her recollections.

She'd always dreamed of being taken without preamble. Khalil wasn't the first man she'd mentioned it to, but others hadn't believed her or perhaps it had never formed a part of their own fantasies. At all events, the most they had done was to smile politely and thrust a bit harder next time, after the usual formulaic foreplay.

There was nothing formulaic about Khalil's approach to sex. He was all she'd ever dreamed of in that respect, right down to demonstrating that it was possible for a woman to enjoy the subtle sensation of a man hardening inside her. Even thinking about it turned her on, the more so because it, too, had happened when she was in a position where she had no choice but to submit.

They'd talked about it beforehand so he'd known she wasn't averse to it, and even talking about it had been a mildly stimulating preparation for the act. Perhaps the afternoon's alarming encounter had been, too. Melinda guessed things like that had served to encourage her ready response to Khalil's possessive technique.

He was a brilliant lover and, unusually in Melinda's experience, one who rated giving her pleasure at least as highly as he rated receiving it himself. She rather thought he might even be a man whose own sexual satisfaction was enhanced by his partner's pleasure. That made him a find to be treasured.

She frowned. It was odd, though. They enjoyed each other's company – though that might be mainly because there were always sexual overtones and undertones to everything they said and did – and they both undeniably enjoyed the games they were playing, yet she knew nothing at all about Khalil the person.

He gave nothing of himself away except the pleasure he got from sex and his talent for giving as much pleasure as he enjoyed himself. His clothes, his car, his self-assurance, all these told her he was as successful in business as he was in bed, but they told her nothing more. She had no idea whether he was married, whether he had children, where he lived, whether his education matched his obvious intelligence; no idea whether he liked music, art, literature or, if he did, what sort. She had no idea of his taste in anything beyond bed, and even there his taste seemed to be to ascertain what she wanted and supply it.

Not that Melinda had any objection to that. When she considered how much he had already transformed her expectations of this holiday, she could only be grateful. It was probably churlish even to think about what else made him tick. Yet not knowing precisely that, not to the slightest degree, was a bit like looking at a picture with one of the primary colours missing, or a bronze without its patina. It was incomplete.

She rolled over beneath the soft embrace of the sheets and glanced at the alarm clock. What the hell, she thought. He's good. Go for it. Enjoy it while it's there – and meanwhile there's a day to kill.

As she began a lethargic consideration of just how to fill it, the thought of that other property she was supposed to own flashed into her mind and all her annoyance returned.

Why was Khalil so unwilling to take her there? He'd insisted it wasn't in a state of disrepair but, even if it had been, it was hers and she had every right to inspect it if she wanted to – and if Khalil was her agent, it was his job to let her do so. She didn't even know where it was, so she couldn't just take a taxi and go on her own. She chuckled. Actually, she probably could. On the evidence so far, there was a good chance the taxi driver's father would have known Great-Aunt Laura.

'I know who does know, though,' she said aloud, leaping out of bed and reaching for her handbag. It would have been stupid to come to Tangier without Khalil's business address, and now she remembered she'd also brought the lawyer's – and hadn't Khalil said he was independent? Maybe he could throw some light on Great-Aunt Laura's history as well.

Ten minutes later she was hailing a taxi and five minutes after that she was standing in the lawyer's outer office.

Idriss Karrouk saw her at once, pushing other work back in the 'pending' tray and coming out to greet her himself, and Melinda wondered if all Moroccan men were going to be in their mid-to-late thirties. He was definitely too young to have any first-hand knowledge of her great-aunt. Pity. She'd hoped the lawyer would be old enough to be a little less vague than most. Still, he should have all the background information in his files somewhere.

'I understand I have another property in Tangier,' she began. 'I've seen the house in the medina and I'm staying in the apartment, but Benani mentioned a third property.'

'That's right. Rather a splendid one, I believe.'

'You haven't seen it?' Melinda was surprised.

He shrugged – a gesture Melinda was fast coming to accept as a Moroccan characteristic. 'I've seen it, naturally, but I've never been inside. My job doesn't require it.'

'But you can tell me where it is? Give me the address?'

'I can do that, yes, but why haven't you asked Benani? He's your agent.'

'I have, but all he says is that he'll take me there when he's got it ready.'

'And I'm sure he will. He's a very conscientious man. I dare say it will take some time. Why don't you find your way around Tangier until it's ready? There's plenty to see. The shops in the Rue Mexique are interesting – they're not tourist oriented. There's a very good modern art museum, too. Of interest to someone in your line of work, I'd have thought.'

'Why are you stalling me?' Melinda demanded.

'I'm merely advising you that you would be better advised to leave it in Benani's hands for the time being. I assure you, he will let you see it. He has no reason not to.'

'I don't suppose you can fill me in on my great-aunt's history in this town, either,' Melinda said sarcastically. She was being stalled and she knew it, and this man was supposed to be an independent professional keeping an eye on her interests.

Again the shrug. 'I'm sorry. I never knew Miss Carr.'

'Let me guess. Your father dealt with her.'

He smiled. 'They had a long and successful business association. I hope that will continue in the next generation.'

'But you're not actually going to tell me anything, are you?' Melinda was furious but letting rip at him would be counter-productive. 'At least you can give me the address,' she demanded.

Another shrug. 'I'm afraid I don't have it to hand but it's up in the area called the Mountain. Dj'bel in Arabic.'

'Then I'll take a taxi and find it myself,' she snapped. An address should take less than a minute to look up in any reasonably efficient office. She guessed he probably knew it by heart, anyway. So why not tell her? Why was he presenting her with a brick wall?

'Be careful,' the lawyer warned. 'Not all taxi drivers are trustworthy and Dj'bel is a wide area of scattered, isolated mansions. Not a good place for a woman to go on her own.'

'Thank you for your advice,' Melinda said bitterly. 'I'm sure you'll add the time I've wasted on to my bill.' And she stormed out into the street.

Sod him! she thought. Sod him, sod him, sod him. She raised her hand to summon a taxi and then lowered it again. OK, he was an uncooperative, unprofessional bastard, but that didn't make him a liar. Taxi-drivers were notorious the world over. They could be bloody marvellous – or not. And he had no reason to lie about the general location.

Melinda frowned. Then she noticed that a tiny kiosk selling postcards and newspapers had a girl in a *hijab* behind the counter. She chose a couple of cards at random and paid for them. 'There's a district called Dj'bel,' she said. 'I've heard it's very pretty. How do I get there?'

The girl looked concerned. 'On your own, madame?'

'Yes.'

The concern deepened. 'Dj'bel is very beautiful,

madame. The houses there are palaces. But don't go alone. You need a man with you for protection. Or take one of the tourist buses to Cap Spartel. They pass through it and you'll see how beautiful it is. All forest and trees.'

Melinda sighed. She supposed that had to settle it. The shop assistant had no axe to grind. Her advice had been entirely disinterested and her concern genuine, even if it was probably a bit exaggerated. Common sense told her to swallow her pride and work on Khalil. If he was really obdurate about it, then she'd find another way of skinning the cat, but it was early days yet – and she would prefer not to be discovered with her throat slit in some benighted forest. With or without trees. Remembering the girl's phrase made her smile and went some way to restoring her good humour. It looked as if there was nothing for it but to follow Khalil's advice and head for the medina. She'd hunt for a handbag. That would be more interesting than wandering aimlessly, looking at this and that.

She soon realised that Khalil's presence had protected her from being hustled by the youngsters outside each small shop whose job seemed to be to get the tourist inside to spend money. When she found a shop she liked the look of, she went in, making it clear to the first man who approached her inside that she was only looking. If she didn't want to go in a shop, she just ignored the touts outside, having cottoned on quickly to the fact that a polite 'No thank you' only made them follow her with exhortations to think again.

The area in which she lingered, and in which the men sitting on chairs were there to protect the shop-keeper, not to encourage customers, was the gold-smiths' soukh. The shops were minute, with room for only one customer at a time; possibly with a friend as well, if they both breathed in. Their windows were a revelation. Wedding belts at the top and then necklaces; below that, pile after neat pile of bangles, seven bangles in each pile, each individual bangle quite narrow but all the ones in one pile of the same design. She suspected there was some significance in the number, that they represented some tradition, like the belts. She'd ask Khalil. He'd know.

The shops selling leather wouldn't have looked out of place in Bond Street, so cleverly were their goods displayed, so welcoming the lighting, and Melinda was soon engrossed in examining the bags an attentive assistant was producing for her now that he realised she was seriously intending to buy one – and could very possibly be persuaded to buy more if he played his cards right.

She was so engrossed that at first she didn't even hear her name.

'Melinda? It is you, isn't it? Melinda Upton – I mean Carr.'

She spun round at the sound of so unexpected a voice. 'Clive?' she asked. What on earth would Clive be doing here, for God's sake? Tangier was just the sort of place he hated. Sun, sea and sand, only let's not move away from the hotel pool. That was Clive's idea of a holiday.

He grinned. 'You weren't expecting me, were you?' he said, his tone making it clear how delighted he thought she'd be.

'No, I wasn't. What are you doing here?' A perceptive man would have realised that delight wasn't at the forefront of her reaction. Clive, she knew, had never been the most perceptive of men.

'Well, right now I'm finding my way around. Seeing what's what. I must say, I didn't expect to bump into you quite so soon. In fact, I was prepared for quite a problem finding you.'

'Are you telling me you came to Tangier to find me?' Melinda demanded.

He laughed fondly. 'What other reason could I possibly have?'

'I can't imagine,' she said curtly. Clive was the last person she wanted to see. True, she now had an escort to Dj'bel if she wanted one, but Clive's company was too high a price to pay just yet. Besides, she thought she'd made it perfectly clear that she didn't want him back. 'How did you know I'd come here?' she went on.

'Your mother told me. She said she knew you'd be glad of my company in a place like this.' He glanced around. 'Obviously she's right. This is no place for a respectable woman on her own.'

'Yes, well, I've stopped being respectable. I'm enjoying Tangier and I certainly don't want you trailing around after me.'

Clive's smile was sympathetic but a bit forced. 'Now you don't mean that, Mel. It's just the surprise talking. I suggest we get some coffee somewhere and have a chat. Then you can tell me where you're staying. I'm at the Rif, by the way. It's quite nice. I know you're not because I asked, but your mother did say she thought you might even be silly enough to stay at one of the places you inherited.'

'That would be silly, would it?' Melinda demanded.

'What? Self-catering in a strange country where you don't even speak the language? Of course it is. Look, why don't we go and get that coffee? Then we can talk and you'll have a chance to get used to the idea.'

An idea had already occurred to her that certainly wasn't what he had in mind, so she smiled and agreed that coffee would be very nice indeed. But first she was buying a bag.

Melinda knew that Clive's French was limited to 'please' and 'thank you', and she remembered the name of the *salon de thé* up near the kasbah where she had

67

gone with Khalil so, while the assistant was wrapping her chosen handbag, she asked him in French the easiest way there.

His instructions were crystal-clear, which was a relief, and she was also rather gratified to see that Clive found the steadily uphill route hard going.

'You really ought to keep fit, Clive,' she said, unable to suppress a smile.

He didn't answer, but his face made it clear he didn't share her amusement.

Clive was not happy when they reached their destination. The only indication that there was a *salon de thé* there at all was a weather-worn painted sign, and when they entered, the contrasting dark inside made him nervous. He wasn't reassured by the sight of the little traditional room in which Melinda had enjoyed an anticipatory interlude with Khalil. In Clive's opinion, this was too much like going native. He almost sighed with relief when they emerged at the top of the stairs into the main room with its depressing decor of the sort more often associated with factory canteens. Only the windows making up three of the walls with their superb views of the straits and the harbour made the plastic-topped tables and metal-framed stacking chairs tolerable.

'Will you order for me, Clive?' Melinda said, smiling pleasantly. 'Mint tea and a selection of pastries. They're delicious here. I need to go to the loo.'

Clive looked doubtful. 'Will they understand?' he asked. 'Your French is better than mine.'

'Of course they'll understand,' she replied. 'Serving tourists is their business. Just so long as you don't want to discuss philosophy or the meaning of the Universe, English will be fine.'

He nodded, albeit doubtfully, and Melinda left him to it. She'd seen the sign for the lavatories on the next

68

floor down, but that was purely academic because she had no need to use them anyway.

Once outside the main dining-room, and safe in the knowledge that Clive wouldn't be able to understand her even if he heard her, she intercepted the waiter and pressed a ten-dirham coin into his hand.

'Can you get me a taxi – fast?' she asked. 'Take that man's order and don't hurry with it, but give me plenty of time to get well away and then act the fool. He has almost no French at all.'

The young man grinned. 'And I speak no English, madame,' he said. 'I'm well known to be stupid – ask anyone. Give it two minutes and a taxi will be at the door. You'll be safe in it: the driver is my brother-in-law.'

Melinda thanked him and was delighted to discover that his 'two minutes' had been no exaggeration. Thank goodness the building spanned the narrow road past its entrance in order to capture the view to best advantage, she thought. It meant no one in the dining-room could see anything at all of what went on in the street below.

It was a bit mean to leave Clive in the lurch like that, she reflected as the taxi drove into the square in front of the kasbah to turn round before driving back out as fast as safety allowed, past the *salon de thé*, past Great-Aunt Laura's gloriously painted house and back into the new city. Still, it served him right. She hadn't asked him to come after her and he certainly wouldn't have chosen to come to a place like Tangier off his own bat.

When he had reappeared on the scene after their perfectly amicable split, she didn't imagine that it had been pure coincidence that the size of her inheritance had so recently become known and his 'hypothetical' questions left her with few illusions about his real motives. Perhaps her mother had tipped him off about that, just as she'd tipped him off about where she'd gone. Mrs Upton had always approved of Clive – and why not? Melinda had liked him, too. He was good company and a useful escort and, if they'd married, they'd probably have rubbed along together better than most. Yet, even at the height of their partnership, she hadn't wanted it to extend to living together. She was quite sure those were reins it would be disastrous to try to pick up again. Khalil Benani had seen to that.

Odd that, she thought. I can't imagine being shacked up with him, either, but already he's given something no one else has, and I don't want that to grind to a halt, not yet – and not for the foreseeable future.

So why give Clive the slip? Why not do the honourable thing and tell him to go away and leave her alone? It had been mean just to disappear and it was likely to be inconvenient because he would stay in Tangier for a few days at least, trying to track her down, and she had no desire at all to bump into him again. She knew Clive well enough to know that she'd used the only strategy likely to work. He was an obstinate man and as conceited as most of his sex. He simply wouldn't believe she meant what she said. He'd think she was just playing hard to get.

No, she'd done the only practical thing. She just hoped there was no way he could find out exactly where she was. Thank goodness her mother had had no interest whatsoever in being told precisely where she was going.

Khalil pulled up outside the apartment block, his expression serious, deep in thought. Who would have thought Miss Melinda Carr would be quite such a beauty – and, as far as he could judge, such a chip off the old block. He hoped he was right about that bit. The long legs, the long blonde hair – those alone were enough to turn any man on. She wasn't coat-hanger thin, either, like so many European women these days.

She was slim, certainly, but lusciously curved in all the right places – a connoisseur's item, if ever there was one. He smiled to himself. He was going to enjoy helping her to realise her potential, a potential that, he guessed, was going to prove substantial. He had already realised how much she enjoyed sex but she had a long way to go before she had realised it in all its manifestations and he couldn't help wondering where she'd eventually draw the line. In the meantime, he was going to enjoy himself working on that potential. He glanced down. The very thought of the pleasures that lay ahead were already making the blood flow faster into his previously flaccid cock and already it was tingling in anticipation.

He opened the car door and reached across to pick up a single camellia from the passenger seat. He smiled. A single bloom. Women liked that. They thought it significant. He hoped it would make her even more receptive to some suggestions he might have for her. He'd have to play it by ear. He nodded to the concierge as he made his way to the lift.

Melinda opened the door. She was wearing her lustrous satin kimono, unsure what his plans were and even more unsure whether it would be a good idea to eat out with him yet. If Clive caught sight of him, would he create a scene either because she was with someone else or, more probably, because she'd made a fool of him earlier?

Khalil looked her up and down. 'Hmm. Interesting,' he murmured. 'An indication of how the evening is to proceed?'

He brought his hand from behind his back and presented her with the camellia.

Melinda smiled with genuine pleasure. It might be a hackneyed gesture but that didn't make it any the less welcome.

'Lovely,' she said and kissed him on the cheek. 'Thank you, Khalil.'

He returned the kiss, but firmly on her mouth this time. As he did so, his hands undid her loosely tied sash and slipped beneath the softly draping folds of the kimono to the bare skin of her waist, his fingers slipping down beneath the elastic of a minute black G-string.

Desire immediately flooded Melinda's veins and she opened her lips so that their tongues could meet and mingle, teasing each other in the dark, moist little cave of her mouth. She sighed with pleasurable anticipation and was rewarded with the feel of his hands stroking the cheeks of her buttocks as he eased the skimpy G-string over them so that it was free to slip to the floor. He reached for the hand that was still holding the flower.

'Put it in water,' he said softly.

'Now?' It seemed an odd thing to be asked to do at this precise moment.

'Yes, now.' His smile was enigmatic.

Melinda frowned briefly, puzzled, wondering if she would ever work out what went on in his mind. When she returned from the kitchen, she realised there was no great mystery about it on this occasion.

Khalil was waiting for her, sitting on the chair over which he had thrown her the night before. He was fully clothed but his legs were wide apart. 'Kneel down,' he commanded her.

She did as she was told, her kimono forming sensuous silken folds around her as she did so, concealing and then revealing first one part of her semi-naked body, then another. Guessing what he had in mind, she unfastened his belt and then the catch at the waist of his trousers.

'Now you get to enjoy your stick of sugar candy,' he murmured, reaching for her breasts and lifting each

72

one out of its half-cup so that each rested, invitingly available, on the wired fabric beneath.

Melinda soon freed his rapidly engorging cock and, as it sprang free, she ran her tongue up its length to tantalise, with a delicate, butterfly touch, the swollen bulb at its tip. As her tongue flicked away the first beads of pre-come, she could feel his prick twitch with delight and hear him catch his breath. Then he reached for her nipples, pinching, tweaking and pulling them into the hardness of receptivity.

'This really turns you on, doesn't it?' she whispered. 'Do you want me to bring you off completely?'

He shook his head. 'Later, maybe. For now, just do as you're told. Get up.'

As Melinda obeyed, his tongue, obliged to leave her breasts, retained its contact with her body until it was able to probe the divide between those other lips, to play with them, teasing the nerve endings with the promise of entry.

Melinda's head was thrown back, her eyes closed, the better to enjoy the sensations of her mounting sexual pleasure – and then the mood abruptly changed.

'Enough,' he said. 'I want you on me. Now. Stand astride me and lower yourself on to your piece of candy.' His tone was rough, his hands already pulling her across him.

Melinda tried to pull back. 'Not yet,' she begged. 'Play with me some more. I need to be more moist. If I'm not, it hurts.'

'Not that much. Trust me. It will be no more than you like, I promise you. And relax.'

Melinda knew she had tensed and she knew that that alone would make penetration painful. She made the effort of will it needed to relax and was rewarded by Khalil's smile of approval.

She held her breath as she lowered herself on to his erection, exhaling a gasp of pure delight as it forced itself into her. The lack of her juices had produced a sensation all its own, slowing the rate of entry and generating a friction which carried its own excitement. It was a transitory enjoyment, for the very excitement it provoked was all it needed to stimulate her lubricating juices to an unprecedented degree.

'Was I right?' Khalil asked.

Melinda smiled her satisfaction. 'Oh, yes. You were certainly right.'

He held her close to him, his hands on her buttocks, enabling him to play around the sensitive rim of her opening while she bore down, clenching her muscles as she did so, the better to enhance the sensations she was able to give him. When he released himself into her with a sudden, upward thrust, Melinda gasped aloud and instantly, instinctively, screwed herself down upon him so that she could feel every inch of his emptying cock.

She felt him gently withdraw and breathed, 'No. Stay there. Come again.'

He shook his head. 'We've got all night. I said I'd stay. Remember? Besides, we haven't eaten yet. Come – we'll bathe. Together.'

She went willingly into the bathroom with him and, as she bent over to put in the plug and turn on the taps, his fingers inserted into her from behind and gave her the welcome news that this was unlikely to be a purely platonic bath. But when he reached past her to turn off the taps, she looked up at him, surprised.

'We'll use the shower,' he said. 'It would never do to flood the apartment. Come on.'

With the shower playing on both of them, he soaped his hands and ran them gently, caressingly, over her whole body, not for one moment forgetting the cleansing properties of a soap-softened finger high in the recesses of her most sensitive places, delighted to learn that there was nothing sated about her instinctive response.

Then it was her turn to massage every part of his body with the soapy softness of her hands and she tantalised him deliberately by taking her time before letting them smooth the tender skin of his groin, his thighs, before she began stroking and caressing his balls, knowing that his erection wouldn't be long in coming.

She heard him sigh with satisfaction before he turned her round so that she stood with her back towards him, his arms around her, one hand playing with her hardening nipples while the other toyed lightly, teasingly, with her clit.

That was when he turned the shower off and the taps on, and sat down in the bath, pulling her down with him. Now she could feel the tip of his cock against the rim of her pussy.

'You like it like this?' he asked.

Melinda nodded. 'I'd like it better still inside,' she told him.

The buoyancy of the water removed any effort and the time spent mutually washing each other made entry easy. It was another odd sensation for Melinda to be taken from behind in such a way that the force of his thrusting was no less, yet the sense of domination that rear entry always gave her was somehow muted by the water. This was fun, she decided. Maybe it wasn't her favourite way of doing it – she thought she hadn't yet discovered what that was, though she was quite sure Khalil would eventually show her – but definitely fun.

They came together this time and even the orgasm felt different, muted by the water without losing its intensity, and, when he withdrew, she lay back against him, supported in the warm water by his hand between her legs, the fingers still absent-mindedly playing with her clit as if its very presence wasn't something that could be ignored.

'I think you liked that,' Khalil said.

Melinda chuckled. 'So did you, I think.'

He didn't deny it. 'You seem to enjoy new experiences, new sensations.'

'Especially new sensations.' She smiled.

'From what I hear, you seem to be remarkably like your great-aunt.'

'Tell me about her.'

'I've nothing to tell. I never knew her. You know that.'

'But you know what's said about her and I'm beginning to draw my own conclusions.'

'Far better to do that, extending them as you go along, than have someone spell it all out for you in one fell swoop.'

'You're making me wonder if I shan't like what I hear,' Melinda commented.

'I think you read too much into what is only common sense,' Khalil replied. He shifted himself away from her just enough to enable him to reach forward for the chain and pull out the plug. 'Come on. Dinner. If we're not careful we'll be too late – and I've worked up an appetite.'

They were the last customers to enter the restaurant and Melinda had the feeling – and not for the first time – that it was only Khalil's presence that induced the proprietor to allow them to be served at all. She looked around her uneasily and glanced at the clock on the wall. At least they were unlikely to bump into Clive. He had probably been in bed for an hour by now.

Khalil caught her glance and sensed her unease. 'What's the matter?' he asked. 'Something's bothering you.'

'No, nothing. It's really quite late, isn't it?'

76

He frowned. 'Is that a problem? You have something lined up for tomorrow?'

'No.' She hesitated and then decided she might as well tell him about bumping into Clive. 'But at least he can't find out where I am,' she concluded. 'Even my mother only knows I've come to Tangier, and Tangier's a big place.'

Khalil didn't seem so sanguine about it. 'Your lawyer knows, though. At least, he must know the two addresses you already know yourself. Wouldn't he tell your mother if she asked?'

Melinda looked doubtful. 'I suppose he might if she asked. He shouldn't, of course – I imagine it comes under "client confidentiality" – but most people would probably take the view that an address needn't be confidential, especially not if my mother spins him some yarn about needing to get hold of me as a matter of urgency.'

'And you're quite sure you don't want to see this man?'

'Absolutely positive,' Melinda assured him.

'Then it's a good job you'll be changing your address in the morning, isn't it?'

'Am I?'

'You wanted to see your other property, didn't you? Your lawyer certainly got that impression very strongly. Well, it's ready now and there's no reason why you shouldn't spend the rest of your holiday there, if necessary. You said your English lawyer didn't even know of its existence, so he can't tell anybody, can he?'

So Idriss Karrouk had got straight on to the phone, Melinda thought, but she didn't comment on it. Instead she asked, 'Your office won't pass it on if Clive gets hold of them?'

'No.' He sounded positive. 'Mind you, I'll phone in the morning just to underline it. Does that make you feel happier?'

'Much. In fact, couldn't we go there tonight?'

'No. Tomorrow. There's no need to rush it. This Clive isn't going to find you before then and you'll need time to pack your things. Tonight we'll enjoy ourselves. Then tomorrow we can enjoy ourselves in very different surroundings.'

'Intriguing.'

He chuckled. 'That was the intention.'

When they had let themselves into the apartment and the door was safely locked behind them, Melinda turned to him. 'Are you really able to stay all night?' she asked, surprised at herself for feeling shy about it.

Khalil's index finger gently stroked her cheek. 'Tonight and every night until you go back to England – if that's what you want. You can always change your mind. I'll be sorry if you do, but that's your prerogative.'

'I can't imagine wanting to,' she told him.

He smiled. 'That might change. Women's minds tend to.'

'And tonight? Do you have some special delight in store for me tonight?'

'You mean do I have another special delight, I think. Not another novelty, perhaps. If we've got all night, we've plenty of time for a prolonged seduction. I want to feast upon you. I want to know your innermost desires because once I know them, I can set about satisfying them.'

'Even if they're rather shocking?' Melinda asked, glancing up at him speculatively from beneath her lashes.

'Particularly if they're rather shocking,' he replied. 'Where's the fun in things always being the same? I already know you like to be dominated but I'm not sure to what extent.'

Melinda took his face between her hands and kissed

him. 'You could always start by undressing me,' she replied. 'Unless you're a man who is better turned on by seeing his woman do a striptease for him.'

'My preferences aren't the object of tonight,' he said, his fingers already busy with the buttons of her shirt. When she made as if to stop him, he read the signs and gripped her wrist. 'Come with me,' he said, pulling her into the bedroom.

Here he stood her facing the mirror and eased her shirt off as she watched. His hands ran over her neck before descending and his teeth nuzzled the lobes of her ears while his fingers undid her skirt and let it, too, tumble to the floor. He watched its falling reflection. 'When will women realise that skirts, especially long ones, are so much more exciting than trousers? So much more seductively emerged from.' He ran his hands over her body and Melinda leant back against him, her eyes riveted on their reflection as she felt him harden against her.

'Watching it is good,' she whispered.

'I thought you'd find it so, though this can only be a taster. Black, I see,' he went on. 'They say Englishmen are turned on by black underwear.'

'Aren't Moroccans?'

He laughed. 'Moroccans are turned on by beautiful women.' He eased the G-string down, taking full advantage of the opportunity it gave him to caress her hips, her buttocks, to pass almost negligently across the Mount of Venus and feel her press herself against him as her desire warmed her loins into restlessness.

'Look at yourself,' he murmured. 'To see a woman naked below but not above, now that is a hundred times more arousing than just topless.' It might be so, but it didn't stop him undoing her bra and dropping it to join the rest of her clothes around her feet. 'You see?' he went on. 'Venus arising out of the waves.'

79

'I want to undress you,' Melinda told him, 'but I don't want to stop watching.'

'Then do it by touch,' he said, sinking his mouth into her neck and alternately kissing her neck and nibbling her ears while his hands continued their sensuous exploration, interrupted only to make her own task easier.

At last they both stood naked before their reflections. Khalil turned her sideways to the mirror and pushed her down so that she was kneeling before him. 'This time you don't just lick,' he said. 'This time I intend to come.'

And Melinda found she had no choice. There was nothing of gentle seduction in the way he rammed his cock into her mouth, but the very fact that he had chosen to do it like that, forcing her submission to his will, was exciting. She knew her body was trembling as her tongue furled itself around his prick, licking round and over it even as she sucked and her hands played with his hard balls rammed up tight against her mouth.

Suddenly, without having come, he withdrew, seized her by the arm and threw her on the bed. Not completely on, though. Her legs were over the edge and he pulled her roughly forward so that her hips were at the very edge of the bed. With another rough movement, he pushed her legs as wide apart as they would go and rammed his cock inside her with such force that she cried out even as she welcomed it with a shudder of delight that filled her whole body.

'Deeper,' she cried out. 'Deeper.'

Pausing briefly in his thrusting but staying within her so that she writhed against him, he brought each of her legs up in turn so that they were over his shoulders. It left her wide open to his continued pleasure and with no way of avoiding it even if she'd wanted to.

She didn't. Getting away was the last thing on her mind. She was completely in his power now and in the

80

headiness of her subjugation her only thought was to raise her hips still higher, to make possible even deeper penetration. She pushed against every thrust, feeling her excitement building, stroke by stroke and then, when his fingers joined in, playing with the swollen, eager clit, she came with a cry of pure delight, plunging against him, revelling in having no control at all of her ecstatic surges or his own continued thrusting. Then came his own climactic surge and with it the sense of being filled and overflowing and being able to do nothing at all about it.

He lowered her legs gently, without withdrawing, and Melinda knew he was still emptying into her. That was as it should be, she thought, the whole act completed and the juices ready to run out, to trickle warmly down her legs. This was what made a woman a woman.

He kissed her as he finally withdrew. 'Tired?' he asked.

She chuckled with warm pleasure. 'Knackered,' she replied, not caring whether he knew the word. She didn't think it would require explanation.

Khalil smiled. 'We shower, then we sleep.'

Melinda's eyes opened wide. 'Shower together? After that?'

'Together if you like, but only a shower.' He kissed her lightly. 'I think you'd let me, wouldn't you?'

Melinda sighed and moved against the last remnants of his escaping come. 'I think I would,' she agreed.

He laughed. 'A truly formidable woman,' he said. It didn't seem to be a criticism.

The warm shower made Melinda sleepier than she'd expected and she was surprised, after the intimacy she and Khalil had already enjoyed, how shy she felt about sleeping with him by her side. He seemed to have no such diffidence and she lay curled in his lap with his arms round her, finding comfort and security in the warmth of his presence.

'So that was your idea of gentle seduction, was it?' she asked.

Khalil chuckled. 'Not at all, but did you like it?'

'What a silly question. You know I did.'

'You really do like the man to take control, don't you?'

'Did you doubt me? Oh, fair's fair and in a long-term relationship it's a matter of give and take, but if I have the choice . . .'

'And this Clive? Did he give and take?'

'Not really. Well, not at all. He thought it was the mark of a prostitute to want to submit.'

'Do you share that view? Deep down, I mean.'

Melinda thought about it. 'No,' she decided. 'No, I don't think I do. It's just the way I'm made.' She turned to look at him. 'Do you think it is?' she asked.

'All I think is that we'd better go to sleep. You've got to pack in the morning. Remember?'

'A masterly evasion of the question,' she commented, but she couldn't pretend she minded what he thought, just so long as he humoured her.

Melinda stirred. She was lying on her back. She never lay on her back. Then she realised why. Her eyes still closed, she lay there enjoying the delicate touch of something between her legs. Something familiar. Something that had already made her warm and moist while she slept. A hand. Fingers. Khalil's fingers, gently searching, probing.

She stirred again. Should she let him know she was awake? No. The illusion was better. She let her head roll to the side. He could go on doing this till kingdom come, she thought. What a delicious way to be woken up! She allowed herself the luxury of a little groan. She wondered if he was just playing with her or whether

82

he intended to take her. It didn't much matter. This was nice. This could go on as long as he liked.

She was aware of her legs being pushed gently, so gently, apart and knew, without opening her eyes, that Khalil was between them now. She felt the first tantalising touch of his bulbous tip against the fair curls of her pussy, against the small cleft, brushing against her labia, and she moved to increase the sensation, the delicate stimulation. Gentle fingers parted the already swollen lips and held them lightly apart while he found his way in.

He paused at the opening, pressed against it, retreated – but not enough to lose contact – and then pressed forward again until, with a cry of exultation that no simulation of sleep could control, she felt his cock surge over that initial barrier and plunge into the waiting cave of warmth and moisture.

She clenched her muscles round its shaft and heard Khalil's groan of pleasure as he pumped into her, slowly, steadily at first and then with increasing speed that built into a pure frenzy, thrusting, screwing himself into her near-inert body. Melinda knew that, although she was immersed in enjoyment of every movement inside her, her body's reactions were reflexes in which her own desires played little part. Every movement, every thrust, had her crying out for more. She kept her legs stiff, trying to minimise her response, and found that somehow this only increased the excitement.

This really was being taken. This was what she had always dreamed of – and the reality went far beyond the expectation. She had a strong suspicion it was exciting Khalil at least as much as anything they'd done before, and quite possibly more. So the realisation of her own fantasy had satisfied both of them. That, surely, must be perfection.

He came suddenly and left her, not caring this time

whether she had come or not. This in no way left Melinda frustrated: the realisation of a fantasy saw to that.

'When did you wake up?' he asked her.

Melinda shrugged. 'I don't know. There was a sort of half awakening. When you went in, that was when I truly woke up.' She shivered with pleasure. 'You know how much I love that moment.'

'And the rest of it?'

She smiled at him in the darkness. 'Let's just say that I enjoyed it at least as much as you did – and I think that's saying something.'

'You don't hear me complaining.'

Melinda smiled. She'd been right then. She lay there, listening. No sounds from outside. It must still be night. 'Do you know what time it is?' she asked.

'Why? Does it matter? It's still night. Go back to sleep.'

She turned over and closed her eyes, completely happy. She thought she felt him leave the bed; she was sure she heard the shower and she definitely felt him climb back in beside her, but that was all she knew till morning.

Chapter Five
Wednesday

Melinda was the first to wake up. The sounds from outside told her it was late but what did that matter? She turned her head to study Khalil's sleeping body beside her and suppressed an urge to run her fingers through his dark, beautifully styled hair, suppressing, too, the urge to kiss his unsuspecting cheek. No, let him sleep on, she thought, snuggling down again beneath the sheet and revelling in the cosy, companionable warmth.

It wasn't long before the light outside was strong enough to penetrate even the closely fitting slats of the shutters and Melinda glanced at the little travelling alarm beside the bed. Half past nine. Half past nine! She was supposed to be packing to move to her other house today – the one she was so anxious to see, the one that had been called a 'mansion' in an area of houses described as 'palaces'. They had to be overstatements but that thought did nothing to lessen her curiosity.

First, they both had to get up, both had to bathe, and both would want breakfast. Goodness only knew when they'd get to this intriguing property of hers. Not that it probably mattered very much. It was just that the later they were about outside in the city, the more likely they were to bump into Clive.

She studied the figure beside her again. Khalil was still sound asleep and Melinda debated what to do. She could slip out of bed, bathe and dress, get herself some breakfast and take him a cup of coffee. She smiled wryly. Just like a good little wife, she thought, a thoroughly domesticated woman – only that wasn't a role she had ever wished on herself.

It was one of the reasons she'd always shied away from boyfriends, no matter how much she'd liked them, as soon as they began to think in terms of marriage, whether on a general or specific level. She'd always told herself she didn't love them enough, that when 'Mr Right' came along, she'd be as ready to rush to the altar as the next woman. Deep down, she wasn't so sure.

What she was quite sure about was that Khalil wasn't the elusive 'Mr Right'. She studied the line of his nose, the curve of his lips with their permanent hint of a smile. He was charming in the social sense and he was the most brilliant lover she'd ever had but she had a strong hunch that whoever he married – or was already married to, for that matter – would become little more than a cross between an unpaid housekeeper with home comforts on tap and a decorative object to be trotted out from time to time when it suited him. Taking care not to wake him up and then bringing him coffee in bed would send out quite the wrong message. Even if it reflected her own underlying desire (which it emphatically didn't), it was more likely to make him grab his trousers and run than to appreciate the gesture for what it was – and that would be a pity.

So she gently kissed the smoothly muscular curve of his shoulder and slid her fingers on to his leg, softly, delicately, letting it tiptoe up the sensitive skin on the inside of his thigh, returning the compliment of the night before. Her fingers played, oh-so-gently, in the little valley of skin between his balls, straying from there to the penis lying limply across the other thigh.

She could feel life begin to stir within it, barely perceptibly at first but with its strength increasing with every tiny touch of her fingertips, and she wondered how much of these small, preparatory surges he was conscious of.

As her fingers felt the blood begin to flow with a more determined strength and his cock grew and stiffened, Melinda slid beneath the sheet, half turning her body, the better to enable her tongue and her lips to take over from her fingers. She kissed and she licked the full length and circumference of his shaft and was more than half of a mind to take it fully into her mouth. But was that the most sensual pleasure she most wanted right now? Was it the one that would pleasure Khalil most? She remembered with a smile the way he had taken her during the night. She had little doubt each had drawn as much pleasure from that as the other. Perhaps a minor adjustment to the template would create a rewarding experiment.

She glanced at his face. Khalil still appeared to be sleeping but she knew from her own experience that he must be at least half conscious of his stirring desire, maybe more. Maybe he was just intrigued to discover how she intended to proceed.

Melinda knelt across him, taking care not to touch anything except his still-swelling cock, which she continued to stroke with gentle, fluttering fingers. She bent down and kissed its tip, running her lips delicately across the slit.

Simply thinking about it made her own blood run more vigorously, filling her desire and making her more receptive for what was to come. She knew she wasn't yet as moist as she wanted to be but she knew, too, that he was as ready for her as he had ever been. She recalled the brief but exciting sensation of his penetration when it had come early in her readiness. Why not again?

She raised herself on her knees above the erect pillar beneath and lowered herself towards it, giving a short gasp of delight as it brushed the gateway to its goal, sending a tremor of pleasure through her veins. Her hand held it more firmly now, guiding it to its target between her widely straddled legs and lowering herself upon it as she did so. She was still tight but, suddenly, resistance vanished and, with a moan of sheer joy, she sank down on to his cock, savouring the sensation of total fusion.

He must be awake now, she thought, remembering how fucking her that night had so fully woken her. Perhaps he wants to play the same game. She smiled. Playing games was what it was all about. She lifted herself to the point of near withdrawal and plunged herself downwards, and when he was deep within her, she tightened her muscles around the welcome invader, to relax them again before lifting herself once more.

This time she lifted too far and felt him leave her. Her near panic was quickly assuaged when it re-entered without help almost at once, thoroughly coated now with her juices. She needed only to press her pelvis down upon him to induce the fullest sensation for her own gratification. She raised herself and plunged repeatedly, steadily, so that his cock-tip teased the nub of her clit. As it did so, the rhythmic speed changed and Melinda wondered how long she could maintain this. For ever wouldn't be too long. She wanted to prolong it and she wanted to come, and the two goals were incompatible. It was difficult to decide which she wanted the more.

The decision was snatched from her control when Khalil came suddenly to life, gripping her to him at a moment when he was most deeply plunged inside her. He thrust upwards into her while he held her hips close to him. Melinda might have been the initiator but he had overturned the relationship and snatched control.

She knew she was powerless to draw away from him even had she wanted to. He was the aggressor now and she loved every minute of it, her head thrown back and her eyes closed in ecstasy while her lips parted to release her groans of pleasure.

He was coming. She could feel it. She wasn't far off herself and she wondered briefly if he would roll the two of them on to their sides, the better to spurt inside her. The matter was soon resolved when the rapid succession of upward thrusts, so strong she felt they'd come out through her mouth, released his spunk in pulses that matched her heartbeat. She felt him empty in her, the precious fluid then trickling, thickly, down her legs.

He held her fast, even though she knew he was shrinking inside her. Now his fingers played with her, sometimes entering, sometimes teasing, and Melinda could feel herself rising to another orgasm. She didn't care whether he hardened within her or whether she came on his fingers as every nerve responded to their touch. It was to his fingers she came, suddenly, wildly, barely conscious that his dick had been withdrawn.

'My God,' Khalil whispered. 'How much you're going to enjoy yourself from today on. I reckon I could lick you to another orgasm right now.'

'Why don't you?' Melinda asked, smiling. She didn't expect to be taken at her word. But she was.

With one powerful gesture, Khalil rolled her over on to her back and sank his tongue into her without preamble, flicking it across her clit, which was still excited from what had gone immediately before. The result was electrifying. As the tip of his tongue made contact, all the muscles within her reacted. Her hips rose towards his tongue in the rapture of orgasm.

'Again,' she breathed as she came in uncontrollable spasms. 'Please. Again.'

Khalil shook his head. 'Another time, I promise. Now we shower – but not together.'

Melinda chuckled. 'Spoilsport.'

He kissed her cheek. 'Let's just say I'm saving myself. I'll go first.'

Melinda lay on the bed, listening to the water running. That had been amazing. She'd never imagined a tongue could have so devastating an effect. And what exactly had he meant about how much she was going to enjoy the rest of her stay?

'Miss Carr,' she heard him call. 'Come here. I've finished.'

He had, but he was standing, quite dry and quite naked, beside the bath. 'Your turn,' he said. 'I want to watch. Do you mind?'

'Not at all,' she replied demurely. 'Whatever turns you on.'

What might, had she been alone, have been a workmanlike shower became something quite different with Khalil standing watching. It became entirely natural to take her time over it, to soap herself every bit as sensuously as he had soaped her the other time. She noticed – she could hardly fail to – that when her hands fondled her breasts and passed slowly down to clean her pubic hairs and on to the seat of so much pleasure, his cock began to stiffen. She'd always heard it was the visual tease that turned men on. If ever she'd been unconvinced, here was the proof.

She emerged from the bath into the waiting towel he held for her and he wrapped it round her like a sarong, following her into the bedroom where their clothes were waiting. His arm suddenly reached round her and undid the towel. 'Time for a quickie,' he said, thrusting her down so that her hands were on the bed, her buttocks high in the air. He slid his hand between her legs. 'Spread them,' he commanded.

Melinda obeyed without question. She hadn't expected this and her cunt twitched with anticipation. He was in her immediately, driving himself deeper and deeper with a rapidity that suggested the clock was against him. The onslaught was so sudden, the thrusting so deep and fast, that Melinda was barely able to do more than submit. Is this what rape is like? she thought. An animal thrusting into you and eliciting no sensation in return? The very thought was enough to spur her to a brief, intense orgasm which reflected the intensity with which it had been induced.

It was over almost as soon as it had begun but it left her feeling as if it had been prolonged to the point of exhaustion. Had that been fun? Melinda wasn't convinced that 'fun' was the right word. It had certainly been different. Interesting, too. And, of course, she'd been entirely willing.

While Khalil showered again briefly, Melinda packed her suitcase and while she douched and dressed, he took it down to the car.

'A little late for breakfast,' he said when she emerged from the bathroom, clean and elegantly dressed, every inch the cold, classic Englishwoman. 'We'll stop off for an early lunch: they won't be ready to serve a meal at the house yet. After today, restaurants will be superfluous – unless you prefer to use one, of course.'

He took her to a small Italian restaurant not far from the central Place de France where, even this early in their working day, the atmosphere was subdued and intimate. It was just the sort of place Clive used to take her to, Melinda thought ruefully, but not the sort of place he was likely to go to on his own: it was too obviously designed for couples.

She was wrong. As she wound the tagliatelle of her

carbonara round her fork, she glanced up at the opening door and, to her dismay, saw Clive come in. He seemed not to have noticed her and she guessed he had chosen this place because 'Italian' was a degree of foreignness with which he felt at ease, a consideration which would have overcome any wariness about being single in a place so obviously not designed with singles in mind.

Khalil caught the dismay on Melinda's face and turned to follow her gaze. 'Is that the man you bumped into yesterday?' he asked quietly.

Melinda nodded. 'And this is just what I was dreading,' she said.

Khalil grinned. 'Then you shouldn't have been so keen to delay our departure,' he pointed out.

The new arrival had spotted them by this time and came over. 'Melinda! What happened to you yesterday? It was very embarrassing to be left standing like that. It makes a man look ridiculous.'

'And we mustn't do that, must we? I'm sorry but something came up.'

'Something so urgent that you couldn't even stop to leave a message?' His annoyance was clear.

'What would have been the point? You don't speak French and none of the waiters would have been able to pass on a message in English and by the time they'd found me some paper and a pen, too much time would have been wasted.'

Clive stared at Khalil with obvious displeasure. 'Who's your friend?'

Melinda opened her mouth to make introductions but Khalil was there before her.

'I'm Benani, Miss Carr's business agent in Morocco.'

'Business?' Clive sounded suspicious. 'I didn't know she'd inherited business interests here. I'm sure she'd have mentioned it, since I'm excellently placed to give her advice on business matters.'

'Without wishing to be rude,' Khalil said with polite firmness, 'I doubt it if you speak neither Arabic nor French and have no previous experience in dealing with business in our very different culture. Miss Carr mentioned bumping into you yesterday. She was clearly under the impression you knew she had inherited property here. It's the management of those properties that I handle, much like an estate agent in England will manage rentals and so on for absentee landlords.'

'And that business is profitable enough for you to take your client out to lunch, is it?' Clive made no attempt to disguise his scepticism. 'Or is she taking you? I imagine you got in there fast enough when you realised you were on to such a good thing.'

'Clive!' Melinda protested, aghast at his manner, to say nothing of his manners.

Khalil silenced her protest with one raised hand. 'My company handled the properties for Miss Carr's great-aunt,' he said, his voice deliberately level, refusing to be provoked by the other man's antagonism. 'When my father was alive, he was the agent. He handled the late Miss Carr's business personally. I've simply taken over from him.'

'And for the record, Clive, the idea of "going Dutch", let alone allowing the woman to pay, is anathema to a Moroccan,' Melinda interjected.

Clive snorted disparagingly. 'You think so? I dare say you're paying for it through the commission he deducts. How much is that, by the way?'

Melinda flushed, as much with anger as with embarrassment. 'It's none of your business, Clive. Nothing I choose to do, nowhere I choose to go, is anything whatever to do with you. Not now. Not ever. I'll do what I damn well please. I'm answerable to no one and least of all to you. What's more, that's the way I like it. If there's one thing inheriting Great-Aunt Laura's wealth has taught me it's that I like being independent – and that sort of money enables me to be as independent as I like. You get the message?'

Clive was not the sort of man who relishes scenes in public and he certainly wasn't a man to appreciate being made to look a fool two days running. He reddened with mingled fury and frustration. 'I get the message loud and clear,' he said and turned his gaze on Khalil. 'It will serve you right, Melinda, if you wake up one morning and find this man has cheated you out of every penny you own.'

'Yes, it will,' Melinda agreed. 'Only if there's one thing I've discovered it's that he's a very shrewd businessman – far too shrewd to risk killing the goose that lays the golden eggs and is likely to go on laying them for the foreseeable future. Now, if it's all the same to you, I was enjoying my lunch.'

Clive looked as if he hoped it would choke her. 'I'm going,' he said. 'I'll be on the first available flight back to England.' He glanced at Khalil again. 'But first I shall have a word with the police about this man. I don't think you should trust him and for old times' sake, if nothing else, I'd like to see your interests protected.'

'Very magnanimous, Clive,' Melinda said. 'Quite unnecessary, though, I assure you.'

Khalil, clearly unmoved by the threat, smiled. 'Then to save you the hours and hours they'll keep you waiting in police headquarters – which would seriously hamper any early departure you had planned – the officer you will need to contact is Commissaire Larbi. He's very senior and if you ask for him by name, you'll be able to miss out several of the lower rungs on the ladder.'

The Englishman made no reply but turned on his heel and stormed out of the restaurant.

'I wonder if he will go to the police,' Melinda mused as the door slammed behind him.

Khalil shrugged. 'It doesn't matter. Sooner or later he'll end up with Larbi, and Larbi's a friend of mine. A very useful friend.'

'Will you warn him about Clive?'

'No need. Larbi's no fool. He'll get his measure easily enough and send him packing. I'm only trying to hasten his departure. You can forget this Clive now. Let's finish this and be on our way.'

The black Mercedes drove deeper into the city and then out again, past the Grand Mosque, steadily climbing hills clothed with the sprawl of newly developed housing, each block with its accompanying range of neighbourhood shops. The further they went, the better the quality of the houses, until the signs of construction gave way to open country where sheep and goats grazed among groves of rustling eucalyptus and the occasional flash of pink oleander, the Moroccan substitute for the elder.

Houses now were few and far between. Some were isolated small farmsteads but others were large – certainly mansions, if not quite palaces, Melinda thought. They were set back behind high walls and metal gates, the wrought iron of which was backed with black-painted metal sheets to ensure total privacy. Only the top floors of these white-washed houses gave a clue to their size and, while some were flat-roofed in the traditional style, others seemed to owe more to the styles of France and Spain a hundred years before. Apart from the unavoidable impression of size, there was nothing remotely ostentatious about these mansions.

Nor was there anything outwardly ostentatious about either the gates they finally entered or the house ahead of them at the end of a tree-shaded drive. Melinda got out of the car and looked back. The man who had appeared from nowhere to open the gates was bolting them closed again. She wondered whether he was a caretaker or a gardener.

A gardener there must surely be to maintain the coarse grass which was obviously tended with great care in the vain hope that it might eventually resemble the close sward of a bowling green or an Oxford college's quad. There were plenty of trees and shrubs. Some, such as hibiscus, bougainvillaea and daytona, she knew from visits to the south of France; others were less familiar. More surprising were the peafowl. She counted six straight away, the two males perched on the green pantiles of the roof, their long tails decoratively breaking the horizontal line of the guttering as they rested against the white walls.

'This is it?' Melinda asked incredulously. 'Are you telling me this is the third house I've inherited?'

'This is it,' Khalil confirmed, smiling. 'You like it?'

'If the inside matches the outside, I shall love it,' she replied. 'And yet Great-Aunt Laura chose to live in that house in the medina? It's a charming house and I loved it but there's no comparison, no comparison at all.'

'I imagine it had something to do with the other house being more ... more private. No visitors were ever invited there, I believe. This house is well suited to entertaining visitors, as you will see. If things go as I hope, I think you'll begin to understand why Miss Carr chose to live elsewhere. Come. You'll want a tour of inspection.'

The indoor staff, a cook and two maids, were curious to meet their new employer but they also struck Melinda as being discrete to the point of unobtrusive. They had very demonstrably kept the huge house in excellent condition. Great-Aunt Laura might not have been there for years but it was very apparent that nothing had been allowed to fall into any degree of disrepair – and that its present state owed nothing to any last-minute restoration her sudden arrival might have provoked.

The rooms were as spacious and luxurious as the outside had intimated. The two sitting-rooms had been decorated and furnished, one in the Moroccan style, the other in the European and both with thick Rabati carpets on the marble floor and rich brocade upholstery and curtains. This was a house, Melinda observed, where the curtains could be drawn across as well as the shutters closed. The kitchen was the biggest and best equipped she had yet seen and the dining-room was heavily formal in the French style.

One room on the ground floor puzzled her, though. It was oval and, being in the centre of the house, windowless, though this was more than compensated for by mirrors round the walls above the crimson-brocaded divans that lined them, broken only by the doors. Low circular tables of intricately carved cedar-wood stood at intervals on the densely woven Fassi carpet so that no matter where anyone sat, a table was within reach. In the centre, a larger but equally low table was itself covered in a matching carpet of lighter weight.

'What a strange room,' Melinda remarked. 'What's it for?'

'This is a *majlis*,' Khalil replied. 'Traditionally it was used as a sort of council chamber. Everyone sat round, each equal with his fellows (which is why there's no table that anyone can be at the head of) to discuss and decide what was to be done in whatever situation had arisen.'

'But only men?' Melinda asked.

He looked surprised. 'Of course only men. Unless there was a female dancer or something like that. Now you need to see the rest of the house.'

'Why would Great-Aunt Laura have wanted a *majlis*?' Melinda asked.

Khalil shrugged. 'It had its uses. I dare say you'll

discover them soon enough.' He grinned at her. 'I hope so, anyway.'

Whoever had designed the house's interior had liked chandeliers – and mirrors, Melinda noted. The former were huge, ornate and would undoubtedly glitter magically when they were switched on. The effect would be enhanced and multiplied by the lights' reflection in the mirrors, some plain, some far from it, which took up almost every wall in every room, particularly the bedrooms. Here, they also formed a huge circular central panel in the ceiling immediately above the bed, of sufficient diameter to reflect beyond the bed, each punctuated by the huge chandelier at its centre. The biggest room of all was dominated by an ornate and gilded four-poster, whose curtains descended not from its own framework, but from the perimeter of the mirror. Each post was a heavily carved wooden pillar, further embellished with cords of golden silk wound round it, tassels dangling.

Each bedroom had its own bathroom, again characterised by the generous use of mirrors, but the bathroom attached to the room with the four-poster was particularly splendid, like something out of an Alma-Tadema painting. Melinda wondered whether it was one of those pseudo-classical scenes of naked ladies emerging from a richly tiled mosaic bath, deep enough to be sunk into the floor while at the same time being raised two steps above it, that had inspired Great-Aunt Laura to have it decorated like this. Great-Aunt Laura was turning out to have been a most unusual woman, Melinda decided. She would have been unusual today. Fifty, sixty years ago she must have been ... well, something else again.

'Which room will you have to yourself?' Khalil asked. 'I wouldn't recommend this one. I think you'd find it too vast to be able to relax in.'

'No, this isn't it. I can't really imagine who'd want to

98

spend a whole night in it. Well, a king or someone like that, perhaps, but I don't know an awful lot of kings.'

He laughed. 'Oh, it has its uses,' he said. 'I know which one I think is best for you – but you will, of course, feel free to choose another.'

Melinda saw no reason to disagree with his choice. The mirrors were disconcerting but they were unavoidable because every room had them. What she particularly liked about this one was the view over the gardens from the little iron balcony outside the full-length windows.

'I think you're right,' she said.

'Good. Then we'll go downstairs and have some mint tea while they busy themselves in the kitchen and then I'll ensure you're duly and properly installed.'

Melinda glanced up at him. She was beginning to realise that even his most mundane phrases often held another meaning. 'That sounds interesting,' she said.

'For both of us, I hope.'

No servant was in sight as they climbed the stairs, Melinda leading the way. Khalil was close enough behind her for his hand to glance across her bottom as if by accident but, brief as the gesture was, it was sufficient to disclose a small detail that he had previously and uncharacteristically missed. When Melinda had finally dressed that morning, she hadn't put on any panties under her dress. He chuckled and his hand slipped beneath the soft fabric so that, as her legs parted as each stair was ascended, he couldn't fail to provoke a twitch of excitement.

Melinda paused and looked round at him. 'Don't,' she said. 'Not here. Someone might see us. I'd be embarrassed.'

'The staff are discretion itself,' he replied, unmoved. 'They won't appear until they're sent for.'

'But this isn't like being in one of the rooms,' she

objected. 'They might have to cross the hall below at any time.'

'I thought you didn't mind the idea of being watched?' he replied.

'That's different,' she said, but made no attempt to analyse why.

Khalil laughed softly but his hand stayed where it was. 'Then the sooner you get to a room where you can close the door, the better.'

He closed the door of her chosen bedroom behind them and turned the key. 'That should put your mind at rest,' he commented. 'You'll soon learn that those three women really are the very souls of discretion. In the meantime, turn round. I want to look at you.'

She turned to face him, relaxed, her hands at her sides, and was unsurprised when he undid the buttons of her dress slowly, one by one. His hand toyed briefly with her unprotected breast and he smiled. 'I wonder what your friend Clive would have thought had he realised you wore only a dress.'

'He wouldn't have approved – not in public, that is,' she told him. 'In the privacy of the flat he might have found it quite a turn-on. I wouldn't know. It never crossed my mind to try it out.'

'But now, I think, you've learned to enjoy living a little more dangerously.'

Melinda laughed. 'I've found I like the idea that things aren't necessarily what they seem.'

'And that someone might decide to take advantage of them?'

'There's always that chance. That's where the risk lies.'

'And what if the someone isn't one whom you want?'

'Like I said, that's where the risk lies.'

'A dangerous game.'

'Perhaps, but it adds spice.' Melinda made as if to step closer to him but his hand stopped her. He gestured to the surrounding mirrored walls. 'This is how mirrors should be used,' he said. 'For the moment, looking at you – really looking at you – is what I want.' And with these words he slipped her dress off and folded it neatly across a chair.

He stood behind her and turned her slowly in front of the mirrored walls so that he could study her from every angle. His fingers crept round from behind her to tease the nipples of each breast and he watched them harden in reflection, standing close enough for her to feel that he was hardening, too, against the curve of her naked buttocks. It was instinctive to push them out towards him. Is this how he wants me this time? she wondered. It was something she'd thought about, read about, but she wasn't at all sure it was something she wanted.

If buggery had been in Khalil's mind, it didn't seem to be something he was ready to pursue just yet for, his inspection apparently complete, he lifted her in his arms and laid her gently on her back on top of the bed. So gentle, so symbolically romantic, was this gesture that Melinda was anticipating a gentle, seductive possession of her body and expected him to undress in preparation while she watched. Instead, he knelt in front of her at the foot of the bed, and an excited shiver went through her as she recalled the electrifying licking she had experienced earlier. He surprised her again.

With only a passing flutter across her sex, he parted her legs and pushed them up so that her feet were flat on the bed and her knees fell naturally apart, revealing still more of her most intimate parts. Melinda realised he was examining her as closely as any doctor, occasionally enjoying the reflection of her rapidly moistening pussy. She caught sight of herself in the ceiling mirror and was surprised how much it revealed. But touch was what she wanted. This was nothing but a tantalising tease and she wanted more. 'Go in,' she breathed. 'Make me come.'

He shook his head. 'I want to see you bring yourself off. You're ready for it. If you don't, you'll be left without.' His voice left her in no doubt that he meant it.

Melinda had no objection to wanking herself. She'd done it before when she had no man to relieve her frustrations, but she'd never before had one standing there watching her do it. She'd heard that some men were excited by it. She found the whole idea pretty exciting herself.

She ran her fingers lightly along the sensitive skin on either side of her pussy and across her now swollen lips. These she tweaked as she ran her fingers around the rim of her moist opening before sliding her long middle finger between them, exploring the space within which even her splayed legs and the enveloping mirrors didn't reveal. She closed her eyes, the better to enjoy the myriad sensations her other hand could induce as she played with her lips and her clit. And then she could control herself no longer, thrusting herself against her finger in a rapidly accelerating rhythm until suddenly she was drained. Finished.

Or so she thought. No sooner had she collapsed, exhausted, than she felt her legs being raised and she opened her eyes to find Khalil, naked now, his cock rampantly swollen and rigid, lifting them on to his shoulders, the better to obtain the widest, most generous access.

Believing she must be exhausted, Melinda moaned, 'No,' and was ignored. Khalil pushed himself easily into her well-moistened cavity, provoking another moan, this time of pleasure at the moment of entry. She recognised that the pleasure was twofold: there was the immense bliss she always felt at that magic moment of penetration, and the realisation that any exhaustion had been purely transitory.

She raised her legs still higher, crossing them behind his neck so that her hips were raised, her sex more easily available, his thrusting deeper and more satisfying. 'Harder,' she breathed. 'Harder. I want it to hurt. I want to be taken so hard that I'm finished. Till I ache to the point of madness – and then to be taken again.' And as she said this, she climaxed in a convulsion of shattering satisfaction, as if the very expression of such desires were all it needed to bring about their realisation.

Perhaps they had the same effect on Khalil. She couldn't know for sure but, whatever the reason, he climaxed with her, two bodies in perfect unison and when, the pinnacle of their orgasms reached, he lowered her legs while still pulsing into her, she still found herself raising her hips, the better to receive him.

He relaxed on to her without withdrawing. 'You need more than any one man is likely to be able to supply,' he said. 'Such a man may exist but as rarely, I think, as another woman like you. Many men dream of an inexhaustible woman but few can satisfy one on their own.'

Melinda studied his face, expecting to see signs of self-mockery – but there were none. He was entirely serious. 'What are you saying?' she asked. 'Exactly, I mean.'

He slid out of her then and pulled the edges of the satin coverlet over them both as if modesty was now a requirement. 'I've learned a lot in a very few days about your sexual desires and needs, and a bit about your fantasies. You thoroughly enjoy sex and you prefer your partner to be dominant to the extent that you fantasise about being forced, although you know you'd hate it if it happened for real. You're willing to give

103

pleasure, too. You're willing to experiment. And so far you seem to be virtually insatiable.'

Melinda chuckled. 'I can't quarrel with any of that,' she said. 'I can't really be insatiable, though. It's just that when I feel I can't go on, it only takes a touch to change things. There must be a point at which that touch will stop working.'

'Why don't you set out to find out?' he suggested.

'What a happy thought!' she replied. 'But you've already made it clear that you're not the one to do it. Do you know someone who is? They'd have to be very good indeed to be better than you, though.'

'A nice compliment. I'm glad you enjoyed me. I've certainly had great pleasure in making myself available to you. No, I don't know any one man but you've already indicated that you'd have no objection to being watched. What if the watchers took their turn?'

Melinda was silent while she thought about it. It must have definite attractions for her, she decided, because even the thought of it was making her cunt moist again. And what an opportunity it would be for variety – at least, there would be variety if they were interested in something beyond a quick and boring fuck.

'As long as those turns were each designed to achieve mutual satisfaction and not just instant gratification for them. With that proviso, it might be good fun.'

'You'd be willing to try it?'

Melinda hesitated. 'In theory, yes, but what if I found I didn't want to go on? Would I be able to call a halt?'

'If I'm truthful, that could be difficult because a lot would depend on how aroused you'd made them by letting them watch what had gone before, but they'd be here at my invitation and the ground rules would be explained to them. I think I could ensure several days of pleasure for all sides.'

'Here?' Melinda made no attempt to hide her surprise.

'Can you think of a house better equipped for that sort of entertainment?' he asked.

Melinda grew thoughtful. 'No, I can't. Didn't you say Great-Aunt Laura kept it for entertainment, keeping the other house for privacy?'

Khalil smiled but said nothing.

'Are you telling me that Great-Aunt Laura ...? No wonder the family never spoke about her! No wonder there were winks and nods galore when I inherited!' She laughed. 'Well, who'd have thought it? All the same, I don't quite see ... I mean, how did it work? There are aspects I don't quite understand.'

Khalil shrugged. 'You don't need to. Understanding will come soon enough and while I'm around, you'll be in no real danger. Do you want to change your mind?'

Melinda shook her head, a mischievous smile on her face. 'I don't think so. It could be fun.'

Khalil unwrapped himself and made for the bathroom. 'It could indeed.' He looked down at her speculatively. 'Some genes seem to be very persistent, don't they?'

He turned to go but Melinda caught his hand. 'There is one thing I want to ask you,' she said.

'Yes?'

'When I was sucking you –' Melinda could feel herself warming at the very thought and wondered if he was, too '– you said you wanted to come like that but, before you did, you took me in my pussy instead. Why? Wasn't I sucking you the way you like?'

He laughed. 'You were perfect,' he assured her. 'It wasn't that at all. Your mouth is the size of every woman's mouth but your cunt isn't. It's a tight fit even for me. I'm not small by any means but many are bigger. To force oneself into you is like taking a virgin, and when you tighten yourself around a man's prick as

105

well . . .' He gave a little shiver of delight and Melinda saw that just thinking about it made him ready for more. She reached up a hand.

'Then take the virgin again,' she suggested softly, rolling over on to her stomach and spreading her legs invitingly.

She heard him gasp at the unexpected invitation and thought he was going to decline, but then his clothes were tossed on to the floor and his hand was inside her, demanding access, then guiding his cock to its goal. As he plunged forward, Khalil pulled her towards him, holding her so tightly that she could do nothing but receive thrust after thrust, her loins tingling with the need to come. How she enjoyed the frustration of not being able to do more than receive; how much more exciting the orgasm would be when it came – and how much more she felt possessed when he came inside her. He thrust a finger down against her clit and Melinda came with a shriek of pure delight at the double stimulus within her. He eased the pressure straight away, relaxing his thrusts into a steady, rhythmic pumping that once more filled her with delight.

Then he withdrew without preamble, without apology, and disappeared into the bathroom, leaving Melinda shaking with both pleasure and surprise.

When he emerged, he kissed her briefly on the cheek. 'I'm exhausted, even if you're not,' he joked. 'Don't look to see me again today. I may be back tonight but probably not. I've too many men to see, too much to arrange. When you're ready, the women will have a meal for you.' He glanced at the bed. 'You'd better get them to remake this, too.'

'But then they'll know what was going on!' Melinda protested.

He laughed. 'Of course they know what's going on. Why else do you think they need to be discrete? Believe me, you pay them enough. Now don't suddenly turn back into a little bourgeoisie. Tell them to remake the bed. You'll sleep more comfortably and it will allow you to restore your energies to the maximum. You'll need plenty of energy if you're going to test yourself to your limits.' He paused with his hand on the door and turned to study her for a few moments. 'Have you ever been buggered?' he asked suddenly.

Melinda flushed. 'No.'

'Fancy the idea?'

Yesterday she'd have said no. Remembering her suspicion a little earlier this afternoon when she'd thought he was going to do exactly that, she wasn't so sure. 'I might,' she said cautiously.

He laughed. 'I'll take that as a yes,' he said and let himself out.

Chapter Six
Thursday

Melinda was woken up by the sun streaming on to the peach satin of her coverlet as someone rolled up the shutters. She turned her head, more than half expecting to see Khalil and seeing instead one of the maids.

The woman must have heard the slight movement for she looked round and smiled when she saw Melinda was no longer asleep.

'Good morning, madame. I hope you slept well.' She nodded towards the decoratively painted bedside table where Melinda now noticed a delicate porcelain matching breakfast set. 'Benani said English tea was probably what you'd like best but I can bring coffee if you prefer.'

'No, tea will be fine,' Melinda told her. 'You are . . .?'

'Latifa, madame. When would you like breakfast?'

Melinda considered. It wasn't often one had the choice. There was a definite appeal in this degree of luxury. 'I'll have a bath first,' she decided. 'Let's say an hour. By then I'll be ready for coffee and croissants.' At home she preferred tea for breakfast but somehow tea and croissants didn't seem a fitting combination, and she fancied croissants.

Latifa inclined her head in acknowledgement and left, closing the door quietly behind her.

The tea was delicious. Someone had certainly been taught how to make English tea. As for the china, Melinda wondered whether it had been Great-Aunt Laura's choice. Since it was Royal Worcester, that seemed highly likely and her late relative had certainly had a good eye. It began to look as if she had inherited more than just her great-aunt's property on the one hand and – apparently – her sexual appetites on the other. Melinda chuckled. How very distressing it must be for the rest of an ultra-conventional family to have a strain running through it of such very different inclinations.

She was halfway through running her bath when it occurred to her that this was probably one of Latifa's jobs. Did one call her back to do it? There was a bell-push beside the bed. Or should she have told her while she was there when she was going to want her bath? Melinda smiled to herself. She'd had no idea that having servants presented one with this sort of dilemma. Had she been brought up to this sort of life, she supposed she wouldn't even have had to think about it. I dare say it's a problem I can learn to take in my stride, she thought. Definitely.

She didn't hurry over her bath. There wasn't any rush and it was the first time since she'd been here that she had felt really free just to wallow in the warm, scented water without having to think about appointments or catching the bank while it was open or having to allow time to dress for breakfast in Havana.

She could eat her breakfast here in the nude if she'd a fancy to. Not that she had. That would seem very peculiar, especially on her own. *Déjeuner sur l'herbe* – now that was a very different matter, she decided, calling to mind Manet's very strangely matter-of-fact painting of a picnic where all the men were fully clothed and all the women weren't.

What did they do when they'd eaten? Dress and go home? Or share and share about? Perhaps they just touched and felt so that by the time they actually got home, the foreplay had been accomplished and they went straight into full-on sex. Were they respectable people playing games or were the women . . . what was the phrase at the time? Pretty horse-breakers. Yes, that was it. So much nicer than 'high-class whores' or even the almost respectable-sounding 'courtesans'. 'I rather like the idea of being a pretty horse-breaker,' Melinda said to herself aloud, and laughed. Perhaps that's just what I am – or what I'm becoming, she thought. Goodbye little bourgeoisie and hello pretty horse-breaker. And I just don't give a damn.

She climbed out of the bath and wrapped herself in one of the huge, enveloping bathsheets, revelling in the feel of the soft, dense pile against her bare skin. What had happened to the object of her horse-breaking experience so far? Khalil. Had he slept here or else-where? It was odd that, although she had spent several days longing for him to sleep with her and having been able to enjoy him for just one night, his absence last night hadn't really bothered her. He'd been right, though: she'd needed her sleep. It was rather more mortifying to her ego that he hadn't chosen to wake her up himself but had arranged for a maid to do it instead.

At the thought of the handsome Moroccan waking her up, she reached down to dry between her legs and decided she would have preferred it to have been Khalil's hands drying her all over. She had slept well, she was fully refreshed and few things would give her greater pleasure than to prove it to someone. Even the thought of this made her breathe a little unsteadily and

110

she decided it was probably a very good thing that she could hear Latifa with the breakfast things.

When she emerged from the bathroom, still wrapped in the bathsheet, the maid took one look at her and opened the large and very French ormolu-encrusted wardrobe and took out a dainty lawn and lace *peignoir*, which she handed to her employer. Melinda had seldom seen anything so beautiful and when she held the fabric against her cheek, the better to enjoy its delicate softness, the heady smell of exotic flowers filled her nostrils. She closed her eyes to inhale the perfume without distraction and when she opened them again, Latifa was watching her, smiling.

'Give me the towel, madame. I think you will find the *peignoir* more *comme il faut*.'

Melinda studied her reflection in the surrounding mirrors. The garment was surprisingly subtle. The light, dainty cotton weave was almost as transparent as the voile at the windows but it was cut with so much fullness from the lace yoke that it concealed the body beneath – until she moved. When she did, the fabric revealed brief and tantalising glimpses of her femininity before the folds rearranged themselves to conceal once more. It was, Melinda decided, one of those rare garments in which one couldn't help feeling sensuously seductive. Englishmen might prefer black stockings and suspenders, but for her money, this left them standing.

Latifa had laid out breakfast on a small table beside a deeply upholstered armchair, placed so that while she ate she could enjoy the sunlight as it filtered through curtains too closely woven to be described as 'net' but not so close as to obscure the view completely. The coffee was excellent, the croissants perfection and Melinda could only regret that she was already nearly halfway through her holiday. With luxurious treatment like this, it would be easy to regard sex as nothing more than an enjoyable bonus.

111

She moistened her finger to pick up the last flaky crumbs from the plate and then parted the curtains to stand on the small balcony overlooking the gardens and the sea. Such was the effect of the floating lawn touching first one part of her body, then another in the slight morning breeze, that she could almost have believed herself to be ethereal and not at all the woman of flesh, blood and sensual desire that she was beginning to recognise herself to be. She took a deep breath, inhaling the fresh breeze with its hint of a salty tang overlaid by the perfumes of the garden below. She knew herself to be a paradox and as she threw her head back, her eyes closed, allowing the sun to kiss her neck, she was entirely happy that there was nothing contradictory in this particular paradox.

The kiss on her throat that opened her eyes was not from the sun. Khalil was standing behind her, one strong hand on her waist.

'You were miles away, I think. Latifa says you slept well.'

'Yes, I did. Very well. I didn't hear you knock.'

'I didn't. I wanted to take you by surprise.'

'That could have been embarrassing for both of us,' Melinda pointed out.

Khalil shook his head. 'Interesting, perhaps. Not embarrassing.'

His hand was resting on her hip now, his longest finger laying negligently along the crease of her loin and as Melinda arched her back so that the cheeks of her buttocks could touch even more of him, she knew the paradox had vanished. There was nothing ethereal about what she felt now – neither what she felt nor what she wanted. Her need was rising fast but she determined to hold it at bay a little longer. What was it they said? To travel hopefully was better than to arrive? Balls, of course, but a tantalisingly long-drawn-out

112

journey might make the moment of arrival a hell of a lot more exciting.

'I haven't got my bearings here,' she said. 'Is that the bay or the Mediterranean?'

'Neither. You're looking at the Atlantic.' He pointed to the right. 'The straits are over there. Some days you can see them from here but not often. The Med is the bit beyond Gibraltar. This bit of the ocean is very sheltered but a few miles to the left and you'll be in the open Atlantic.'

'I can't see a single house from here,' she went on.

'You can't see any other buildings from any room in the villa,' he told her. 'You have total privacy. You can neither see nor be seen except from within the house.'

'I've never lived so totally cut off from the world before.'

'It has its advantages. Disadvantages, too. Does it bother you?'

She thought about it. 'I don't think so. It might if I were living here permanently but I'm not, am I?'

'I wouldn't recommend it.' He paused and Melinda could feel his breath stirring her hair. 'I need to ask you something,' he said at last, and she thought she detected a note of reluctance in his voice. 'It's personal. You may consider it too intrusive.'

Melinda frowned. This sounded too serious. She forced herself to keep her voice light and unconcerned. 'Well, if it is, I can always slap your face, can't I? Or just refuse to answer.'

She couldn't see his face but she could almost hear the grin in his voice. 'The latter option is the one I'd prefer – if you don't want to answer, that is.'

'You'd better get on and ask it, then, hadn't you?'

His hesitation was only brief. 'Do you think you've fallen in love with me?'

The question was such a surprise, so far removed from whatever ideas she might have had about what

113

he was going to ask, that Melinda could only spin round and stare at him.

'No!' she exclaimed, and immediately clapped her hand to her mouth, her aghast eyes looking up at him from above it. 'Oh, Khalil, I'm sorry it came out like that. I didn't intend to hurt your feelings, really I didn't, but . . .'

He pulled her hand down, smiling. 'You're not, I promise you. If I'm surprised, it's only that the answer came out so quickly, so unequivocally.'

She flushed, not entirely convinced that she hadn't inadvertently damaged a fragile ego. 'It's just that, well, we're so suited in bed that I'd already wondered about it, so I knew the answer. You're the best lover I've ever had and I like your company, too, but I can't delude myself I'm in love with you. I'm sorry if that isn't what you wanted to hear, but it's the truth.'

'It's exactly what I wanted to hear – and I suppose it's my turn to hope that saying that doesn't offend you, either. I asked because I've been setting up . . . certain arrangements for the next few days and nights and it would be quite wrong of me to let them go ahead if there was the least chance you were going along with them just to please me.'

'Do you think I would? Is that how you read me?'

He looked at her speculatively. 'I'm not sure. I don't think so, but then I remind myself that you have a preference to being dominated by the man.'

Melinda chuckled. 'Only in bed – and I've a feeling there would come a point at which I might even jib at that.'

'Really? What point?'

'I don't know and for the moment I'm not interested in finding out. But if I were in love with you and if you'd been making arrangements along the lines of some of the things we've been talking about, then I don't think I'd want to go along with it. It wouldn't be

114

compatible with love – not for me, anyhow. What's more, I've a feeling that if you were in love with me, you wouldn't even suggest it.'

'You understand me better than I'd realised,' he commented.

'As it is, I'm looking forward to some of the best nerve-tingling experiences of my life. I hope I shan't be disappointed.'

'I hope so, too. Come with me.' He took her hand as he spoke and led her back into the room and then along the corridor to the mirrored room with the enormous canopied four-poster.

'The rest of your holiday starts now. Here. With me,' he told her, undoing the small pearl buttons at the yoke of her *peignoir* and sliding it off her shoulders. 'On the bed,' he said.

She lay looking up at him. He seemed in no particular hurry to undress and she soon discovered why when he took her hand and swiftly, efficiently, tied it to one of the bed posts by means of the silken cord she'd assumed to be purely decorative.

Fear sprang into her eyes. 'What are you doing?' she asked.

Khalil smiled down at her. 'A superfluous question, I'd have thought,' he said as he did the same to her other wrist.

Melinda pulled against them. The cords binding her weren't painful but they weren't loose, either, and even as she made this discovery, he had tied her ankles to the posts at the foot of the bed. She lay spread-eagled on the rich brocaded silk.

Now Khalil undressed. He was in no hurry. Why should he be? Melinda thought. After all, I'm not going anywhere. She lay very still, part fearful, part excited. She watched his every move. Would he seduce her with hands and tongue? Or would this be a more violent taking? The bonds suggested that it wouldn't be gentle. She'd never been tied for it before and the thought of it made her cunt twitch and swell.

She remembered when he had taken her in the night and the different excitement of not allowing herself to respond. Now she wouldn't be able to, not outwardly, at any rate. Just thinking about it sent a shiver down her spine.

Khalil saw the tremor and smiled. 'If that's fear, you're being very wise,' he said quietly. 'I could do anything to you now. Anything at all, and there's not a damn thing you could do to stop me.'

She could see that the thought of that was exciting him. Already his cock was filling, lifting, and she stared at it, fascinated, unable either to accelerate her fate or delay it. She wasn't even sure what form that fate would take, and shivered again.

A huge vase stood on the floor a little distance from the bed and someone had cleverly arranged a display of peacock feathers in it. These were not just the beautiful eye-feathers of the tail but also the longer, two-pronged ones behind them and the shorter, bronze-green plumes that curved over to one side or the other; close to the rim of the vase were the short, soft feathers that made up the cushion of down which in life supported the displayed tail. Khalil took one of the eye-feathers and ran his hand along it.

Melinda watched, warily. 'You're not superstitious?' she asked. 'It's supposed to be unlucky to bring peacock feathers into the house. It's like bringing in the evil eye.'

'We regard it as fending off the evil eye: quite the reverse. Do they bother you?'

She was still looking askance at the feather. 'I hope your superstition is the right one,' she said and caught her breath with a sudden gasp as he ran the feather lightly across her breasts.

She knew fear had made the nipples harden and now

116

she felt the aureolae harden at the light, ephemeral touch of the magic eye. They must be darkening, too, she thought as the delicate sensation drifted down across the curve of her belly and played in the crease of her loin where Khalil's finger had lain. It induced a reflexive desire to move towards it, to enhance the sensation and draw it towards the more sensitive places below, but the cords held her firm. Such movement was impossible and the frustration only heightened both the sensations and the desire.

Melinda turned her head and could see that her torturer – for this was definitely a form of subtle torture – was aroused to the point that most men would have chosen to enter, so when he climbed on to the bed, she prepared herself for what she expected – and was confounded again.

This time Khalil lay beside her and took her hardened nipples between his lips, between his teeth, each breast in turn. He licked and caressed them while at the same time he sometimes bit, sometimes sucked at the nipple, evoking well-nigh unbearable sensations as she tried to thrust herself closer to him – and all the while, the feather touched, tickled, tantalised her groin, her thighs, her cunt.

The frustration of being able to enjoy but not respond, except in ways over which she had no control, drove Melinda into something close to an inner frenzy. She felt her lower lips swell and moisten and knew she was ready to be satisfied, even though she wasn't sure what sort of satisfaction was possible when she could barely move. She was soon to find out.

When Khalil had teased her breasts into maximum arousal, he let his mouth wander downwards, kissing and licking her body as it went, lingering over her belly and the smaller curve of her pubis, taking care to tantalise her loins on the way down to its true goal.

God! she thought. If his tongue does what it did

before, and I can't move ... I don't think I can bear that. 'No,' she moaned. 'Not your tongue. Not while I can't move.'

He took no notice. His tongue flicked over her lips, made easily accessible now that her legs were stretched as far apart as they would go, and touched briefly the space between. It left then, and Melinda gave a small sigh of relief that he had listened to her. Such relief was premature for, even as she sighed, the tongue was inside her, fully this time, then darting out, seeking and finding her swollen, sensitive clit. It was as if an electric current had been passed through her to make the whole of her pussy convulse with ecstasy while the bonds that held her firm ensured that all that sexual energy could only be expressed inwardly, intensifying the sensation still more.

Melinda cried out with pure, frustrated, pleasure. She longed – needed – to thrust towards the source of such ecstasy, but it was impossible. She couldn't even move her hips for release and then, when she felt she could bear no more, Khalil's tongue left her as he forced his stiff cock into her without preamble. Melinda's pussy was so small that, even with her legs asplay and her juices running, she knew that he would feel the extreme pleasure of her tightness.

She moaned and longed to wrap herself, arms and legs alike, round him, the better to feel him plunging inside her, but she couldn't. She could only be taken, possessed entirely, at the speed, the intensity, he chose, but her very lack of choice heightened every sensation he induced.

After his initial deep penetration, Khalil deliberately, calculatingly, regulated his invasion of her body, ensuring that his swollen cock brushed against her clit with each thrust. She could feel the whole length of him inside her, every nerve of pleasure rising to the sensation that passed and withdrew, passed and withdrew, until he had reached her physical limit. Then he thrust hard and fast until he came.

As if he knew she had only partly come herself, Khalil made no attempt to withdraw but lay there, his tongue playing with her breasts once more, his fingers feeling, stroking and caressing her still-swollen sex. Instinctively she responded the only way still available to her: she clenched and relaxed those inner muscles, which even on their own could excite a man to hardness once more.

His response was immediate and she felt him gradually stiffen and swell within her. Had she had a hand free, she thought, she could have stroked him into life as well. This way was slower but that didn't make it any the less pleasurable, and neither did the knowledge of her total helplessness.

As he grew and stirred within her, she felt her own intense desire for orgasm rising. She visualised the swollen, bulbous tip of his cock as it pushed its way into her like a thick snake. Again she had the frustrated urge to respond with the rest of her body but this time she channelled it in a different direction.

'Screw me,' she breathed. 'Screw me hard.'

And he did, rotating his slim hips against her with such force that she almost wondered if it were possible for his balls to enter her as well. He could penetrate no further, but the feel of his shaft inside was more intense than ever as the pressure of his cock rubbed hard up against her clit as well.

She came suddenly and, as she was still bound, the exquisite torture of orgasm was an unimaginable delight. She felt her release wash over his cock and knew she was entirely at Khalil's disposal, whether he chose to take her again or to withdraw, or whether he would leave her here, safely bound, until he was ready to possess her once more.

It was entirely up to him now. He had no need to

119

ask her what she desired and it didn't bother her at all. Maybe he'd leave her here like this until such time as he chose to put her at the disposal of others, as they'd discussed. Just thinking about that, even so soon after coming, caused Melinda's pussy to twitch in anticipation. She had no idea what was in store – and that suited her just fine.

But Khalil simply slid out of her, coating her inner thighs with warm juices as he did so, and knelt over her. 'Was it as good as you'd imagined?' he asked.

'Better by far,' she told him, 'and quite different. I'm intrigued to discover what you've got lined up for me next.'

He smiled. 'Oh, I think I've one or two things up my sleeve to try out.' His hand slid between her tied legs. 'I take it you're not finished yet?'

'You know I'm not. Isn't that the object of the game?'

He leant back and studied her face. 'Game? You've used that word before. That and "fun". Is that how you see this?'

'In the present context, yes. I'm developing an appetite I had no idea I had, and I'm loving it. I can't take it seriously. It's something I shall leave behind when I board the plane home and, meanwhile, I intend to enjoy it to the full.'

'Do you think you'll be able to leave it behind when you go?' he asked doubtfully. 'Isn't it the sort of appetite that could become an obsession?'

Melinda considered the matter. 'I suppose it could,' she admitted. 'This needn't be a one-off, though, need it? I mean, if I own these properties, there's nothing to prevent me from returning for another fortnight of self-indulgence, is there?'

'Not if that's what you decide you want,' he agreed. 'But will that be enough?' He leant across as he spoke and began to untie the cords of golden silk.

Melinda sat up beside him, rubbing her wrists and

ankles. They didn't hurt but she was conscious of the restricted blood flow. 'I think it has to be,' she told him. 'I've never met anyone in England with such an adventurous approach as you.'

'Such men must exist.'

'I suppose they must but I don't know how one finds them and, besides, there are other considerations to take into account.'

'Such as?'

'I'm no one here in Tangier. Just another English tourist. I suppose you could say just another English tourist in search of a sexual adventure. Not a compliment, I suppose, but a judgement that isn't likely to give rise to much more than a shrug of the shoulders. In England, however, once word got round among friends and colleagues, it would be much more difficult to live with. Men would view me salaciously, their wives and girlfriends would see me as a threat and bang would go my social life. Here I haven't got a social life. I can do what I like – within the law, I suppose – and leave it behind when I go. A very different situation.'

'Do you think what you're doing here is lawful?' he asked. 'Be under no illusions. Fornication is illegal.'

Melinda looked at him, surprised. 'What are you talking about?'

'Fornication,' Khalil said, 'is a legal term for an illegal practice. A woman can't fornicate inside marriage. If she has sex outside marriage, it's either fornication or adultery. Interestingly, men can only be found guilty of adultery.'

'Its illegality doesn't seem to bother you,' Melinda pointed out.

He shrugged. 'Discretion is all. Your great-aunt knew that as well as anyone.'

Melinda chuckled. 'It's all right so long as you don't do it in the street and frighten the horses?'

121

He seemed taken aback. 'Something like that, yes. An odd expression.'

'A quotation. Some actress or other, I think, a long time ago. Before Great-Aunt Laura's time, even.' She looked at him, her head on one side as if trying to work out what he was thinking. 'All this talk of legality,' she went on. 'Does this mean you want out?'

'Not at all. It was you who raised the matter, remember? Not me.' He picked up her *peignoir* off the floor and handed it to her. 'I'll use this bathroom,' he said. 'Can you find your way back to your own? Call Latifa and when she's run the bath you can tell her we'll have lunch on the terrace.'

Recalling her thoughts about the Manet, Melinda giggled. 'Not on the grass?' she asked.

'A picnic, you mean?' He seemed surprised. 'I wouldn't have thought that was your scene at all, but if you want one . . .'

'A joke,' Melinda said hastily. 'I was thinking about something altogether different. You're quite right: picnics aren't really me. The terrace will be fine.'

By the time they had finished their leisurely meal, the afternoon was well advanced. Khalil glanced at his watch. 'A good time to catch people back at work,' he said. 'I have a few matters to attend to and then I'll be back. I'll be gone two, three hours at the most. Will you mind if I bring a friend back with me?'

'A man?'

'Of course.'

She hesitated. 'Someone you can vouch for? I've learned to trust you, you see.'

'Good. You may rest assured that anyone you meet in this house through me is, as you put it, someone I can vouch for.'

Which, Melinda decided as she wandered round the garden in the afternoon sun, certainly removes a degree of anxiety from an otherwise intriguing prospect. The odd thing was that she really did trust Khalil. It was as if he had her interests at heart, or at least on a par with his own. This was unusual, to say the least, and Melinda couldn't help wondering to just what extent their interests marched side by side. She trusted him, yes, but she had a suspicion that if ever their interests diverged or, worse, were directly opposed to each other, then it would be hers that would be dumped. She'd been pretty good in the past at keeping her own best interests in the forefront of her mind and it would be very silly to let that slip now, just in the name of fun. She'd be well advised to remember the risks if they diverged, but in the meantime she'd go with the flow. She smiled to herself. Let's hope we go on seeing eye to eye, she thought.

She was sitting in the upholstered swing on the terrace, just beginning to think about going indoors out of the early evening chill, when she heard the sound of not one, but two car engines at the gates and by craning her neck – it was just too much effort to get up and go to look – she could make out the black Mercedes being admitted, closely followed by a smaller, dark blue car of not quite such ostentatious value. She glanced at her watch and smiled. Khalil had kept to his promised timescale. She rather suspected this made him unusual among Moroccans. She went indoors to greet him.

There was something familiar about the tall, distinguished man in his forties who followed Khalil into the European-style *salon*. As slim as most Moroccans seemed to be, he moved in a way that suggested that the body under the beautifully tailored suit was muscularly well-honed and she guessed his physical strength might well be greater than Khalil's – but where had she seen him before?

'You've heard me mention Larbi,' Khalil began.

'Allow me to introduce him. This is the late Miss Carr's great-niece,' he went on.

Melinda frowned. 'Larbi? Isn't that the name you gave Clive? The high-ranking police officer?'

'Miss Carr and I have met,' Larbi said, shaking her hand, 'though in less pleasant circumstances.'

'Of course!' Melinda exclaimed. 'You came to my assistance. I seem to remember you said something about your father having known my great-aunt.'

He inclined his head in salute. 'And now I have the pleasure of extending the acquaintance to the next generation.'

Latifa appeared in answer to Khalil's summons – this room, like every other, had its own bell – and shortly returned with a silver tray on which a silver teapot was surrounded by gold-rimmed glasses.

'Not in here,' Khalil said. 'The Moroccan *salon* is more suitable.'

Melinda led the way and sat in the corner of the divan that went round three of the four sides of the room. The two men sat on either side and Latifa, having poured out the first three glasses, disappeared discretely.

'And how are you enjoying Tangier?' Larbi asked. 'Apart from that unfortunate incident, I mean.'

'Very much indeed,' Melinda told him. She could play the game of social courtesies, too. She wondered how soon he'd drop them. She was quite sure there was a lot more than that behind his arrival. 'Khalil has been initiating me into some of its delights.'

'So I understand.' He looked at her as he spoke and Melinda knew he was mentally undressing her. 'Our friend seems to think you'd welcome my assistance in a similar capacity.'

'I didn't realise he had you in mind.'

'Does it change things?'

Melinda laughed. 'I don't see why it should, do you?'

'Of course not.' He reached across to put his glass back on the tray and Melinda wondered whether it was entirely by chance that his hand brushed against her breast as he did so. She glanced up in enquiry and his strong, long-fingered hand touched her neck, his thumb on her throat. 'Our friend tells me you prefer not to take the initiative.'

She shot Khalil a glance but he seemed to be studying the wall opposite. 'In general, yes.'

'Why don't you show me this house?' he said, getting to his feet and holding out his hand to her. 'I've heard a great deal about it and I'd like to see it for myself, especially the great bedchamber.'

'Take him,' Khalil said. 'I'll follow later.'

Melinda led the way, her heart pounding with excitement at what might be in store. She had the distinct impression he probably knew the house better than she did. When they entered the room, he closed the door carefully behind them, though she noticed he didn't lock it.

He drew her towards him and raised her chin, gazing down into her hazel eyes before sinking his mouth on hers. As his lips and his tongue fought with hers, his hands ran slowly down her body, feeling, enjoying, every curve. Melinda knew she was enjoying it as much as he and moved sensuously against him before he pulled away.

'I thought my instincts were right,' he said.

'What do you mean?' Melinda asked.

'Undress and I'll tell you.' He watched her remove one garment after another until she stood before him in her bra and thong. 'Stop there and come over here.'

Melinda did as she was told and when she was right in front of him, he pulled the orb of each breast out of its restraining cup so that it rested, prominent, on the wired support of her bra. A long-fingered hand slid down the back of her thong, pulling her towards him while it sought from the rear to finger her most private place.

'I was right, I think. When I came to your aid on the beach, I had the feeling that part of you might enjoy what those men had planned.'

'No woman enjoys rape!'

'True, but had the circumstances been different, I don't think you'd have been too unwilling. I think there was a part of you that might wonder what it would be like. Just a bit.' He caught sight of her shocked face in one of the mirrors and laughed. 'Are you shocked that anyone could think like that? Or shocked that they've hit the nail on the head? But don't worry – that's not my line. Undress me.'

Melinda obeyed and, as she knelt down to lower his trousers and his underpants to remove them completely, she gasped at the sight of his cock. Khalil hadn't been unduly modest when he had said there were plenty larger than his. This was certainly one of them and she wondered what it was going to feel like inside her. Not subtle, that's for sure, she thought, unable to repress a shudder of anticipation.

'Lick it now you're down there,' Larbi commanded. 'Just enough to make it ready. I'm told that you're so small it's a pity to waste oneself on your mouth.'

The door opened as he spoke and Khalil came in to sit quietly in a chair, watching. Melinda had never been watched before and that simple fact, together with the fact that they were reflected on all sides, made her flush with embarrassment.

Larbi pulled her to her feet. 'Take no notice of him. By the time he's watched us from every direction he'll be ready himself.'

With one forceful push she was face down on the bed, her legs over the foot, and before she realised what was happening, he had secured her ankles to the bottom of the bed's legs. Until this moment she hadn't been entirely sure she wanted him, especially with Khalil watching every move from every angle, but as she realised what Larbi had in mind, she could feel her pulse racing, feel the quickening in her groin and the growing, swelling warmth between her legs.

He used neither fingers nor tongue to extend her access to its fullest but teased her opening with his massive cock, feeling her rapidly increasing moist readiness. When he finally plunged it into her, the power and size of that huge thing forcing itself through the disproportionately small opening wrenched from her a scream of pure shock.

'Ssh,' Larbi said softly. 'I'll be more gentle from now on. You are, indeed, tiny. All the more exciting for me, of course, but I've no wish to hurt you more than I must.' True to his word, his thrusts didn't go as deep or as hard to start with as they might have done.

The fit was as tight as Melinda had ever known and every drop of her juices was needed to lubricate his cock as it pushed ever deeper and then ever more strongly inside her. It still hurt, but with the pain came an unexpected pleasure. The fact that her hands had been left free meant that this time she was able to pull herself back against him to enhance the depth of his penetration. As he went deeper, the pain increased, but now Melinda welcomed the pain as she felt him climax, every jet of his come squirting against her tight pussy, leaving no fraction of it unexplored.

He slid off her as soon as he was empty and she relaxed against the brocade coverlet. That had been frightening, but good, she decided and wondered whether he would want to take her again and whether it would be easier next time. She'd enjoyed the sheer force of that but she'd like to be taken to orgasm by that fearsome dick.

These thoughts had barely had time to race across

her brain when she realised she was being taken again, but not by Larbi this time.

'Oh, God,' she moaned. 'So soon.' Just for a moment she thought she couldn't stand it but it seemed as if Larbi's massive invasion had but cleared the ground for a more subtle incursion from Khalil, an incursion whose excitement was enhanced when he caught up both her wrists and held them behind her. Now she was fully helpless again until he should see fit to let go. She felt the tingle of rising desire as this smaller cock more subtly found her delicate places and worked them into the same frenzy she'd experienced earlier. Perfection, she thought, would be this frenzy coupled with the pain so recently withdrawn.

Holding her wrists with one strong hand, Khalil slid the other round to tease the nub of her clit, knowing that she would enjoy being made to come when she was under such severe control.

Melinda gasped. This was really being possessed and even as she gave herself to the spasmodic plunges of orgasm, she wondered what Larbi would feel like if he entered her again now that she had been so fully opened. Even as her excitement subsided, she knew she was ready for it to rise again and it was almost a disappointment when both men untied her legs and lifted her on to the bed, turning her over with gentle hands. They lay beside her, one on either side, caressing her, first one, then the other, and flirting with her sex.

'Was that what you expected?' Khalil asked gently.

She shook her head. 'I don't know what I expected, especially from a man like Larbi.' She turned her head to look at him. 'You hurt,' she said. 'Oh boy, did you hurt.'

'Inevitable, given our differences, but was it too much?'

'At first I thought I'd die. For a few seconds I even wanted to, but then ... Now I can't help wondering

128

what it would be like now, when I've been so stretched.'

'Let's watch you bring yourself off,' Khalil said softly. 'There's something exquisitely arousing in watching a woman do that.'

'I've never done it to an audience before,' Melinda objected.

'You've never had two men while they watched each other before,' Khalil pointed out. 'Show us what really turns you on.'

Each man raised himself on an elbow and watched as, eyes closed, Melinda ran her fingers down her body, raising her knees and splaying them wide, uncaring that the surrounding mirrors detailed every touch of her fingers. The spot of her most extreme satisfaction was just inside her pussy, and she supposed that was why Khalil's tongue had had so devastating an effect. She knew her fingers would work almost as quickly and she sought the spot that could bring her to her peak. Part of her wanted to feel a cock up against her, and not a finger. Imagining that was all it took, and she came with a moan of satisfaction. Then Larbi was on top of her, taking full advantage of her already parted legs, drawing them up and over his shoulders.

His entry was more gradual this time and the moment of penetration as satisfying as it was painful. This was indeed being taken, possessed, becoming an object of desire. Now she could respond, raising herself as high against him as she could, suddenly conscious that a pillow had been pushed beneath her. They came together this time, Melinda's legs tightening over his shoulders, the better to receive the full force of that gigantic, satisfying cock.

When he withdrew, she knew she was exhausted and looked for Khalil. Would he, too, want more? But there was no sign of him, only the sound of the sunken Alma-Tadema bath filling in the next room. Khalil, still naked, appeared in the door and both men led her into the bath and joined her there, soaping themselves and her clean while she gently played with them beneath the surface and then, while the three of them lay there in the warm, scented water, Khalil brought her to another small peak of happiness with his fingers.

'You see,' he said to Larbi, 'she must be exhausted yet she's still ready for more. I truly believe she must be well-nigh insatiable.'

Larbi's fingers replaced Khalil's and Melinda squirmed with delight. The water made everything more gentle, more relaxed, and her legs parted wider, the better to enjoy the delicate game.

'Benani's right,' Larbi whispered in her ear. 'Taking you is almost as good as having a virgin, even on the third successive entry. You're better than I expected and I'm glad I came – in every sense.'

'Will you come again?' Melinda asked.

'You enjoyed?'

'Oh, yes. It hurt but somehow that seemed right, especially from behind.'

'Khalil has formed the opinion that that's how you like it best.'

Melinda smiled and glanced at Khalil. 'He's a very astute man,' she said, 'but you haven't answered my question. Will you come again?'

'In both senses, I hope. I don't think Benani will dare to refuse me.'

'And I shan't want to,' she told him, wriggling against the last touch of his fingers inside her as if she knew they would soon be withdrawn.

When she stood up to be wrapped in another thick bathsheet, Khalil said as he secured it around her, 'Go to bed now. Tomorrow a doctor will come. You must be rested.'

'A doctor? Why? Does this mean you won't be sleeping with me?'

'Neither of us will. You wanted to discover the limits of your appetite, remember?'

Melinda nodded.

'It crossed my mind that Larbi might prove to be your sticking point, but I was wrong. If you want to go on, it is arranged. Not so firmly that it can't be cancelled, but I'm taking no chances. A doctor will decide if you're fit. Don't worry. He's a man who can be trusted.'

'Do as Benani says,' Larbi interrupted. 'Believe me, his advice is good.' He took her damp hand and raised it to his lips. 'I look forward to the next time,' he said.

Melinda smiled demurely. 'So do I,' she said.

Chapter Seven

Friday

Melinda woke late next day to find the weather was unusually warm and windless for the time of year, prompting Latifa to suggest she might like breakfast on the terrace. Melinda hesitated. She wasn't a fan of eating out of doors, and she had never been able to understand the British holidaymaker's passion for pavement cafes. However, the terrace was sheltered and the wind that was such a feature of Tangier had gone somewhere else for the time being. Although it was warm enough to eat *al fresco*, it wasn't so warm as to attract unwelcome insects. She decided to give it a try. Who knows, she thought, I may be able to see what other people go into raptures about.

She was joined by Khalil, who kissed her fleetingly on the cheek before he sat down. It was a completely passionless kiss, Melinda thought ruefully. The sort one saw exchanged by long-married couples or between brother and sister. She and Khalil came into neither category and, although she certainly wasn't in love with him, she fancied him rotten and had no reason to suspect he felt otherwise about her, so why was so little of that passion injected into his kiss?

'You decided not to sleep with me,' she said, taking very good care not to sound miffed.

'It wasn't easy,' he replied, and Melinda wasn't sure whether he meant it or whether he was a very good actor. 'I woke during the night and very nearly came along to you as a matter of fact.'

'I wish you had. What stopped you?'

His grin was not unsympathetic. 'You're greedy. Hasn't anyone told you that before?'

'Do you blame me when you represent sexual haute cuisine and you're just around the corner? You haven't answered my question.'

'There were two reasons. The main one is that you're seeing a doctor today to determine whether you're fit to participate in the test of your sexual stamina in the way we've discussed. I don't think sex with me immediately beforehand will help because, believe me, if I share a bed with you, I certainly shan't be holding myself back. I think you found Larbi hard work – I'd have been surprised if you hadn't; your sizes are so disproportionate – but it was bound to be tiring, and he may inadvertently have done some harm. Nothing major, but you're probably a bit tender as a result. Are you?'

Melinda considered the matter. 'I was last night,' she admitted. 'I don't feel so this morning.'

'Good. I don't want to aggravate it – and you'll need to be completely rested for tomorrow.'

'Tomorrow? Not until then?'

He laughed. 'Tomorrow is the start of the weekend. Men from a certain social level can expect to be free over a weekend. Some can extend it beyond that but Friday is not generally felt to be a good day to begin.' He leant across the table and his voice became confidential. 'You do realise what's being lined up, don't you? You must be under no illusions. You're intrigued to find out where your limit is. So am I, as a matter of fact. Larbi has the same curiosity coupled with a great willingness to achieve his own satisfaction in the course of helping you to reach yours. I doubt if there's a man alive who wouldn't jump at the chance to participate in the whole thing. You'll be tested to the limit, you may be sure of that. What I've got lined up for you is, to be blunt, little short of an orgy, with the difference that instead of a selection of women, willing or otherwise, you'll take the brunt of it alone. Just you and them.'

Melinda's hazel eyes sparkled. It was an exciting prospect. A daunting one, too, and it was the sort of thing that could all too easily become dangerous. It was a good thing she could trust Khalil.

He was watching her reaction. 'You're not deterred, I take it?'

Melinda shook her head. 'Not so far. How many are you expecting?'

'Difficult to say for sure. Some will drop out, others will bring friends they can vouch for. I've been thinking in terms of about a dozen.'

Melinda blanched. 'So many?'

'How many were you thinking of?'

'I suppose I'd assumed three or four; maybe as many as five or six. But a dozen! That's a lot.'

'It can be changed if you insist,' Khalil told her, 'but if it's brought down as low as that, I don't think you'll be tested to your limit. Most men are going to need quite a long interval before they can get it up again.'

'You don't seem to have a problem,' Melinda pointed out. 'Neither did Larbi.'

He laughed. 'True, but I'd have a job to find another four equally vigorous – and neither of us, even together, is going to be enough. You're a very unusual woman, you know.'

'Hmm. I'm not sure that's necessarily a compliment,' Melinda commented. 'I take it you can vouch for these men?'

134

'I know them all. I know their sexual proclivities. Their tastes are varied. Some like it rough, some like it gentle. All of them prefer to be dominant – there wasn't much point in inviting the opposite sort, given your own tastes – and between them, they'll certainly ring the changes in how you're taken.'

Melinda gave a small, pleasurable shudder. 'It sounds good.'

He frowned. 'Providing this doctor gives the go-ahead.'

'"This doctor"? That sounds as if you don't know him.' Melinda couldn't suppress her anxiety.

'I've met him and he's very well qualified. He's an up-and-coming young gynaecologist.'

'But . . .'

'I've not used him before. His professionalism isn't in doubt. Larbi says he can guarantee his discretion. He's Larbi's suggestion, so I had no hesitation in calling him in. I imagine Larbi has some hold over him to enable him to be as positive as he was.'

Melinda frowned. 'What did you mean when you said you hadn't used him before?'

His surprise seemed perfectly genuine. 'I'm a man. Men don't use gynaecologists.'

'Of course they don't,' Melinda said impatiently, 'but that wasn't the inference.'

'A poorly expressed figure of speech,' Khalil said, shrugging. 'One of the problems when one converses in a foreign language.'

It wasn't a problem he'd had before, Melinda thought, but she'd had enough to do with him by now to recognise when she wasn't going to get an answer. She had her suspicions, fuelled both by the condition of this house – theoretically unused since Great-Aunt Laura had left Tangier – and by the very nature of the house itself. Sooner or later she'd find out. She was already well on the way to deducing just why Great-Aunt

135

Laura's name had been such anathema to the rest of the family. 'When's this doctor coming?' she asked.

Khalil consulted his watch and Melinda didn't think it was imagination that she saw relief in his expression.

'You've got about an hour.' He stood up. 'I'll tell Latifa to run you a bath. Don't worry. I'll be here when he comes.'

She was taken aback, unsure quite what he meant by 'here'. 'In the house, I take it – not in the room while he examines me,' she said in case he was labouring under any misapprehensions.

He looked surprised. 'If you wish.' He chuckled. 'A little inconsistent, don't you think?'

'No. Women don't usually want another man present when a doctor examines them, and I dare say he'll bring his own nurse.'

Khalil shook his head in a gesture of incomprehension. 'Yet you raised no objection yesterday at the presence of one man while another fucked you,' he pointed out. 'In fact, I had the distinct impression it added spice to the exercise.'

'That's quite different,' Melinda said flatly. 'There was nothing clinical about it. An unqualified observer during an internal examination . . . that's just voyeurism plain and simple.'

'The difference escapes me, but it shall be as you wish. I shan't be far away, though.'

Melinda shrugged. 'If that makes you happier,' she said. 'If he is, as you say, a well-qualified gynaecologist, I'm sure the precaution will be unnecessary.'

The bath Latifa ran was much deeper than Melinda was accustomed to run for herself, perhaps because it didn't have to be snatched before getting ready for work, catching a train or grabbing a breakfast. The maid had used perfumed oils lavishly so that, as Melinda lay there, their scents drifted into her nostrils to relax and penetrate her whole body. She felt sensuous as well as relaxed under their influence. She ran her hands slowly over the soft contours of her body, her eyes closed, the better to savour the luxury.

It was a pity Jacuzzis hadn't been invented in Great-Aunt Laura's day, she thought. Perhaps not here so much as in the Alma-Tadema room. She smiled to herself. She could afford to have one put in now. It was a pity she had only another week here. Even if she suggested its installation to Khalil, he couldn't possibly get it done before she left but if, when the time came to go back to England, she'd decided to return here, then that was something he could take care of before she came back.

She frowned. She recalled that peculiar turn of phrase – that this doctor wasn't one he'd used before. Not, 'He isn't one who has treated my wife/sister/mother.' That wouldn't have been out of the ordinary. The implication was that he was in the habit of using the services of a gynaecologist. Melinda could think of only one explanation and it wasn't one she liked. If it was the right one, it would explain why this place had been so well looked after. If this house had been used since Great-Aunt Laura's departure as a brothel – and a very high-class one, to judge by the accoutrements – and Khalil were the pimp for it, then from time to time he'd have needed just such a physician.

It wasn't a brothel in the ordinary sense because it was quite evident that no one other than the staff actually lived here, and there was no sign of a Madam, but it would account for the mirrors, the silken cords and goodness only knew what else that she hadn't yet discovered. Khalil, as agent, could be expected to be familiar with the property but she'd formed the impression that Larbi hadn't been exactly a stranger here.

What she didn't like at all was the thought that Khalil

was just a pimp. If he was, then he was of a very different sort from those she'd seen portrayed on TV and in films, her only other acquaintance with the breed. He was thoughtful and considerate and she believed him when he told her she could call a halt at any time. Surely that wasn't behaviour characteristic of a pimp? And if he was one, where did that put her?

She had always enjoyed love-making, fucking, call it what you will, but until now it had always been less than entirely satisfying both in terms of quality and – although she was only just realising it – quantity. She had never been paid for it and she wasn't being paid for it now. So what did that make her? She couldn't make up her mind but she did decide she was extremely glad she was enjoying this interlude somewhere other than in England. It was definitely an illustration of the desirability of keeping the two halves of one's life quite separate.

The water was no longer so warm now and she glanced at the chair on which Latifa had carefully draped, not her clothes, but a freshly laundered negligée. Melinda reached for a bathsheet and stepped out. If a doctor was coming to look at her, she didn't need any other garments, and this one would be a joy to wear, she decided, holding it against her. The heavy lace was virgin white, backed with a white voile that gave it the weight to drape her body to perfection and gave the tantalising impression of revealing far more than it actually did. She studied herself in the mirrors and liked what she saw, but it did cross her mind that a plain, old-fashioned terry-towelling wrap might have been more appropriate to a medical examination.

She'd been prepared for a fairly young man, but this one was younger than she'd expected. She had no doubt that Khalil would have checked his qualifications but they must have been of fairly recent date. His

138

serious face was made more serious by his gold-rimmed spectacles, his lips were fuller than Melinda admired in a man, and his nose was flatter. She'd noticed several examples of the same physical type in the city but she had decided she preferred the sharper, more Arab features of the majority. Nevertheless, most women would have described him as handsome, and she could only wish there was rather more indication of humour. She wondered if he really was as serious-minded as he seemed or whether, given his profession, it was a demeanour he'd adopted because it was more appropriate. He hadn't brought a nurse with him.

He put his case down on the small breakfast table and glanced at Khalil.

'If you're sure you're happy about it,' Khalil told her, 'I'll leave you both to it, but I shan't be far away.' He spoke in English and Melinda wondered why.

'Does he speak English?' she asked.

'No. He doesn't understand it, either. His French is – naturally – fluent.' He turned to the doctor and told him, in French, that Melinda understood that language. The young man smiled but it was a polite smile and she noticed it didn't involve his eyes.

Once Khalil had closed the door behind him, the doctor opened his case to reveal the shining steel of his instruments. He looked Melinda up and down and told her to take off her negligée.

She wondered if he was embarrassed by what must be a rather peculiar situation for him. That would account for his avoiding her face but, as she untied the two satin ribbons that secured the negligée at neck and breast, she realised that his avid gaze at the body gradually being revealed was hardly that of a disinterested physician. She wondered whether he was going to be one of her visitors. She hoped not but she supposed it was too much to hope she'd fancy all of them.

* * *

When the examination was over, Latifa came quietly in from the bathroom and beckoned her mistress in.

'Thank you, Latifa,' Melinda said. 'I need this.'

Khalil entered as she spoke and, with a nod in the direction of the bedroom door, dismissed the doctor and followed Melinda into the bathroom. 'I'll help you,' he said, taking off his jacket and rolling up his sleeves.

Melinda looked doubtful. 'Is that a good idea?'

'Don't worry. I'm not going to make love to you. Just think of me as your . . . body-servant. Yes, I think that's the right word.' As he spoke he gently lifted the negligée from her shoulders and held it between them, a screen between her nakedness and himself that enabled her to step into the aromatic water with no loss of modesty. The fact that he had scrutinised her naked body many times distracted not one jot from the consideration he was now showing.

Once she was submerged with total modesty beneath the scented bubbles, Khalil knelt beside the bath, thoroughly soaped his hands and began with gentle firmness to wash her neck and shoulders. 'Wash' was too prosaic a word, Melinda decided, tipping her head back to feel his fingers on her throat, and 'massage' was too energetic. 'Wassage', perhaps? She smiled at the thought, her eyes closed, an unconscious indication of the extent of her relaxation.

Realising this, Khalil suggested softly that she should sit up, his strong and soothing hands following the waterline as it receded to just below her nipples, which now rested upon it as if it were some aqueous half-cupped brassiere. Soft with soap, his hands cupped and stroked the two spheres, gently pressing them before wandering over her shoulders to massage every inch of her exposed back. He let them drift softly and sensuously across her shoulders to touch, to rinse, to stimulate again the senses stored so close to the surface of her breasts. He noted with pleasure that those senses

140

were undiminished and the nipples were hardening before his eyes. Good, he thought. She's still got the taste for it.

'Lie back again,' he murmured.

She did so, closing her eyes in perfect relaxation, aware of his hands descending, circling, caressing her whole body. It was automatic, instinctive for her to part her legs beneath the water as his fingers made their descent and when, as if by accident, they flickered across those lower lips, Khalil was happily conscious that they were beginning to swell with desire – a desire he hadn't the slightest intention of gratifying.

The greater that unsatisfied desire became, the better.

He sat back on his haunches and reached for a towel. 'Do you feel better?' he asked. 'Cleaner?'

Melinda sighed with undisguised regret. 'Much,' she said. 'I'm sorry it's come to an end. Must it?'

He chuckled. 'I'm afraid so. The water's getting cold.' He reached for the deeply soft bathsheet Latifa had laid out and stood up. 'Come on. Let me dry you.'

It was Melinda's turn to chuckle. 'Like a nanny, you mean? Not a role I'd associate with you.'

'Don't you have a saying about needs must when the devil drives?' he asked, unperturbed. 'You'll have to tell me if I've any shortcomings as a nanny.'

Melinda stepped out of the bath into the enveloping folds of the towel and let him pat her dry, enjoying the sensation of being an entirely passive partner in the experience. He'd make a very good nanny, she thought, except that she hoped no nanny would kiss freshly dried nipples in quite that arousing way.

When he judged her to be completely dry, Khalil wrapped her in another, dry, bathsheet and led her into the bedroom where she noticed that not only had Latifa remade the bed, but she had done so with a complete change of bed-linen from virgin white to Madonna blue.

'Lie down,' Khalil told her. 'Face down. I'm going to give you a massage. By the time I've finished with you, you'll feel a completely new woman.'

Melinda did as she was bid. She wondered just what would be the extent of this massage and more than half hoped and anticipated that it wouldn't only be her external muscles which would be stimulated.

Khalil was far too wise to make the psychological mistake of removing the huge towel. Instead he simply moved it down so that her buttocks were still covered and then he reached for the perfumed oils Latifa had set out. With a firm, professional touch he massaged her shoulders and spine, his fingers just occasionally brushing the sides of her breasts in passing.

For Melinda, who was almost asleep, there was a frisson of anticipation in such accidental brushes, and when Khalil gently turned her on her back, she expected the anticipation to be realised. She thought it odd that he covered her lower body again because his hands, gently kneading her breasts from below, soon provoked not just the hardness of her nipples that implored his mouth to kiss, to suck, to bite, but also that instinctive parting of her legs that was the most obvious indication of what she yearned for.

He resisted the temptation. Neither her gratification nor his own was the current order of the day and, instead, moving the towel upwards across her waist, he began to massage the gentle curve of her belly and then downwards to her thighs.

As his hands descended and his thumbs pressed, rotating, over each muscle in turn, Melinda felt her unsteady breathing betraying the intensity of her desire. As if Khalil's hands held a glowing ember, she felt the heat they stirred in her loins free her inner juices and knew that he must be able to feel the moisture lubricating her cunt.

But it was not to be. The satisfaction must wait.

142

Khalil knew his business well. He knew that he could take her now to his heart's content. Right now, Melinda was ready to accept any man – and very likely any kind of dildo, too. Khalil was more concerned to make sure she wouldn't want to cry off from their original plan. In fact, she needed to be gagging for it – and there was nothing quite like sexual frustration to guarantee that.

He spread the towel across her so that she was completely covered and laid the duvet on top of that. 'Now you need to sleep,' he told her.

Melinda's eyes flew open. 'Sleep?' she queried.

'Sleep,' he repeated firmly. 'Latifa will look in on you from time to time and she can bring you something to eat later on, but I suggest you stay where you are. After all, the next few days are likely to be rather busy.' He straightened up and looked down at her. 'Or have you changed your mind?'

Melinda took a deep breath and let it out again before she answered. It was the deep breath of total relaxation that signals a readiness to sleep.

'No, I haven't changed my mind.' She smiled sleepily. 'No way.'

'Good.' Khalil bent down and deposited a chaste kiss on her forehead. 'Sweet dreams, then. I'll see you tomorrow.'

Chapter Eight
Saturday

When Melinda awoke next morning to the flood of sunlight that surged into the room as Latifa rolled up the shutters, she felt fully refreshed. She stretched her arms and yawned like a cat, and felt instantly ready for anything.

Just as well, she thought, remembering that Khalil had plans. She need do nothing more now than give herself over to her own enjoyment and gratification. What she didn't know for sure was just how long this sexual debauchery was expected to last. One day? Two? Two seemed more likely. Then she recalled its purpose. If the idea was to find out how long it took to satiate her, it had to be open-ended but, since she'd never been put to the test before, she couldn't help doubting whether she could go on for longer than the weekend – and quite possibly not even that long.

Latifa had brought her breakfast on an elegantly inlaid tray and indicated, by plumping up the pillows in a thoroughly nurse-like manner, that today breakfast in bed was scheduled. Melinda had no quarrel with that. She couldn't remember when someone had last brought her breakfast in bed. It wasn't the same if you had to get up, make it yourself and take it back to bed. This was yet another slice of pure luxury. She should have asked for it before.

While she buttered croissants and poured coffee, Latifa was running a bath, and when Melinda had brushed the last crumbs from her fingers, it was clear that today her ablutions were going to be supervised by an expert.

Latifa twisted Melinda's long hair into a knot on top of her head and saw to it that it stayed completely dry. Then she washed her with the thoroughness and objectivity of a true nanny – quite an achievement, Melinda decided, since she could hardly miss the fact that her mistress's sexual excitement was rising by the moment in anticipation of the hitherto unknown – possibly even unimagined – delights in store.

When she had been patted scrupulously dry, Latifa worked perfumed oils into Melinda's skin so that it was soft and smooth to the touch. Her hair was released from its restraints and brushed till it, too, was smooth and gleamed in the sunlight filtering through the voile curtains. She turned Melinda round, studying her reflection and then nodded with apparent satisfaction and wrapped her, not in some sexy negligée, but in a very practical terry dressing gown, just the sort of thing Melinda had wanted the day before.

The garment was totally unexpected and Melinda's surprise showed in her face, but Latifa only smiled and pushed her gently down in a chair, telling her to wait just a few minutes. Then she left, closing the door behind her.

With nothing else to occupy her mind, Melinda became aware of the arrival from time to time of cars at – she assumed – the front door. There was the crunch of tyres on gravel, the pause, the sound of car doors closing – that particularly discrete 'click' that only very expensive luxury models manage to achieve – and then the quiet purr of the engine and the diminishing crunch of gravel as the vehicles drove away again.

She was tempted to crane her neck out of the window to see what sort of person had arrived, but she resisted. These must be her ... what? Audience? Customers? No, not that. The inference was unwelcome and must surely be inaccurate. Partners, perhaps? No. None of these words was quite right. She shivered, but more with excitement than with fear or uncertainty. Not being able to define the roles made it more of an adventure, an experiment.

When Latifa returned, it was with another tray of coffee, this time accompanied by petits fours. She left Melinda to get on with her elevenses but returned shortly with two padded hangers from each of which hung a garment that could have been called a *peignoir* or a negligée but by no stretch of the imagination merited either dressing gown or house coat. Melinda looked at them and chuckled. How ironic, how revealing it was that the English words for these particular garments of undress should be so prosaic and unalluring, and she wondered which had come first, the prosaic names or the practical fabrics and design.

There was nothing practical about these. One was a delicate silken gauze shot through with gold and sparingly embroidered with exquisitely executed sprigs of golden flowers. The other was heavier and opaque; the phrase that sprang to mind was 'cloth-of-gold', though she guessed it was something more modern like gold lamé. The fabric was generously gathered into a heavily beaded yoke and the sleeves fell wide to halfway down the lower arm, not unlike something clerical or a magician's robe. The gauze *peignoir* was of a similar style, of equal fullness at the yoke but with pearl buttons to the hem and longer, narrower sleeves. Melinda guessed that she wasn't intended to choose between them but to wear the one over the other.

146

She was right and, when Latifa had dressed her in them, Melinda realised how effective the combination was. At every step, the heavy gold over-garment parted to reveal the semi-transparency of the one beneath. Her hair was brushed smoothly down her back and, the final touch of stylistic perfection, her finger- and toe-nails were painted gold.

Latifa stood back, her arms folded, a smile of satisfaction on her lips. 'I think Benani will approve,' she said. 'Yes, I think he will like it. Wait here. I fetch him.'

Approval was writ large on the Moroccan's handsome face as he took in his protégée's appearance. He made just one adjustment.

Taking the silver-backed hairbrush from the dressing table, he brought Melinda's thick, honey-blonde hair over one shoulder and brushed it smooth again.

'Leave it like that,' he said, 'and when each garment is removed – whether by you or someone else – return it so that one breast is completely covered. Very sexy. Very enticing.' He said something to Latifa and then turned to Melinda. 'I've told Latifa we're nearly ready for you. She'll bring you to the top of the stairs in a few minutes. You'll hear the music. Give it a few seconds to get under way and then go down the stairs and into the *majlis*. Remember your approach can be seen from there. From the moment the music strikes up, you're on your own.'

Melinda stared at him in alarm. 'On my own? Won't you be there? Where will you be?'

'Of course I'll be there.' He laughed. 'I've your welfare at heart and, besides, I wouldn't miss it for worlds. I mean that Latifa won't be there to arrange your hair, your clothes, or anything else. From that moment all that becomes your guests' prerogative.'

He left, and this time the bedroom door stayed open behind him and Latifa stood in the doorway, listening for the first sounds of music from below.

Melinda's heart was beating nineteen to the dozen. Actors must feel like this when they're waiting in the wings, she thought. It wasn't a nice feeling, mingling, as it did, expectation, excitement and, she realised with a shock, sheer naked fear.

It wasn't a fear for her own safety: she had every faith that Khalil's presence would safeguard that. It was the fear of the unknown. There were so many unknowns down there. Her 'guests', as Khalil had called them, for a start. She didn't even know how many of them there were, let alone their identities.

And how, exactly, were they planning to test her to the full? A glorified gang-bang or something more subtle and varied than that? Would they introduce as many variations as they could to stretch her to her limits and to encourage her to go on and on? And just how many variations could they devise? Years ago she'd read the *Kama Sutra* – who hadn't? – but at the time a lot that it described had seemed scarcely practical to anyone who lacked the suppleness of an athlete – and Melinda knew she was no athlete.

She heard the first beats of the *tabla* and the chief musician set the rhythm. Well, she thought, this is it. This is where I find out.

Latifa took her by the hand and led her to the top of the staircase where she arranged her golden robe and her golden hair in much the same manner that a bride's train is arranged before she enters the church. Satisfied that all was perfect, the maid nodded and smiled at her mistress, her glance towards the staircase telling Melinda to descend. The insistent beat of the *tabla* set the unhurried rate of Melinda's descent, her bare feet cold on the white marble.

The dozen or so men waiting below watched her descent with a mounting excitement that stilled all conversation. They sat or reclined on the exotically upholstered divans of the *majlis*, drinking in the slow, rhythmic revelation that unveiled itself before their fascinated eyes. The bare white feet spoke of an erotic promise which was enhanced a few *tabla*-beats later by tantalising glimpses of long shapely legs through the semi-transparent gauze of the under-robe and then, as the woman they'd come to test reached the bottom of the stairs and stood, momentarily still, the outer-robe fell back into place, concealing once more the all-too-brief glimpse of thigh that caught their breath and stirred their willing organs into life.

Melinda walked to the open doorway and paused there briefly before entering. She looked around, barely aware that someone had closed the door behind her.

There must have been a dozen men there in addition to Khalil. So many! she thought, undecided whether the realisation brought heightened excitement or apprehension. They ranged in age from their mid-twenties to some thirty years older and were dressed in a variety of styles from which anything as casual as jeans was noticeably absent. A few were in superbly cut Western-style suits; most wore the traditional *djellabah* and the backless *babouches*, the leather slippers that were men's traditional footwear both indoors and out. None wore beards, though some sported the heavy black moustache associated in every European's mind with a certain Iraqi dictator.

As she stood there, dauntingly conscious of the scrutiny of a dozen pairs of eyes, Khalil stepped forward from behind her – it had been he who had closed the door – to introduce her to her 'guests'. Out of courtesy to their hostess (and to avoid the hassle of having to translate) he spoke in French, a language he was to use throughout the following hours.

'Gentlemen, permit me to introduce Miss Carr – Miss Melinda Carr, great-niece and heiress of the late Miss Laura Carr who was so well known to our fathers and, in some cases, to our grandfathers. This is Miss Carr's first visit to Tangier and her first opportunity to step on to a path set out by her great-aunt. I'm sure we all hope it will prove the first visit and the first step of many, just as I'm sure we all hope she will prove to have inherited much more from her great-aunt than that lady's wealth.'

His audience smiled and nodded and then clapped their appreciation of the sentiments expressed and Melinda found herself sinking into a curtsy of acknowledgement, like an actress at the final curtain.

Except that this was the opening curtain, and she was completely taken aback by the odd formality of it all. She didn't know what she'd expected, only that this wasn't it. Being referred to as 'Miss Carr' and the oblique and respectfully worded references to Great-Aunt Laura and what now appeared to be the cause of her black sheep status – the inference of which she was sure she fully understood – was certainly an improvement on, 'This is Melinda and she's here for the shagging,' which might be the bald truth but not so elegantly expressed. But there was more to it than that. It was as if Khalil had set the tone, had established that no matter what was about to take place, Melinda was entitled to respect. She rather thought it was designed to set her above the common whore. Which, she thought, apart from the surroundings, the wardrobe and the fact that I'm not being paid, is just about what I am.

She didn't understand Arab music and could find no melody in what was being played but the rhythm was compulsive and it was the most natural thing in the world to follow the beat and circle the huge, low, carpet-covered central table, turning as she did so like some gleaming gold planet rotating on its axis as it circles its sun. All her audience could see of her femininity was the long swathe of thick blonde hair over one shoulder and a hint of gauze-covered leg.

The second time around, she began unfastening the buttons at the yoke and then, remembering Khalil's instruction to keep her hair where it was, let the golden robe slip from her shoulders on to the marble floor. The intensified interest was almost tangible as she circled in front of the assembled men once more, instinctively using her arms and her upper body to introduce an element of voluptuous dance to her progress.

Suddenly a man stepped forward and barred her way.

This is it, she thought. Now we begin in earnest.

With assured hands, the man stroked the sides of her body and on down her thighs, her legs, to her ankles. He lifted one foot to his lips and kissed the golden toenails before undoing the three lowest buttons. Then he took his seat again among the others on the divans.

Melinda resumed her semi-dance, taking care that every twirl she made revealed as much as possible of the unveiled part of her legs.

Another man stepped forward to undo two more buttons. When the third man seized his chance, it meant that the translucent robe was now open to a point just below her navel. His fingers brushed across the short blonde curls of her pussy and her sharp intake of excited breath caused him to glance up at her face. He smiled in full understanding of what she was feeling.

Her audience was no longer watching in silent appreciation. They were studying her avidly, heads together in close conference without removing their gaze from her body.

Melinda wondered if it was her imagination that the beat had quickened. It seemed the right moment to start unbuttoning the rest of the robe, to let it slip to the floor as the other one had. Now her hair completely covered one breast like some sexual Amazon. It

151

fascinated her audience who reached out to stroke the hair and feel the hardening of the nipple beneath. Soon she was in the centre of a small group. As one man fondled her breasts from behind, she could feel his rising erection against her buttocks and as another knelt to place kisses from her navel downwards, she could see his excitement rising under his *djellabah*.

Something was said in Arabic and the men stepped back as her hands were taken by Larbi. He led her to the table where the carpet that covered it was now hidden under a white sheet.

The tall policeman lifted her in his arms and laid her gently on to the sheet. 'Lie still,' he commanded her. Someone handed him a skein of scarlet and silver cord and she was swiftly and efficiently bound, spread-eagled on the low table.

Melinda was excited but unconcerned. Already she could feel the warmth of anticipation between her legs. An element of relief, too: if Larbi was to be the first, she knew what to expect.

She realised her confidence had been misplaced when two men approached, one with a small towel over his arm and holding a metal bowl, the other with a cut-throat razor in his hand.

She gasped with horror and cried out in protest but Khalil stepped forward to reassure her. 'Lie still,' he told her. 'Our women remove all bodily hair but they do it in the privacy of their own bathrooms. These men want to watch it being done – and to do it to you themselves. Only those I trust absolutely have been allowed a turn.'

Melinda's fear while she was being soaped up was naked in her eyes but, even as she shivered involuntarily at the first stroke of the razor, she knew the fear and the sensation were merging into desire, and that desire was steadily mounting as the razor progressed with infinite care on its downward path. Her eyes were

152

closed now, the better to enjoy the delicate sensation with its terrifyingly possible consequences. She held her breath and lay rigidly still as each barber held first one and then the other of her outer lips to one side in order to strip them of every last vestige of blonde curls. One slip of the razor was all it would take and, if she wasn't even breathing, there would be less to make them slip. It was small comfort that the onus was in the hands of a stranger who might – or might not – be as careful as Khalil thought.

Then it was over. As the last barber stepped back to allow the man with the towel to wipe her clean, she exhaled with relief and suddenly the warmth of unsatisfied desire flooded over her with undiminished urgency.

As if someone recognised this, fingers replaced the towel, stroking her burning loins to establish that they were now smooth enough. She moved against them as well as she was able against the silken restraints and groaned.

'Take it soon,' she moaned. 'For God's sake, take it soon.'

She heard Khalil translate and the appreciative chuckle that followed and then she realised they were drawing lots to see who would be the first.

The winner was a well-muscled man of about her own age. As he stripped off his *djellabah*, she saw he was naked underneath and already his cock was well on the way to being fully erect. He stood over her, his eyes raking every inch of prostrate, spread-eagled body. It was a look so lascivious that even without so much as a touch from him, she could feel her breath shortening and her heart drumming with the beat of the *tabla*. This wasn't a man who would feel obliged to be gentle – and the way she felt right now, gentleness wasn't high on her list of requirements.

He placed a strong hand on the curve of her belly

and Melinda caught her breath, expecting him to move it straight away to her naked mound and plunge his fingers into her. He didn't. Instead, he said something in Arabic and several of the other men came forward with the heavily stuffed pillows that had made up the back of the surrounding divans. Hands slid beneath her buttocks and raised them so that cushions could be pushed underneath to support her lower body. They achieved this without loosening her bonds so now she had even less leeway to move, to react, to respond than she'd had before. She didn't delude herself that it had been by accident that the cushion-bearing hands had, as they left, brushed against the rapidly moistening gateway to the weekend's enjoyment.

She glanced at her first ravisher. His gaze was fixed with open greed on the totally revealed delights of her bald cunt, now swollen with still unsatisfied desire. His own organ must now be at its peak, she thought, seeing how it curved upwards, swollen with the same desire. It was bigger than she'd expected it to be. This was going to hurt. Her breath shivered. Right now, that was what she wanted.

He climbed on to the table between her legs, carefully positioning himself for maximum physical effect. He parted her exposed lips with surprisingly gentle fingers but then, gentleness abandoned, rammed a finger as far inside her and as hard as he could, as if he were not only discovering her readiness but also her physical extent. The grim smile that flickered across his face suggested he was pleased with what he found.

No sooner had his finger left than his thickened cock took its place, ramming itself into her with such force that she cried out with shock. He pulled back almost, but not quite, to the point of withdrawal, then rammed himself forward again before repeating the process over and over again, the base of his cock slamming up against her clit with each thrust.

This hurts! Melinda thought. My God, this hurts! But even as she thought this, there was at the back of her mind the fear that each partial withdrawal would be the last, that the next one would be complete and, painful as his fucking was, she didn't want it to stop.

Perhaps because of the pain, perhaps because of her position, her orgasm was longer in coming than usual but when it came, it did so with a power that made her regret that the restraints on her legs stopped her acknowledging her sexual ecstasy with her body.

Her partner seemed to have developed the power to withhold the usually inevitable ejaculation and, as her orgasm faded, he withdrew without releasing himself either inside or out. It was the first time she'd encountered a man who could do that and she couldn't help wondering whether the fault was somehow hers: was she the reason he hadn't come, despite his almost demonic thrusting? Or could a man train himself to that degree of control, especially if he expected to fuck a woman several times in a relatively short space of time? Every woman knew that a man's sexual strength ebbed with his ejaculation. Khalil was the first she'd come across who could manage it several times in an evening. Her previous lovers had regarded themselves as sexual athletes if they managed it the morning after as well as the night before.

He shrugged himself back into his *djellabah* and disappeared, Melinda guessed, to find a bidet. Someone untied her bonds and her previous partner's place was taken by an older man, who soon made it clear he liked his sex in a very different manner.

He pulled her towards him, making her kneel on the carpeted table while he stood before her, his hands fondling her breasts until her nipples hardened enough for him to bite and suck them while his hands slid down to her hips. As one hand moved behind her, the

155

middle finger descended into the cleft between her buttocks and entered her cunt from behind.

Melinda moved on the finger and smiled, guessing he was going to take her from behind as well. Good, she thought. I like it like that. I relish that feeling of total possession.

The man didn't miss the smile of enjoyment as his finger worked her quietly, seeking, finding, exploiting the nub of her clit. 'Turn round,' he said softly. Melinda did as she was told, still kneeling and now very conscious that the exploring finger could reach satisfyingly deeper inside her.

He pushed her down so that she was on all fours and his finger withdrew. She readied herself to receive the cock she had seen rising beneath the fabric of his striped *djellabah* but instead felt the electric surprise of a tongue.

Another new experience, she realised with delight. No one had ever used their tongue on her from behind and within seconds it had found the most sensitive part of her sex and teased her to a convulsive orgasm the like of which she had never experienced before – and which, judging by the onlookers' faces, they had never seen before. But Melinda was oblivious to this. Such were the extremes of her ecstasy that her eyes were closed even as her lips parted in groans of delight.

It might have been an anticlimax when his tongue was withdrawn to be replaced with the real thing. It might, but it wasn't. This man was much more subtle than his predecessor. Brute force didn't seem to be part of his armoury, not at this stage, anyway, and the softer approach, coming so soon after the welcomed violation by his companion, was a contrast which blew away any fatigue.

Despite his dominant position, he began gently enough, making no attempt at this stage to plunge in to her absolute limit. Gentle thrusts, each stronger than the last, each reaching deeper than the one before, were an unavoidable contrast to her previous invader and Melinda found that that alone was enough to lend an enjoyable frisson.

He held her hips tightly up against his body, reinforcing her instinct to push her backside against him. She wondered how soon – or how long – it would be before he began to make his final fulfilling thrust and she hoped he would empty himself inside her rather than employ his predecessor's technique.

Now she was aware that this man was subtly changing his technique and at the end of each near-withdrawal there was a brief, tantalising hiatus when she wasn't sure what he was going to do. Her heart began to beat harder and she tightened her internal grip on the weapon inside her as if to prevent its slipping out.

Almost as if that were a signal to him, the man's strong fingers slid across her groin and quickly reached the moist entrance to her sex, now swollen with desire. He played with her until she felt she could bear the frustrating suspense no longer. She wanted to come. Orgasm was imminent but she was desperate to reach it at the same time as he shot his load inside her.

As she recognised these fundamental desires, one finger left its delicate teasing to push its way into her cunt, despite the constriction of the fat stalk already there. Melinda held her breath in the intoxicating antici-pation of the moment when he would find it.

She cried out with a deep, guttural moan as the finger found its goal. She could hold back her orgasm no longer. The man knew it too and, as she thrashed uncontrollably against him, the finger was gone and he climaxed powerfully within her, his spurting thrusts timing themselves to complement her own.

Melinda neither knew nor cared whether what he did was instinctive or the result of experienced calculation.

She knew it to be one of the best, most satisfying experiences of her life so far and it was difficult to imagine that the weekend held anything better in store. When this man withdrew, she was going to be exhausted. Would she be forced to admit she was satisfied? It would be ironic if just two men – admittedly two formidable sexual performers – were all it took to make her holler 'enough'.

Suddenly he was gone, withdrawn without warning and departed. Melinda sank, exhausted, face down on to the table beneath her, her whole body trembling with the satisfaction of consummated desire. Her deep, uneven breaths spoke volumes to her audience.

Hands turned her over on to her back. She raised no more resistance than a rag doll and barely noticed that the hands that had turned her over were opening her legs. She was just conscious enough to reflect that it would be the first time she'd been inert when someone fucked her.

But another fucking wasn't what was in store for her just yet. A warm and scented moistened cloth was wiping her bare cunt, cleaning each lip in turn and Melinda gave herself up to the soothing care it offered. She enjoyed the contrast with what had gone before. She wouldn't much mind if it went on for a long time.

So she was half asleep when, with no preamble, no foreplay, someone entered her strongly, firmly but without the force that others had used.

Startled, she opened her eyes and found herself looking into the handsome face of one of the youngest men present. It was odd, she thought, that he wasn't hurting her. Perhaps he was less generously endowed than the other two. Then, as he pushed backwards and forwards with consummate and practised ease, she realised that she was so well lubricated that in all probability a cast-iron girder would have worked as smoothly.

Now there was an interesting comparison, she

thought – and her fatigue suddenly dropped away. She'd almost forgotten the pleasures of an uncomplicated position like this and gladly gave herself to its enjoyment. It wasn't long before she felt an excited arousal that reminded her of snatched moments of sex in secluded beechwoods when she was a teenager. The spice of the fear of discovery was missing, but the unexpectedness of the entry more than made up for it. She abandoned herself to the sheer enjoyment this handsome man was provoking.

Perhaps he was more of a master than she had thought, for there was no doubt he was playing her as a violinist plays his instrument, bringing her to a crescendo of desire and then, at the exact moment she reached her peak, he withdrew as totally as his forerunner and stood back to watch the consequence of his sudden and unexpected withdrawal. The other men moved closer to watch, too. Melinda was only vaguely aware of their interest, though she saw that some were more interested in the image in the mirrored ceiling than in the flesh before them. It didn't matter. From exhaustion she'd been brought to another climax and she lay there, her legs akimbo, her pelvis thrusting in the frustration of having nothing to rub up against.

As her sexual tension began to subside, a hand brushed the inside of her thigh, raising her excitement again, and then something cold and unyielding was forced into her, the very contrast it presented with what had gone before making her gasp with surprise.

'Take it,' someone said. 'Do it yourself.' And her hand was pushed between her legs to grasp the metal dildo.

'Bring yourself off,' another voice said, and Melinda was perfectly willing. She was desperately ready to come again and this was better than doing it with nothing inside her, nothing to rub against her clit. There were her fingers but this reached further than they did. A lot further.

Her pussy tightened around it so that, as she pushed it further in, there was a slight resistance. She wriggled against it, the better to enhance the excitement and, as she did so, she couldn't fail to see the rising excitement in the bodies of the onlookers.

Her own sexual needs then overcame any thought of gratifying their curiosity and she turned herself over so that the pile of the table-cover pushed against the dildo and her hands were no longer needed to push it back and forth. She screwed and pushed against it, biting her lips against the pain caused by its sheer size in her small cunt but, despite the resistance of the carpet, she found herself moving back towards the edge of the huge table.

Suddenly the metal dildo was wrenched out of her and she heard it clatter on to the marble floor. As the sound registered, Melinda was aware of being seized from behind by a man whose cock must have been at least as big as the dildo and full of the vigorous life the metal had lacked. It was so big and thrust so deep, so hard, that there were moments when she wondered if it would come out through her mouth. And it hurt. It hurt like hell. She didn't understand why pain like this was not only welcome but actually enhanced her sense of satisfaction.

She felt the man come, ramming into her with a quivering force that she guessed could only be followed by the disappointment of withdrawal. No one could have been better pleased than she to be proved very wrong indeed.

As the force of his orgasmic pumping lessened, he rearranged himself so that his legs were outside hers and hers were pushed together, holding his prick tightly inside her, grazing her clit with every thrust. Then, slowly at first but accelerating, he built up to another climax, bringing Melinda with him.

As they climaxed together, Melinda shouted with

160

pure delight, tinged with regret that he must soon withdraw. She was steeling herself to accept the inevitable and was rewarded instead with a sudden thrust which, combining both surprise and pain, made her cry out. How long would this man – whoever he was – go on? Was this perhaps the one man capable of leaving her sated?

If he was, she wasn't about to find out for, with three more heavy thrusts inside her, he withdrew as suddenly as he had entered and Melinda's disappointment showed. She was enjoying this. She'd never been brought to so many orgasms in so short a space of time before. How many more could she manage? And did it matter? She suddenly realised that she was enjoying the fucking at least as much as the climaxes that followed. She was being dominated with a vengeance – and she loved it. If she was honest with herself, it was the domination she was enjoying. The orgasms were the icing on the cake.

Khalil said something in Arabic and the men standing round the table withdrew to the divans. Khalil himself came forward and threw a soft white bathsheet over her.

'Latifa will bathe you now, and then give you something to eat.' He led her towards the door.

Melinda stared at him, nonplussed. She hadn't expected this and it certainly wasn't what she'd been psyching herself up for. 'Is that it?' she demanded. 'Is it over?'

Khalil chuckled at her dismayed tone. 'Do I take it you're ready for more?'

Melinda grinned sheepishly. 'I think I've only just got started,' she confided, and was rewarded with a shout of laughter from her escort.

'Glad to hear it,' he told her. 'Believe me, the weekend is young yet and I don't doubt it can be extended if needs be. A short rest won't do you any harm – and

161

some of your guests will be very grateful for a chance to recharge their batteries. They'll be bathing, too, and then fortifying themselves with an invigorating *seksu tanjaoui*.'

'Isn't that just another kind of couscous?' Melinda asked.

'Indeed it is, but the amount of ginger in it makes it particularly valuable in situations like the present.'

He handed her over to Latifa, who had a steaming aromatic bath ready for her mistress, and Melinda, her long hair twisted, Lautrec-style, on top of her head, slid gracefully and gratefully into the water, aware for the first time today that her muscles – and particularly those inner muscles which had had so much exercise – were in the mood to start to ache. That would never do, not while there were still undreamed-of pleasures awaiting her.

She closed her eyes and sighed deeply. Should she speculate upon their possible nature or let them come as a satisfying surprise? She hadn't the slightest doubt that, whatever they turned out to be, she'd find them immensely satisfying. A surprise, she decided. A sort of sexual Christmas present. She smiled to herself. A whole sackload of them if she was lucky.

She surrendered to the warm sensuality of the perfumed waters, enjoying the way in which the caressing warmth relaxed her body and prepared it for further enjoyment, while the perfumes worked their subtle magic on her mind. She lay there with her eyes closed and such was the influence of the aromas wafting up from the water that it wasn't long before she wasn't only ready for the next step in her sexual education but almost desperately anxious for it to begin.

As if the waiting were part of the whole strategy, Latifa, after helping her from the bath and patting her dry, massaged aromatic oils all over her before letting her sit, generously enveloped in soft towels, at the little

162

table. A silver pot of mint tea and gold-rimmed glasses were waiting here with a plate of marzipan-stuffed dates and gazelles' horns, small Moroccan pastries calculated to restore any flagging energy. Melinda didn't think there was much wrong with her energy but she knew the cakes would be delicious. It was certainly no hardship to eat them or to wash them down with the delicately sweetened tea.

The clothes Latifa brought out this time were quite different from their gauzy predecessors. Now it was the turn of sumptuous silk brocades in unsubtle combinations of emerald and vermilion, shot through with gold and heavily embroidered with freshwater pearls. It was theatrically pure *Arabian Nights*, Melinda decided as she studied her reflection. From the upturned gold toes of slippers that owed nothing to Moroccan culture to the equally foreign cloth-of-gold turban with its single peacock feather secured in place by a brooch that glittered suspiciously as if its stones were real diamonds. The brocade of the puffed trouser legs was heavy enough to stand out unaided and support the cleverly flared skirts of the matching coat so that it, too, stood out below the single button securing it beneath her breasts. The style was Persian and it might easily have been copied from a Dulac illustration.

She looked like an Englishman's idea of a woman in a harem, an effect underlined by the fact that she wore nothing else, so bare flesh was tantalisingly revealed between the fastening of her jacket and the unusually low-slung waistline of the trousers and Melinda wouldn't have been the least surprised had Latifa suddenly produced a large stone – ruby, emerald or diamond would have co-ordinated nicely – for her navel.

Nothing so crass as such cabaret-kitsch was forthcoming, however, Latifa wisely deeming it better to let a perfect skin speak for itself.

The maid was surveying the mistress with an

approvingly critical eye when a tap at the door announced Khalil. He scrutinised Melinda's appearance, approval evident in his eyes. She was certainly a stunner, he thought, and it looked as if she was going to prove every bit as much an asset to him as her great-aunt had been to his forebears. He wouldn't be at all averse to reserving her for his own exclusive enjoyment but that would be very short-sighted when, as it was, he could have her whenever he wanted.

He had only to look at the faces of the men in the *majlis* to know he was pressing the right buttons there: he knew them all well but he had never seen them as sexually aroused as they were now. The chance to test to the limit the sexual appetite of a woman whom one man couldn't possibly hope to satisfy wasn't one men often found available. Indeed, women as sexually avid as this delicious creature seemed to be weren't often come by. Melinda Carr was a sexual treasure in more ways than one.

'And her hair?' he asked Latifa in Arabic, without taking his eyes off Melinda.

'She has only to take off the turban complete and shake her head as she does so and her hair will tumble down in a natural manner. She mustn't unwind it.'

He nodded and repeated the instruction to Melinda. 'It will look very sexy. Believe me, men will find it so.'

Melinda nodded and fingered the brooch in her turban. 'These look like diamonds,' she said. 'The real thing, I mean. Are they?'

Khalil looked surprised. 'Of course.' He held out his hand. 'Come now. I escort you. Your guests are waiting, refreshed and bathed and, as you say, raring to go.'

Melinda smiled up at him, her eyes sparkling with excitement. 'Then don't let's keep them waiting,' she suggested.

This time she wasn't taken down to the *majlis* but

along the carpeted corridor to the extraordinary bedroom whose purpose seemed far removed from sleep.
As the door closed behind her, she noticed that the
mirrored door leading to the Alma-Tadema bathroom
was open and a steamy haze suggested that the mosaic-
tiled bath was ready for use.

Then she realised she was the only person in the
room, apart from Khalil, who sat quietly on guard by
the door, who was actually clothed. The men watching
her come in were all stark naked, some sitting on the
huge bed itself or on the divans under the mirrors,
some standing by the high bedposts with their golden
cords. Music, softer than that in the *majlis* but just as
Arab in feel, came from hidden tapes and once again
Melinda circled the room in time with the slower, more
sensual music, enjoying the brush of fingers against her
visible skin. She noticed that as the heavy brocade of
her clothes brushed against one of the onlookers in
passing, his cock hardened, so she made a point of
tantalising them still further by brushing her fingers
against their stiffening rods as she passed, enjoying the
sharp intake of delighted breath as she did so.

This spurred them on to less passive enjoyment and
it wasn't long before someone's fingers undid the solitary golden button so that her breasts were sometimes
partially visible, sometimes covered as she moved.
Then two men stepped forward, one on each side, to
catch hold of the bottom of each sleeve so that, as she
progressed, the jacket stayed behind.

The room was warm but, even so, the sudden loss of
the heavy brocade provoked enough chill to harden her
nipples and their surrounding aureolae into darkly
inviting peaks. Thrusting her breasts forward and arching her back, Melinda reached up to remove the turban
as Khalil had suggested, shaking her head as she did
so, so that her thick, honey-blonde hair tumbled over

her shoulders, partly concealing what had so recently been revealed.

That was when she discovered the harem trousers weren't quite what they seemed but had rather more in common with the frilly 'knickers' worn by can-can dancers a hundred years before. The total absence of any sort of join between the legs became apparent when two long fingers were suddenly thrust inside her, her obviously genuine surprise sparking laughter from those around. The next she knew, a dozen pairs of hands were forcing her to the floor – not on to the warmth of the thick rug but on to the cold marble tiles so that her hips squirmed in the effort to get away from it and the cold hardened her nipples still further. Someone held her arms firmly above her head and two men knelt down, one at each side, to suckle her breasts with a teasing, tantalising force that compelled her to open her legs still wider. Immediately, they were pulled even further apart by two more guests and the young man whose fingers had started this welcome onslaught thrust his stiff cock inside her while the men who had pulled her legs apart now forced them down and held them so that she could enjoy the full pleasure of being taken on a cold, hard surface without the freedom of movement to respond. It was a frustrating enjoyment but none the less exquisite for that.

The young man – he was certainly younger than Melinda – lacked both the self-control of the older ones and the ability to pace himself. The energy with which he thrust to a climax and then released himself into her in uncontrolled spasms indicated to Melinda that it was likely to be several hours before he would be ready to perform again. Nevertheless, she'd enjoyed the uncontrolled enthusiasm of his youth and couldn't help wondering just how good a lover he might turn into in a few years' time.

His dripping and rapidly shrinking cock had barely

withdrawn before it was replaced by that of a master, a man who knew the value to both participants of a slow and gradual build-up. He was still happy to have Melinda's hands and feet held but this time she was deliciously conscious of every inch of cock as it slowly, calculatingly, penetrated and drew back, never to the point of total withdrawal but always to a point where she feared total withdrawal might follow. This was a technique she had learned to enjoy with every nerve-ending in her body.

She longed to respond with the full abandon of a free woman, but with her wrists and ankles so firmly held, any movement she could make was minimal, limited almost entirely to clenching her vaginal muscles round the welcome intruder. When she did that, the man sunk his teeth on to her breast, already made tender by the bruising of the other two men, and bit the nipple hard enough for the pain to make her wrench her pelvis into the air – as if those few inches would bring respite from his teeth. That was not the effect. As her hips rose, her partner thrust deeper inside her until she was unsure which she was enjoying the more: the pain of the bite or the thrill of penetration.

The man said something to the others nearby. The hold on her ankles was released and he rearranged himself so that her legs were pushed together by his on either side before her ankles were held again. All this was accomplished without his cock being withdrawn.

Melinda was happily aware that she'd lost count of the number of times she'd been fucked. Completely and utterly lost count. She only knew she'd never, absolutely *never*, enjoyed herself as much as she was right now.

Such satisfying reflections were swept away as he thrust upwards within the narrow confines of her legs. She could feel the moist skin of his cock against the sensitive skin of her inner thighs where the nerve-endings tingled with pleasure close to the surface. It was the most deliciously sensual counter-balance anyone could have contrived: her thighs were stimulated as he half withdrew and then, as he plunged with deliberately calculated force, it was her sex with its unusually narrow confines that tingled to the sensation.

Melinda had always known her 'sexual equipment', as one doctor had called it, was much smaller than average. At one time she'd been told it might be unwise to try to have children. This advice was later withdrawn but since then she had been far more excited by the idea of shagging as often as possible than by that of disturbed nights and dirty nappies; the changed professional opinion made no difference to her at all. What she had learnt, though, was that when a man discovered it, he was immediately excited and, the larger his own organ, the keener he was to shove it into her. She guessed his excitement was enhanced by the thought that she would be as tight as a virgin.

As to whether she enjoyed that pain – even welcomed it – she'd never been entirely clear until today. Now she knew she could enjoy it very much and she was almost sorry that pain didn't come into the current equation. This man was big and he was undeniably skilled. Melinda could feel her orgasm building and knew from the very nature of his thrusts that they were in full harmony with each other. She tried to raise herself to move in time with him but the hands holding her down made it impossible and, at the very moment she stopped trying, she felt him release himself into her.

He must have given a signal to the men holding her feet, for suddenly they were no longer restrained and she could enjoy to the full the diminishing force of their mutually coordinated spasms of release. She'd be sorry when this man finished and she wondered whether, if there had been just the two of them, he would quite simply have gone on and on.

He seemed to feel he had had his turn for the time being and Melinda sighed with regret as she felt him slowly withdraw. He smiled into her eyes and bent down to kiss and then bite her nipple. 'There will be more,' he told her. 'If you want it, that is.'

'Oh, I want it all right,' she replied. 'I don't think you've given me the half of it yet.'

He grinned. 'Not even a tenth,' he replied, turning away and disappearing into the steam of the bathroom.

Melinda's hands were released and she was pulled to her feet and pushed back towards the bed. Its deep softness was a welcome change from the cold marble and she prepared to luxuriate in the comfort, initially oblivious to the fact that her wrists were being secured to the gilded bedposts and then surprised that her feet were left free. Someone climbed on to the bed beside her, tenderly kissing her sore nipples before his lips travelled downwards towards her shaven pussy. She closed her eyes, the better to appreciate the feel of his lips and tongue. She was happily conscious of the increasing heat of her sex and, as his mouth approached her pussy, her legs parted for him. She caught her breath as his tongue flicked lightly across her clit and she cried out with delight as it entered her. I can come to this, she thought, and I want to – and soon!

But then things changed. The tongue disappeared and its owner sat astride her to plunge his cock deep into her throat. The vacancy below was unexpectedly filled by a man who lifted her legs over his shoulders and plunged his dick into her well-lubricated and very willing sex. Melinda gasped. Two men seriously fucking her at the same time was a fantasy realised. This made her the sex toy her fantasies had always wanted, and the added spice of her tied hands gave her no option but to submit. And the idea of submission to men's demands had always been what turned her on.

Both men came simultaneously and Melinda found herself coming in orgasm to the one, while accommodating the orgasms of both. As both men unceremoniously withdrew, their juices trickled out from either end. Her wrists were untied and she was led into the mirrored splendour of the bathroom.

No longer aware who was doing what to her, the men had ceased to have separate identities. They were simply the inventive source of sexual pleasure. Far from having reached a limit yet, she felt pleasantly fulfilled, perhaps a smidgen tired, but she wasn't even within sight of having had enough. Simply thinking about where her limit might lie was enough to stir her lustful inclinations into further action.

Once they reached the side of the bath, one of the men twisted her long hair expertly into a coil and, with two or three deft moves, pinned it on top of her head before he and several others accompanied her down the steps into the depths of the cleansing, steaming water.

Some of them were already there, ensconced on the brightly coloured mosaic tiles over which the water lapped, one or two of them were on the floor of the bath and others reclined against the rim like naked Romans in Pompeii. Not so much Alma-Tadema, she thought, chuckling to herself, as Fortunino Mantania – not nearly so much collected and a lot less subtle, but much naughtier.

The quiet chuckle changed into a sudden gasp as her foot touched the step that brought the water almost, but not quite, up to her crotch. Someone at that moment must have flicked a switch because a spray of water shot up, targeting with flawless aim the shaven area between her legs. It had already given her so many previously undreamed-of pleasures but this was stimulation of a different kind and she paused on that step to savour the way the continuing spray played with an area that the last few days' activities had honed to a fine and willing receptivity.

Then strong hands drew her further into the bath, which now became a seething turmoil of tumbling waves created by submerged jets at all angles. The bath had become a far more sophisticated Jacuzzi than the one she had been thinking about having installed. Those enjoyed by friends in England paled into insignificance compared with this.

Someone came behind her and slid his arms beneath hers so that his hands cupped her breasts. In this position, he was able to pull her gently off her feet so that she floated against him and could feel his erection brushing against her as she moved with the waves. Her legs parted in a silent and symbolic invitation.

The invitation was immediately accepted – but by someone else, who took her without preamble while she was being held. The impact of his entry was deliciously cushioned by the steaming water which surged into every cranny, increasing the stimulation of the man's thrusting. When he had had enough, a man with the biggest dick she'd ever seen seized her wrist, pulled her to her feet and plunged it into her.

As soon as she saw it she feared that this time the pain would be too much even for her to bear but the effect of the water was to make it slide in so easily that it could almost have been made to measure. He was a master of sexual skills and when, holding her tightly to him, he sank on to the bottom step so that she straddled his lap and his huge cock pushed into her still further, his orgasm was immediate.

Melinda threw her head back in ecstasy and closed her eyes, enjoying the sensation of being so thoroughly and completely fucked and, as she did so, the ready hands of others supported her in the water, under her thighs and shoulders so that the man taking her with such force and skill could continue to expend himself inside her until he was ready to withdraw.

Then there were hands everywhere, soap-covered hands caressing her breasts, her belly, finding their insistent way into her willing cunt. She realised different men's fingers were playing with it in different ways – and then she knew one well-lubricated finger had eased its way into her bumhole. This was something she'd imagined and Khalil had given her a taste for more, but she'd never gone the whole hog. The initial shock was soon overcome by a feeling of guilty pleasure. Then the finger was gone. Another taster, she thought.

Before she had time to be disappointed, she was drawn to the side of the bath and pushed across the rim so that her buttocks stood high and proud above the water and her pussy was available to all.

Now I'll find out what it's like, she thought. Good. She was ready for it.

And then a towel snaked down across her backside. It was warm and damp – and it hurt. She cried out, partly in surprise, partly in pain and it struck her again. This time a corner of it reached between her legs and, as it was pulled through, she felt her cunt twitch with lust and she raised her buttocks to receive the next blow.

But none came. Instead, the ease of entry she was displaying was fully utilised by a man kneeling on the steps below. Skilled fingers parted her lips and sought her enlarged clit to tease it before his red and swollen cock entered slowly, seeking that magic spot that tongues had found, the further to excite her before plunging in. His fingers added to her excitement by playing with every accessible part of her cunt as his own pleasure mounted and Melinda screwed herself against him. He was deep and he was satisfying. She shuddered with delight as he came and she heard herself murmur, 'Don't stop. Go on. I want it to go on for ever.'

Face down as she was, she didn't see the lascivious glances exchanged by her guests. As the man's cock slid out of her, she was pulled back into the water and sensuously soaped all over, no crevice overlooked, before she was guided out of the bath. As she stood on the warm tiles, looking round for a towel, a spray of ice-cold water shot up to rinse between her legs. Her gasp of surprise had barely subsided when the spray was followed by an unsophisticated ice-cold rinse of her body from the silver jugs which every man seemed to hold.

She could feel the sudden hardening of her nipples with the impact of the cold douche and knew from the men's glances that they'd noticed it, too. Not until then did they produce an all-enveloping towel and take great pleasure in patting her dry as if she were a child.

When they led her back into the bedroom, she saw that the blinds were down. It must be night, she thought, and she wondered what time it was. She glanced round and realised for the first time that there was no clock in the room. She looked at the men. None was wearing a watch. Khalil would be, though, and Khalil was still sitting, fully clothed, by the door.

Melinda turned to him. 'What time is it?' she asked.

He grinned but he didn't look at his watch. 'It's a few hours into Sunday,' he said. 'You're doing fine.'

Chapter Nine

Sunday

*A*s Melinda was led into the adjacent sumptuous bedroom, she sensed that the atmosphere had changed. The previous light-heartedness had gone, to be replaced by purposeful determination, and she guessed that from now on they were going to set about their task in earnest.

She shivered with delighted expectation. Good, she thought. Now the fun really begins. She glanced at the faces surrounding her. These were definitely not the faces of men seeking a dominatrix; Khalil had chosen well – she could look forward to hours of domination. It might not be politically correct but it promised a lot more fun. She hadn't the slightest intention of being reduced to a lump of shaggable flesh. That wasn't her idea of fun at all. Even when she was held down or secured to the table in the *majlis*, she hadn't been inert, only limited to a response less vigorous than her body wanted. This was the second day of the experiment and Khalil had said the weekend could be open-ended. Her pussy clenched itself expectantly and she wondered whether her sexual appetite would be as open-ended as the calendar.

As she approached the bed, she saw that Larbi already lay there, his enormous scimitar of an erection impatient to impale a woman's cunt and ram her to distraction. He watched her approach with lascivious eyes and, as the towel slipped to the floor, his eyes raked her naked body as if he were seeing it for the first time.

He beckoned to her. 'Here,' he said. 'I want it in you. Now. And I want you to put it there without help from me.'

Melinda climbed on to the high bed and straddled him. He had a hard-on and she knew he'd be happy to enter her right now, but she preferred to heighten his enjoyment as well as her own. She bent over his swollen cock, red with the blood that was racing into it, and flicked her tongue around it, taking care not to miss the slit through which he would soon be filling her. She heard his sharp intake of breath and knew she'd surprised him, but also that the surprise was a welcome one.

When she judged he was close to coming, she clasped his stiff shaft and guided it into her. The cold douche had tightened her up again – perhaps that had been its purpose – and now she was increasingly ready to be enjoyed. It was still too tight to admit Larbi's huge prick so Melinda straddled him wider and parted her sex with her fingers, taking care to brush her clit so that the juices that would speed his penetration were encouraged to flow.

As her tightness gave way and she screwed his cock deep inside her, she moaned with the pleasure of a woman who knows this is just the beginning. God, how she enjoyed being possessed! She leant forward so that her breasts hung, round, full and temptingly available for his tongue, his teeth, his hands to raise her desire to new heights.

But hands pulled her back so that the penetration

was greater and she cried out with the pain even though it would be that very pain that would lash her to an orgasm. Larbi plunged upwards into her and she forced herself down upon him, her cries now a mixture of pain and delight. Her tongue had felt his cock's slit and now her imagination could see it widening, ready for his release.

They climaxed together, his powerful convulsions adding to her pain and her pleasure and, as they diminished and he shrank inside her, she knew she didn't want him to.

'Again,' she pleaded. 'Don't come out. Take me again.'

Those words were enough to make him harden again and, when she reached behind her to finger his balls, she knew it wouldn't be long before he was ready to indulge her again.

This time he pushed his legs outside hers and drew them together so that she was in a vice-like grip. Held tightly like this, Melinda flexed her pussy muscles round his cock and felt it harden even more as he gasped in surprised delight. Holding her tightly to him, he rolled her on to her back, pumping into her as he did so. Then he started in earnest, slowly, delicately at first so that she raised her hips as high as she could beneath his weight to get a fuller penetration. He wanted it, too, and pushed her legs apart to screw himself hard inside her with mind-blowing intensity. His cock was brushing against her hard clit and the sensation lashed her into an uncontrollable frenzy of sexual delight. Larbi was the most perfect sexual partner she'd had so far but, even as she writhed in ecstasy, she still wondered whether a better one might not yet be found.

She climaxed again and as her orgasmic explosion diminished, she felt him reach his peak. He groaned with satisfaction as he came with such power that her own spasms of relief revived to harmonise with his. She wished they'd been alone. Who knew how often and in what manner he could shag her before he was exhausted?

'Pass her on,' a peremptory voice said, and Larbi withdrew, smiling down at her as he did so.

'This needn't be the end,' he murmured. 'You and I have a lot more to try.'

Now Melinda found herself being grabbed roughly from all sides. She was pulled off the bed and made to stand at the foot, where two men unwrapped the golden cords from the bedposts and tied her hands to the topmost finials while two others tied her ankles to the bottom. There was no 'give' at all. She could only move her head. Perhaps it would be sex without finesse from now on. Her pussy tingled at the prospect. In her present mood, being nothing but a sex toy suited her just fine.

Before she'd had time to wonder what was next, someone's cock forced its way in with no attempt by its possessor to move her moist lips out of the way first. It was painful and it was soon clear that the man was only interested in his own satisfaction, not hers. Domination with a vengeance, she thought happily. Her assailant seemed to get most of his pleasure from the fact that she was physically prevented from responding to his onslaught and she wondered if he'd have enjoyed it quite so much if she'd been free. As it was, his fucking had an exhilarating edge of violation, which was by no means unwelcome. Only those inner muscles were free to do as they pleased, and they did. Melinda could see the surprise on his face and guessed he wasn't sure whether she realised what she'd done.

She felt someone get behind her on the bed. Strong hands stroked her smooth body, brushing her breasts and sliding across her spine, her buttocks, to play with her cunt from behind so that a finger competed with the cock. Her inability to respond became even more frustrating.

Suddenly it dawned on her that he was using two fingers and, while one played with her cunt, the other had slipped into her anus. There was something exciting about the resulting sensation.

Her assailant came quickly. He soon spent himself inside her and withdrew, leaving his come to trickle down her legs. Now the much smaller prick of the man behind was hard against her sex, as if she were riding on the crossbar of a man's bike. She fully expected it to be plunged in from behind, but she hadn't bargained for the fact that this man would take his pleasure another way. She realised he was gradually, insistently pushing it into her anus and, spread-eagled between the bedposts as she was, she could do nothing about it except submit to a new and painful experience. She could call for Khalil but the fact that she didn't want to told her something about her true reactions to this brand-new violation.

She could tell the man was being careful. He must have had a shrewd idea she'd never had it this way before and she guessed he was anxious that she should enjoy it – so that another time he could indulge himself with greater abandon. She suspected that, right now, he'd be content not to reach a climax, that all he intended was to accustom her to the idea that buggery was as much fun as anything else.

He withdrew as carefully as he'd entered and Melinda saw impatience on the surrounding faces. They'd have done it differently.

Now she was untied, but not for long.

This time her wrists were tied behind her and she was lifted on to the bed, face down. Someone turned her face to one side so that she wouldn't smother. Her ankles were again tied to the posts and her body was pushed back towards them so that her buttocks and

178

cunt were forced upwards. Cords were attached to her wrists and tied down to the same posts as her feet. It was now impossible to lie flat or straight on the bed.

Two men were going to take her now. One, she saw out of the corner of her eye, stood behind her, his erection ready for use, maybe in her pussy, maybe in her anus. She shuddered. Time would tell. The other lay beside her, his thick cock against her mouth.

Melinda obediently opened her mouth and began to lick the cock, gently to start with. As she took it into her mouth, she felt fingers pull her moist pussy lips apart and push themselves inside, every nerve-tingling inch of her narrow cunt feeling the pleasure. His long fingers were soon replaced by his cock and she thrust herself towards him with what negligible leeway she had. I like it, she thought, I like it a lot. She gasped with pleasure as his shaft then rammed into her with greater force but this cry was immediately stopped by the other man's dick plunging into her mouth with renewed vigour.

Both men fucked her hard with the unerring accuracy of long practice and Melinda gave herself up to enjoying her enforced submission. It was soon apparent that they were harmonising their thrusts so that they would come together. The very thought of two men climaxing into her simultaneously was enough to spur her to an orgasm in time with theirs. She could only wriggle her buttocks in delight but the man got the message and screwed himself into her so hard that it hurt as much as she could have hoped for. They all three came together in a paroxysm of orgasmic release and both men withdrew together, leaving Melinda to enjoy the taste and feel of their success.

When she opened her eyes, her next pleasure was standing beside the bed. Since he could only enter her from behind, she knew the nature of what was in store. He was one of the younger men, his body honed to a muscular beauty, and she watched as he brought a huge vibrator from behind him and fastened it round his hips so that it sat above his not inconsiderable cock. He held it against her tied hands. Melinda could feel that the hard stainless steel was vibrating gently. She squirmed with delight.

He laughed at her expression and slapped her hard across the rump. The gently vibrating phallus tingled, making her catch her breath as it vibrated over her clit.

If only I were free, she thought. What wouldn't I give to be able to make the most of this? She tightened herself around it, pushing herself as far backward on to it as her bonds would allow. She was rewarded with vibrations so powerful that they were almost unbearable, and their strength was reinforced with the rhythmic pumping of the young athlete behind. She had no idea what sexual satisfaction the man was deriving from this variation and she fully expected the object to be withdrawn. I can't be the only one enjoying this, she thought, or he wouldn't be using it. This weekend may be about testing me to my limits but every man here is getting his own gratification along the way.

As her pleasure eased, so did the vibrations, but the phallus remained plunged inside her up to the hilt. She wriggled against it and felt the young man begin to plunge it back and forth within her. She wondered if it was her imagination that the phallus had now both swollen and heated up. The avid faces around her showed that something had changed and she didn't think it was simply because she was forced to crouch there like some captive animal.

Suddenly the cords binding her to the bed were cut. Her wrists remained tied behind her and the phallus was still inside her, being forced back and forth as strongly as before. She writhed against this intrusion; she pushed her legs straight down behind her as if that would dislodge the hot, hard dildo. But the man held her rigidly in place and took the fullest possible advantage of her struggles. He twisted her long, thick hair round his hand and jerked her head backward and, as her spine threw her buttocks upward, he slapped her hard across her backside.

She recognised once more that pain enhanced her pleasure. The pleasure she was feeling right now was a perverse one – and it was that perversity that thrilled her. She glanced over her shoulder and guessed from the ecstatic expression on his face that the phallus's wearer had been rubbing himself and was close to climaxing. She knew he was completed only when he pulled the vibrating phallus out of her with neither ceremony nor consideration. Melinda let out a yelp of suprise as he came. She now felt exhausted.

Khalil was instantly at her side. 'That was amazing,' he said.

'I'm not finished yet, am I?' she asked.

'Not yet,' said Khalil. 'You need a soothing bath and Latifa's ministrations. I suggest a few hours' rest. It wasn't part of the original deal but we feel a rest will only improve matters later, when we're ready to test you to your absolute limits.' He glanced up at the surrounding faces and all nodded their reluctant agreement.

'No one wants to see her tortured into defeat,' Larbi remarked.

Someone handed Khalil the bathsheet she'd been wrapped in before and he placed it gently round her shoulders.

'If you've no wish to continue after you've had a rest, you must say so,' he told her. 'Do you trust me?'

Melinda looked up into his handsome face and nodded. Oddly enough, she did. 'He's just made me so very sore,' she said. 'I think the inclination's still there, just so long as Latifa knows what to do for me physically.'

181

'If she doesn't, no one will,' Khalil told her. He turned to the guests. 'Once I've handed Miss Carr over to her maid, I'll have a word with the cook. I'm sure something more than half decent can be rustled up. She was talking about *b'stillas*.' He nodded towards the glass panelling of one wall. 'You'll find some robes in there – and you know where the bathroom is.'

With these words he guided Melinda to the door and along to her own room.

Latifa smiled when she saw Melinda.

'She says she knows exactly what you need and she can have your body as right as rain in no time – well, in a couple of hours – but she can't guarantee you'll still want to continue the game. She's no control over your mind, she says, but she's given me a list of food for the kitchen to prepare, which she reckons will do the trick.' Khalil frowned. 'They're not dishes I've heard of, though, which is a bit unusual. She says they're traditional Berber ones from the *bled* – the countryside. That would account for it.'

'Will the cook know them?' Melinda asked doubtfully.

'Oh, yes. They come from the same village deep in the Rif. She'll be on the same wavelength.'

'You look worried. You don't think Latifa would do me any harm?'

'Heavens above, no! No, it's just that ... well, I suppose the truth is I'm a bit of a control freak. I like to know exactly what's what when it happens on my – what's the expression? – my bailiwick. You can't do better than put yourself entirely in Latifa's hands, I promise you.' And with this assurance he bowed to the maid's urging and left the room.

The bath was just the right temperature for comfort; warm enough to ease aching muscles but not enough to flush the palest skin. Its perfume was soft and calming and Melinda suspected it might also be mildly astringent which, in the circumstances, would be no bad thing.

When she judged Melinda to have soaked long enough, Latifa raised her to her feet and began to soap her all over, once again reminding Melinda of a nanny. She rinsed her thoroughly and then reached for a large tub of salve. Pushing Melinda's legs apart, Latifa smeared generous amounts of this cream on to her and worked it deep into her pussy. Already Melinda felt less sore. Perhaps she hadn't been torn as she had feared. Every delicate tissue was covered with salve and, although there was nothing overtly sexual about Latifa's actions, Melinda realised that, once she could be sure the pain and soreness had gone, she would be only too willing to resume what Khalil had called 'the game'.

When Latifa was ready to pat her mistress dry, she took care to avoid disturbing the healing ointment, which must be left to do its job. She wrapped Melinda in a warm robe and sat her down in a comfortable armchair. A cosy, down-filled duvet was tucked round her legs and when a small silver pot of coffee arrived, Latifa opened a cupboard door and, to Melinda's amazement, took out a bottle of Remy Martin. She then added a generous slurp to the coffee. Melinda knew alcohol was available to tourists in hotels – she'd even seen it in some grocers' shops – but she also knew it was forbidden to Muslims, so she didn't expect to come across it in a private house, even if that house had belonged to an Englishwoman for decades. In any case, she thought, that particular bottle hasn't been there since Great-Aunt Laura's last visit, that's for sure. She sipped it. Whisky would have been better, but the warmth percolating down inside her was both welcome and reassuring. It induced a feeling of wellbeing,

which was reinforced by the deliciously different couscous which followed. The warm bath, the brandy and
the warm meal had their inevitable effect and Melinda
soon dozed off in the comfort of the armchair. When
she eventually woke up, Latifa was ready for the next
stage in her mistress's recovery.

She stood her in the shower and let the inverted
showerhead rinse the salve from her sex. Melinda
closed her eyes. It was a very pleasant sensation, she
decided, though she couldn't see her maid's little smile
or her nod of approval. Latifa wasn't averse to having
a chance to prove to Benani that she knew her job. If
she was successful, she could expect a nice little commission from him when it was all over, and she was
gratified to find there was no involuntary flinch of pain
as she patted Melinda dry between her legs. Good. The
salve had done its job.

She lay Melinda on the bed and massaged perfumed
oil over her entire body with strokes that expertly
combined gentleness with firmness in a way which
could only fan her mistress's sexual desires into new
life.

Melinda lay there enjoying the stimulation of the
maid's proficient touch and dreaming of her next bout
of shagging. How would she be taken this time? Would
the men come up with another variation? Or would it
become a case of wham, bang, thank you, ma'am? Or
something more drawn out and lingering. Right now
her vote was for drawn out and lingering.

When Latifa judged she had done sufficient and
knew that Melinda was now smooth and fragrant
enough to arouse the most jaded sexual palate – and
was satisfied that Melinda's own appetite for fucking
had been fully restored – she helped her to her feet. She
helped her into a deceptively virginal *peignoir* and
brushed her hair until it shone. The reflection in the
mirror was that of a young and vulnerable woman. It

could almost, Melinda thought with an ironic smile, be the image of a virgin awaiting her husband on her wedding night.

A tap at the door heralded Khalil's return. He smiled at her evident surprise. 'Every room has a bell. I was in the kitchen so that when it rang from this room, I'd know you were ready. Are you?'

Melinda smiled shyly. 'As near as I can tell,' she said, and then she chuckled. There was nothing shy about the chuckle. 'The spirit is certainly willing,' she added.

He grinned. 'Then we must hope that the flesh doesn't prove to be too weak.'

As she entered the specialised bedroom one more, the men lounging on the bed and reclining on the divans rose to their feet and gave her a standing ovation to which the most fitting response seemed to be a curtsy of diva-like proportions and the skirt of her *peignoir* floated gently down with her like petals of some exotically perfumed rose at the very peak of its beauty. Melinda might be unaware of the image she presented. The men were not. All were wearing robes of one sort or another but, as they stood there clapping, one after another of them let them slide to the floor until they were all once more naked – naked and ready.

It was Larbi who came forward to take her by the hand. 'Don't be anxious,' he said. 'We resolved that your re-introduction will begin gently. You've already proved yourself to be something special. We regard ourselves as, shall we say, connoisseurs and none of us has any desire to let such a diamond slip through our fingers for want of a little care on our part.'

Melinda lowered her eyes and smiled up at him from beneath her lashes. 'M'sieur, the fingers of all of you are organs of the utmost skill – and not only your fingers,' she added demurely. 'I've every faith in your

185

ability – your collective ability – to nurture and polish to perfection anything you regard as a diamond.'

He inclined his head in acknowledgement of a compliment returned and gestured to the front of her *peignoir*. 'I think this time, Mademoiselle Almaas, we'd like to see you disrobe yourself entirely unaided.'

'Mademoiselle Almaas?' Melinda queried, puzzled.

'Diamond. *Almaas* means diamond.'

The *peignoir* was buttoned from neck to hem and undoing the bottom buttons first, as the men had done previously, was not going to be the most graceful way of doing as she was told. So she began at the neck, undoing each button slowly and carefully for maximum effect, making quite sure as she reached her breasts that her audience wasn't denied glimpses of the thrusting white toys that she knew turned most of them on. A glance told her that nothing had changed. Each one of them had hardened and most were craning their necks for the smallest 'accidental' glimpse of tantalising nipple.

With the button below her navel undone, she rotated her hips slowly as if she were about to break into a belly-dance and then, one more button unfastened, she drew the top of the garment across her shoulders so that they no longer kept it in place and it slid slowly to the ground, caressing her breasts, her belly, her hips as it fell. She stepped out of the pool of flower-patterned lawn, her head high, her breasts thrust out and her arms and hands raised in a gentle curve above her head in the triumphant gesture of a circus artiste's response to her audience.

It was Larbi who led her to the bed and gestured to her to lie down, but it wasn't Larbi who lay there with her. Instead he beckoned a man over and Melinda suspected this had been by prior arrangement. The man's cock wasn't small but it certainly wasn't too big. What's more, despite his erection, it didn't look as if he was going to be in any hurry for he had armed himself with one of the peacock feathers Khalil had used some time before – and so, she realised with a delighted little shiver, had all the other men.

The delicate brushing of her neck, her breasts, her belly and downwards, not just towards her naked cunt but further, to the tingling nerves of her inner thighs, was more stimulating than fingers or tongue. The feathers stimulated her in so many places at once that the pleasure amounted to something very close to the most delicious torture imaginable and even if she'd wanted to keep her legs together, it would have been impossible. So the feathers tantalised her there, too, and Melinda knew that unless someone did something soon, she'd come to nothing more substantial than a peacock's eye.

But it wasn't to be the feather after all. As she closed her eyes in tortured ecstasy, she felt a warm tongue licking, teasing, her lower lips. She could feel them swell and moisten so she thrust her legs as wide apart as she could. She wanted his tongue on her clit, not just playing around the edge. Oh, how badly she wanted it!

And then it was. With expert precision it homed in on the hard nub of her clit. One flick was all it took to jerk her into a sudden convulsion of delight. Another, and she was in the throes of full orgasm. There was a murmur of comment from the onlookers and Larbi translated for her.

'We're agreed we've never seen so instantaneous and dramatic an outcome of that particular technique,' he told her.

She smiled at him as her climax subsided. 'And I can't remember ever having been brought to quite so sudden an outcome,' she told him. 'I can assure you, it felt as amazing as it must have looked.'

The man whose tongue had proved so devastatingly effective a tool now climbed on to the bed as she lay there, breathing heavily after the energetic efforts of the last few minutes. His fingers toyed playfully with her breasts, teasing and pulling the nipples until he was ready to sink his mouth on to them, sucking and biting while his hands, now free to explore elsewhere, did just that: a journey of exploration to gauge just how ready Melinda might be to accept even the largest cock.

His exploring hands soon told him she was hot for him and moist with horniness. He parted the lips and slowly, carefully, gently, eased his hard prick inside her. Melinda's little cry of gratitude at the moment of entry spoke volumes. It was the moment that never lost its delight – the best moment of all because it promised the joys still to come.

He paused there to let her savour that moment and felt his consideration rewarded when she tightened her muscles round him so that his cock was held in a firm and unexpected grip. Then he pulled back. He'd observed the pleasure she'd had from others when a partial withdrawal had been carried out with complete control. He would give her the same pleasure. Her sharp intake of breath was his signal to plunge back in, a little further this time. Again he nearly quit her, watching her hold her breath for fear he'd leave her altogether, but this man knew his craft. Once more he hovered on her brink and this time his re-entry was slow and gradual, so that every inch of her cunt could enjoy the sensation. This time he almost reached her end.

Almost, but not quite. His tremendous self-control enabled him to pull back almost too far. He paused there briefly – and then plunged into her with the force he had hitherto avoided. This time he fucked as far into her sex as he could reach and Melinda gasped with pleasure and put her hand down on herself. She was close to coming now and she wanted to prolong the arousal, to delay the explosion of delight.

His hands slid under her buttocks, forcing their bodies even closer as he timed his own explosion to coincide with hers. My God, she thought, this man is good. Really good. I want him again.

They came together in so great a climax that the satisfying rhythmic convulsions were greater than any of the thrusting that had preceded them. They diminished in unison, too, the man still holding Melinda as close to him as any lover.

'Don't withdraw,' she whispered. 'I want it again. Soon. I know you can.'

'Yes, I can,' he replied, 'and few things would give me greater pleasure. With you I could occupy a whole night and never sleep – and I think you'd like that.'

Melinda smiled. 'I think I would,' she agreed.

'Unfortunately, we're not alone here. There are other men as skilled and equally keen to give you the pleasure you lust for.'

'And of taking their own,' Melinda pointed out.

He looked surprised. 'Of course. These things work both ways. The point is, we're not alone and they're impatient for their turn. It isn't only a matter of discovering your sexual limits, you know, but also to discover who will have the distinction of bringing you there. Everyone must have their chance.'

With these words he withdrew, kissing Melinda's glowing pussy as he did so and flicking his tongue provocatively across it at the moment his prick finally left her.

'It seems that you still have plenty of energy,' Larbi remarked as she lay supine on the bed.

'Thank God,' she commented and propped herself up on one elbow. 'Tell me, had that young man intended to tire me out so that he could have the distinction of being the victor?'

The men exchanged glances. 'Something like that,'

Larbi admitted. He hesitated. 'Does the idea revolt you?'

Melinda looked surprised. 'Why should it? I mean, given the nature of the weekend and the goal of seeing how much I can take, I should think it's a natural progression.' She looked from one face to another. 'Tell me, does the one who takes me last of all get some sort of reward for his achievement?'

Larbi looked uncomfortable. 'In a manner of speaking, yes.'

'What?'

'This is difficult because Muslims aren't supposed to gamble, but there is a kitty. The last one takes all.'

Melinda chuckled. Another pinch of spice had just been added to the dish. 'My guess is that the kitty isn't especially small.' A glance around was enough to tell her she was right. 'Well, then, we'd better waste no more time. What have you lined up for me next?'

One of the younger men grinned. 'Don't you have a saying in English about actions speaking louder than words?'

Melinda smiled. 'We do – and it's truer in this activity than in most.'

The laughter was general and her guests descended on her, touching, brushing, feeling, but amongst these rousing sensations were other, more deeply exciting ones. Her last question hadn't been answered so there was a hint of fear because she'd effectively given them carte blanche to use her body entirely as their plaything.

They liked to dominate, she to be dominated, and bondage was the best way to satisfy both. Leather straps fastened her wrists and ankles firmly to the bedposts so she was staked out like a farmer in cattle-country for the ants to sting to death. The bed was a lot more comfortable than Death Valley and she very much doubted whether ants would give the sexual delight she was looking forward to here but the analogy was close enough for the fear to rise higher, to harden her nipples and tighten her cunt even as she was once more moistening with anticipation. This initial penetration could hurt, she thought, shivering with delight at the prospect.

One of the older men, his prick hardening but not yet stiff enough to make an entry, lay lightly upon her, placing his rising cock between her breasts and massaging them towards it to hasten the process. The effect he sought didn't come quickly enough for his satisfaction so he pulled himself forward so that it was dangling across Melinda's mouth.

'Lick it,' he ordered. 'Lick it hard.'

Melinda wanted it elsewhere, and the sooner the better, but obedience was the name of the game and probably the best way of achieving her own goal. She licked him slowly as if his cock were a stick of barley sugar; she wrapped her tongue round it; she let it play lightly with the slit at the top and, as her tongue felt his response, she found the sensation of it hardening inside her mouth a surprisingly arousing one.

He withdrew suddenly and unexpectedly and whispered in her ear, 'I am going to fuck you so hard.'

'Is that a threat or a promise?' she asked apprehensively.

He smiled unpleasantly. 'Oh, it's a promise. Make no mistake about that.'

She shivered and clenched her pussy as tightly as she could as he sought entrance both with his fingers and his cock.

A command to the onlookers led to a loosening of her ankle-bonds and something that felt like a hard, curved stool was pushed under her buttocks, raising her clenched opening to general view. Then the straps were tightened again and she had even less leeway than before.

This time one finger forced its way into her and then, his rod guided to the exact spot, withdrew. There was a brief hiatus while he adjusted his position for maximum effect and then he drove his cock so forcefully into her that she cried out. Once it was there, however, the warm enticing moistness of her sex helped it to drive forward without hindrance. It had behind it the power of a very strong man.

If she hadn't been tied up, it would have been a plain, straightforward, old-fashioned fuck, Melinda decided. As it was, her enforced immobility mixed with her lust for domination gave a charge of almost electric excitement to every savage thrust – and they were very savage. She could feel him deep inside now. It hurt, though not enough to destroy her want for more, but she was tied so firmly that she had no control over her arousal and she would have to orgasm without being able to move. His fingers had moved up to her clit. This would bring pleasures that overcame the frustration. It would be exciting for both of them and his climax couldn't be far off now.

It wasn't. He came with the same strength his fucking had demonstrated, releasing himself inside her with a force that gratified both of them but then, his own satisfaction achieved, he withdrew without preamble at exactly the moment Melinda's own orgasm exploded.

Her eyes were tightly closed, the better to savour the excruciating experience of bondaged ecstasy. She clenched and unclenched whatever muscles she could and knew the bystanders were watching avidly, her inability to react bodily not disguising in the least what she was enduring.

Her body finally relaxed on the hard stool and she barely noticed when the support was removed. She was beginning to tire now. The unremitting shagging and her repeated orgasms were beginning to take their toll, but she wasn't too tired to want more. Not yet.

Khalil stepped forward and, after whispering with Larbi, addressed the room.

'Miss Carr. Gentlemen. I have to tell you that, thanks to Miss Carr's enforced rest after that unpleasant young man's antics, time is running ahead of us. We all expected this trial to last over Saturday and Sunday. Monday has just arrived. It seems to me that neither you nor Miss Carr are really ready to quit yet, but she has time at her disposal if she wants to go on and some of you may not. What do you want to do? Admit defeat or go on?'

'Is Miss Carr willing to continue?' one of the men asked.

Khalil turned to her with an enquiring look. 'Well?' he asked.

'I'm looking forward to it,' Melinda told them.

The men looked at each other and nodded. 'Another day won't be impossible,' Larbi said. 'Most of us are our own bosses. Those who aren't – like me – can always be taken unexpectedly ill. I dare say we all ate at the same restaurant.'

Khalil nodded. 'Then the game goes on,' he said.

Chapter Ten

Monday

*T*he brief interruption did nothing to dampen Melinda's readiness to go on. She hoped the men would come up with more variations to whet her appetite though the absent-minded fingers playing carelessly with her pussy while the exchange went on didn't augur much change.

But when Khalil had resumed his seat and attention was once more fixed on her, she noticed for the first time that one of the men was holding a black leather lash that looked suspiciously like a soft leather version of a cat-o'-nine tails without the knots at the end of each thong.

She tensed. This wasn't a variation she'd bargained for. A good hard slap was one thing. A thorough beating was something else.

She was manhandled on to her belly and the leather manacles tightened. A hand came down hard on her exposed buttocks, the first of a rain of heavy slaps and then, as if this had only been a preparation for what was to come, the man with the lash stood in front of her, his arm raised. She saw he had strapped a leather codpiece over his cock, presumably to protect it from being accidentally caught by the thongs. He meant serious business.

The lashes came down on her unprotected backside. Melinda flinched. She was too tightly bound to pull away from it.

The man was an expert. After that first stroke on her already tingling cheek, the lashes moved up her body until the fear of the thongs lashing the soft, sensitive flesh of her breasts tightened and hardened them. But here his technique was more subtle. The thongs struck her back in such a way that the thin ends trailed across the exposed edges of her breasts, tightening and hardening the concealed tips. Thin red welts across her back recorded his skill and he continued the pain down to her buttocks again. Now he changed his position. Most of the lashes still thrashed her buttocks but some of them reached down into the cleft between or flicked sharply between her legs.

Beneath Melinda's pain was a strong undercurrent of rising desire, desperate to be assuaged. She knew that the feel of a cock inside her while the area around it was hotly tingling would have a thrill all its own.

As if she'd spoken, the man with the whip stepped back. Fingers pushed inside her and another was rammed up her anus; she could feel them playing against the skin between.

Now she saw the man had put down his lash and unbuckled his codpiece. He had a massive hard-on and was playing with it. No, she realised, not playing with it – lubricating it.

He grinned when he saw her expression and went behind her. The fingers were removed and the lubricated prick was pushed relentlessly into her tight, virgin anus. He filled her arse like nothing she could have imagined and, despite the lubrication, it hurt – but she wanted more. He fucked her steadily, purposefully, and the tightness brought its own quivering excitement.

Her cunt cried out to get its own satisfaction but Melinda's hands were tied.

'For God's sake, someone ram the other side,' she cried out.

And instantly someone did. Fingers slid inside her. They played with her lips as they sought the nub of her clit. Melinda trembled with excitement as her arousal mounted. This was some variation on two men, she thought, her mouth opening in a gasp of delight at this exquisite torture. Then her wrists were unexpectedly untied and, as her head was free to move, a third man was there beside her, half kneeling, half lying, his cock rammed into her mouth. Someone held her arms above her to give him free access, automatically preventing her from helping him. She was virtually inert. She was a sex object to be taken, to be used, to be enjoyed: she was being fucked senseless and it was the most exciting thing she'd ever had done to her.

Both men were coming fast and she was already there – the fingers on her clit saw to that. The three of them climaxed almost simultaneously and Melinda knew it was a sensation she'd remember for ever – a mind-blowing explosion of ecstatic satisfaction and pain.

'Turn her over,' someone said.

Her bonds were untied, she was turned on to her back and her arms were pulled together above her head and fastened to the bedhead. Her legs were splayed taut and she was savagely penetrated before she'd had time to draw breath. This man meant to finish her off, she thought, as he rammed hard and then rammed again. He may well succeed, she decided, grunting at every lunge inside her. There was no finesse here. He might have been fucking an animal – or a blow-up doll – and it wasn't easy to have to lie there and take it – but neither did she want it to stop. The sheer violence would bring her off and she had no wish to climax on her own.

Light fingers began to play with the soft white skin of her upstretched arms, travelling lightly down and across her naked armpits to her breasts and then down between her legs. The contrast between the lightness of this man's touch and the other so heavily shagging her was such that it was almost as though she was two bodies, each enjoying itself independently of the other.

She opened her eyes and saw a man kneeling astride her, the scimitar of his prick a hair's breadth from her mouth. It was instinctive to flick her tongue across the glans. She knew he'd want that, knew it would make him harden even though she didn't want her attention distracted from the other cock ravaging inside her.

The man grinned. He guessed what was in her mind, but she was tied. No way could she refuse him if he insisted – she'd already sucked most men's cocks dry and he didn't intend to go without. He moved to plunge his dick into her mouth – and found the passage barred by white teeth.

He swore. It wasn't in French but Melinda had no need of an interpreter: the tone was enough. 'When I've come,' she said. 'I'm nearly there.'

He seemed to accept that, contenting himself with brushing his hard-on against her lips as if he knew she was close to coming – and close she certainly was. She arched her neck and her eyes closed as the man's thrusts pushed her body to the limits of the leather bonds and her orgasm to its climax.

Her mouth opened in a gasp of joyous delight – and was promptly filled by the swollen cock lurking at its edge. She had come and she could feel the other cock coming high inside her. She wanted to feel him come, to feel it trickling out of her again.

But before that pleasure was realised, the cock now plunging against the back of her throat had spurted its load, speeded up by the enforced wait. Melinda had never before wanted to swallow come. She knew there were women who enjoyed it but it wasn't a taste she'd acquired, and so far she'd been able to close her throat. But she gave in this time. She gagged at first, but after a few seconds her throat opened and she felt it slide down like cream.

At the very moment she was compelled to swallow, she felt the other man come, the sheer force of his cock's convulsive release pushing her hard against her bonds.

The violence of that fuck was over too soon and his deliberately slow withdrawal of a still-rigid cock down the full length of her tautly held legs was little short of subtle torture. It had been good and she'd like such a brutal fuck again – but not right now.

She was tired but not yet finished and she guessed they must be wondering how much more she could take. She'd be interested to find out herself. 'Why don't you untie me?' she suggested. 'After all, I'm likely to tire much more quickly if I can use all my muscles.'

They exchanged glances and she knew her surmise had been right. She was rubbing the circulation back into her wrists when the onslaught began.

Pleasure had little to do in the men's minds with the continuous shagging that followed; mutual pleasure, none. That didn't stop Melinda getting pleasure from it, all the same. The sheer sexual violence of their fucking saw to that. She was rammed by cocks of every size. They were shoved into her without preamble from every position they could push her into. They fucked her on the soft bed, the harder divans, the cold marble floor. Every man thrust and screwed until he came and there were so many of them that each had ample time to recover before his turn came round again.

Under such relentless bombardment as this, Melinda could no longer climax and gave herself up instead to the pleasure of submission to such total, violating domination. It was good. She wouldn't want it all the time, perhaps not even very often, but boy, was she enjoying it. Whoever finally defeated her would certainly have earnt whatever was in the kitty.

The men weren't idle while they recharged their batteries. Depending on her position, she could expect her breasts to be fondled, a finger to toy with her arse, a flaccid penis to be licked into another erection and the smallest response from her now couldn't fail to excite her current partner into thrusting with renewed energy and increased satisfaction.

Melinda knew she was tiring fast. She was beginning to feel both sore and 'used' and she didn't enjoy either sensation. It wasn't going to be long before she'd have to call it a day and when the current man withdrew, relief rather than regret was uppermost in her mind for the first time. The time had come to admit defeat.

'Enough,' she said. 'That's it. I've had enough.'

A cheer went up and she could hear the admiring congratulations being lavished on the man who had been the last to take her. A warm blanket was wrapped round her and she opened her exhausted eyes to see Khalil's concerned face peering down at her. 'Are you all right?'

Melinda managed a tired smile. 'I'm sore and I'm knackered and I feel as if my inside has been gouged out into a cavern big enough to hide St Paul's in. But otherwise I'm fine. I dare say Latifa can heal me.'

'No doubt about it,' he assured her. 'She'll be waiting for you.'

He helped her to her feet and was guiding her to the door when their way was barred. A man stepped forward. It was the man whom Melinda would very much have liked to have been able to continue, the man whose skilled and subtle intercourse had pleasured her as much as him.

199

'You're a truly amazing sexual partner, Miss Carr,' he said. 'You seem to have inherited a lot more than just your great-aunt's property. You've taken us to the limit, too. Our manhoods have certainly been tested this weekend – and we've had the benefit of the occasional respite while someone else took you on. You should know that we're unanimously lost in admiration of your stamina – and we all appreciate the fact that you didn't just submit but enjoyed doing so. That makes all the difference, you know. As a token of our appreciation, Mahmoud – the man who finally defeated you – has suggested it would be more fitting for us to give you the kitty.' He handed her a leather pouch as he spoke. It was big, it looked heavy and it both jingled and rustled. 'We take the liberty of hoping this won't be the last time you come to Tangier.'

Melinda smiled and thanked him but she was much too exhausted to take in all the implications of what he was saying. All she really wanted now was a hot bath and a long sleep. Khalil, recognising this, guided her through the phalanx of naked men who were clapping her now as she was led out of the Bedroom of Sexual Pleasure and into the privacy of her own bathroom.

As Khalil had predicted, Latifa was ready for her and so was the aromatic bath, the salves and the perfumed oils. Melinda was too tired to notice the worried look on Latifa's face but the maid knew how much store Khalil Benani was setting by Miss Carr's great-niece. She'd already warned him that he risked overdoing it and that nasty business with the vibrating phallus had underlined her point. If he wasn't careful, this Miss Carr would be turned off the whole idea before it had really got off the ground.

Melinda could feel the salve working almost at once and the maid recognised that her mistress was relaxing more quickly than she'd anticipated. Perhaps matters weren't so lost as she'd feared.

She dressed the Englishwoman in a nightgown of broderie anglais, propped her up in bed against a mountain of soft pillows and brought her a delicate porcelain cup of hot chocolate. Exhausted as she was, Melinda's professional eye clicked into gear and judged immediately that the cup was Sèvres. She turned to Latifa.

'This is very pretty,' she commented. 'Is it one of a set?'

Latifa looked surprised that she found it necessary to ask. 'Of course. About fifty pieces, I think. It was a favourite of your great-aunt, though she rarely used it and often complained that it was incomplete.'

'I rather like it.' Melinda hoped she sounded casual. 'One day, when I feel a bit better, I'll have to have a good rummage through the cupboards here.'

Latifa smiled. 'You'll find it quite an entertainment: the late Miss Carr tended to buy all sorts of things that just happened to take her fancy.'

Melinda could only hope that Great-Aunt Laura's fancy had frequently been taken by pieces of this quality, but that was a thought she kept firmly to herself.

The shutters were down and there was no clock in the room so Melinda had no idea what time it was, only that it was still Monday. It didn't matter. Right now all she wanted to do was sleep and as soon as she had finished the chocolate, Latifa removed most of the pillows and Melinda snuggled down beneath the duvet, closed her eyes and was asleep even before the maid had left the room.

A sudden crash of thunder woke her up. She could hear rain beating on the shutters and thought she detected a sheet of lightning between the slats. Someone – Latifa, she supposed – moved swiftly to close the windows and cut out most of the noise, and Melinda drifted back to sleep, her only truly conscious thought being that she felt completely rested already – rested but perfectly ready to fall asleep again.

When next she woke, she was fully awake and could make out Latifa sitting in the armchair across the room, waiting for precisely this moment. The maid pressed the button that would warn the kitchen to have coffee and croissants ready and came over to the bed.

'How do you feel after that long sleep?' she asked.

Melinda smiled happily. 'Refreshed and renewed. You might almost call me a new woman. Well, newer than I was yesterday, that's for sure.'

'Yesterday?' Latifa looked puzzled.

'Yes. Monday.'

The maid smiled. 'It's still Monday, madame.' She stepped over to the window and wound the shutter up. The sun blazed through but it was coming at the wrong angle to be morning. 'It won't be long before sunset. You've been asleep most of the day. It was barely sunrise when your guests left.'

There was a knock at the door. The maid answered it and returned with a tray. 'This is a breakfast, madame, because breakfast is what your body will be expecting. Later on we'll see you get dinner and then you can sleep again and be back to your normal routine for the morning.'

Melinda sighed and then she chuckled. 'I'm not sure that a "normal routine" is ever going to appeal to me again.'

'Does that mean you've enjoyed the last few days or just that you're feeling a lot better?'

'Both.'

'Benani will be pleased. He was a little worried about you.'

'Really?' Melinda was genuinely surprised. 'He had no need to be.'

The maid smiled enigmatically, judging it unnecess-

202

ary to spell out to her mistress the exact nature of the agent's concern. 'He even looked in on you while you slept. There was a heavy storm – we get them some-times – and he closed all the windows. He was afraid it would have woken you up.'

'It did, sort of. I knew someone was in the room but I assumed it was you.'

'He'd like to visit you when you've finished breakfast and have had a bath. I think from your improved spirits that just one more application of my special balm will see you fully back to normal. May I tell him he'll be welcome?'

'Of course.'

Melinda decided she was definitely getting used to being bathed and rather enjoyed the pampering. The gentle, oiled massage and the application inside her pussy of Latifa's highly effective salve were processes she was enjoying more than she'd have thought poss-ible after that abnormally huge dildo had been torn from her. For her part, Latifa noted that her mistress's involuntary responses suggested that she had, indeed, fully recovered both internally and in her readiness to be roused once more. Benani would be pleased.

A fresh nightgown, close-fitting this time, quite plain and of white satin, was slid over Melinda's head and her arms were slipped into a matching negligée which fastened with a solitary button at the waist. The bed had already been remade with fresh sheets which meant, Melinda realised, that some other maid must have come in because Latifa couldn't possibly have done it. If ever a house ran like clockwork, this was it. It was luxury of the highest order.

She climbed on to the bed and lay on top of the duvet, supported by an almost wasteful abundance of down-filled pillows. She felt like some oriental odal-isque and her reflection did nothing to dispel this entirely welcome illusion. That was how Khalil found her when he came in shortly afterwards, bearing a tooled-leather box of some age and, apparently, of some weight. He also carried a briefcase, which looked fairly heavy too.

He smiled as he looked at her. Melinda decided that his eyes didn't miss much. If it were possible to make an inventory of someone's appearance, Khalil would certainly have been able to produce one for hers. 'You look rested and refreshed,' he told her. 'How do you feel now?'

'Exactly that: rested and refreshed – thanks to Latifa. That woman is a genius.'

'Don't tell her so, for God's sake. She'd expect more money – which is what I want to talk to you about.'

Melinda was taken aback. 'Latifa's wages? Surely you know better than I do what she should be paid – and what can be afforded?'

He laughed. 'It wasn't Latifa or wages I had in mind. It was more a matter of what you want to do with the kitty your guests handed over to you yesterday. While you were asleep, I sorted it out. It amounts to a tidy sum. They put in their stakes in all sorts of forms: dirhams, pounds, dollars, French francs, gold – both coin and ingots – and jewels. Converted into English pounds, it amounts to something over £100,000.'

Melinda stared at him. 'You've done the sums wrong,' she said flatly. 'You must have done.'

Khalil was not amused. 'I don't make mistakes about money,' he said. 'Not ever. And this I have checked and double-checked. Of course, realising these assets won't be that simple. I'd advise against trying to take the dirhams out: you'd have to convert them into hard currency in Morocco and you'll get half their face value. Even if you wanted to risk jail by taking them out, you wouldn't be able to convert them at all in England – and if you were caught, even Larbi couldn't save you from jail. No, they had best stay in your bank here where you can draw on them whenever you're here. The hard currencies you can take with you. You'll have to say you brought them with you to buy – oh, carpets, gold, whatever – and Larbi will see to it there's no further trouble. He'll need a consideration, of course, but I'll see to that and my own firm's commission will come out of the dollars, if that's all right with you. The gold poses a problem, mainly when you get home and have to go through your Customs. Quite a lot of it – the bangles and so on – you can wear. Lots of tourists splash out on a set or two of bangles, so that won't surprise anyone, and a couple of neck-chains won't cause much comment, either. But you can't take ingots either out of here or into England – not without being asked an awful lot of questions, and I doubt if they'd believe a truthful answer so they'd assume it was something to do with drugs. Will you trust me to put them in the bank's vaults on your behalf? They can always be turned into money at a later date.'

Melinda looked at him thoughtfully. 'You've managed my great-aunt's affairs honestly for a good many years. I'm sure I can trust you and this is certainly an area where I need guidance. I do feel uncomfortable about it, though.'

'I assure you I shall be honest in my dealings,' Khalil said stiffly.

'That's not what I feel uncomfortable about,' Melinda told him. 'It's having been given all this money.'

Khalil looked puzzled. 'Are you saying you think Mahmoud should have it after all?'

Melinda gave a rueful laugh. 'I've no opinion on that. It's just that – well, it's like being nothing more than an up-market whore who does it for the money, whereas I did it because I wanted to, because it sounded like fun and because this is the first time I've had any realistic prospect of being sexually satisfied. I didn't do it for money.'

'And were you satisfied?'

'Oh, yes. Well, temporarily, at least. I'm not sure the satisfaction will last very long.'

Khalil laughed. 'I'm glad to hear it. Your guests were entirely satisfied. They were delighted with you and giving you the stake money was entirely their suggestion. Quite different from agreeing the rate for the job beforehand. Besides, I can assure you no whore, however up-market, earns that sort of money – and certainly not over two and a half days. Your guests don't see you in that light any more than their fathers and grand-fathers saw your great-aunt as a whore.'

'So my suspicions about her were correct,' Melinda said. 'She made her money the same way I've just done?'

'She was what used to be called a courtesan,' Khalil agreed. 'She kept a great many wealthy and powerful men very happy and had, I'm assured by my father, a formidable and insatiable appetite for interludes and entertainment like this weekend's. I dare say a lot of wives were secretly quite pleased to be relieved of some of their wifely duties. You needn't feel uncomfortable about this generous gift. Regard it as ... as a spur-of-the-moment gratuity. This, on the other hand,' he said, reaching for the tooled-leather box, 'is their thank you present. You could say, the equivalent of a bouquet of flowers sent round next morning.' He handed her the heavy box and took a small, ornately wrought brass key out of his pocket and gave it to her. 'It's very old indeed,' he said.

'I can see that.' She fitted the key into the lock and realised as it turned with unexpected ease for something so obviously very old that it had been made by a master craftsman.

Inside, on a bed of the darkest of dark green velvets,

nestled a massive gold belt of the sort Melinda had seen on the top shelf of every goldsmith's little shop except that, where they had clearly been stamped out by machine, this bore all the signs of having been beaten, chased and pierced by hand. It was also much bigger than any of them. It must have been some six inches deep at its deepest point and, when she lifted it out, she realised that the gold was absolutely solid: it hadn't been hollowed out on the reverse to lighten it without spoiling the heavy appearance. It looked heavy because it *was* heavy. She looked enquiringly at Khalil.

'Five kilos,' he said. He grinned. 'A quarter of your luggage allowance.'

Melinda snorted. 'You think this is something I'll risk in the hold? No, this is hand-baggage. How old is it?'

He shrugged. 'I can't say with accuracy: we don't have your admirable system of hallmarks but the gold-smith assures me it's at least two hundred years old – which means it's well over a hundred, maybe a hundred and fifty. This is a museum piece, I promise you.'

'Can you get a signed certificate verifying its age?' Melinda's professional training surfaced fast. 'It doesn't much matter what age so long as it's more than a hundred years. Preferably from either a reputable dealer or, better still, from an expert in the field. Given that, I won't have to pay duty in the UK.'

Khalil frowned. 'Tricky. It's the sort of thing they won't want to see exported. It can be arranged, of course, but it will cost. I'll have a word with Larbi. Why don't you try it on for size?'

Melinda stood in front of the mirrored wall and slipped the negligée off her shoulders so that its solitary button wouldn't get in the way of the gold. The belt differed from the others she'd seen in that this one had a complicated arrangement of gold chains hanging from it and each chain had a sort of fob attached halfway down it. It fitted snugly, filling the space between her hips and her ribs like an exotic basque.

Khalil came up quietly behind her to fasten it. It wasn't comfortable but, she decided wryly as she studied the effect in the mirror, it did wonders for her posture.

'It's stunning,' she told Khalil. 'I shan't wear it very often but when I do, it'll knock them cold. I don't see the point of all these dangly bits, though. Quite honestly, it would look better without them.'

Khalil grinned. 'But then it would lose some of its appeal to the connoisseur – and all of its appeal when it was being worn.'

'What do you mean?'

He slid his hands down her body until they reached the belt and Melinda's heart beat a little faster with the expectation his touch aroused. She knew she'd recovered from the weekend's enjoyable excesses – and she knew Khalil would have picked up the signals.

He unfastened the belt. 'You'll have to slip out of your nightgown,' he told her. 'This piece isn't meant to go on top of a woman's kaftan.'

Melinda slipped the narrow shoulder straps off and, with a few sensual wriggles, saw the soft satin slide to the ground round her feet. The mirror reflected Khalil's appreciative expression – and Melinda's answering smile.

The Moroccan fastened the belt round her again and the effect on her naked body was, she knew, as inviting as ever suspenders and stocking-tops were to the average Englishman. Then Khalil was on his knees before her. 'Open your legs,' he said. As she did so, he ran his fingers up the inside of her thigh as if to tease her sex and realised at once how ready she was to be aroused again. He brought the heavy links of the suspended chains between her legs and the action let them play with her eagerly twitching pussy. He held them tautly

208

in place as he fastened them back to the belt, taking care to ensure that the 'fobs' were securely inside her. One chain went straight down between her legs and up the cleavage of her buttocks; others were taken out at an angle so that the firm white cheeks of her arse were encircled by gold chains. Finally, he inserted a golden key in the back of the belt and turned it.

He held the little key up to the mirror so that Melinda could see it. 'You're locked in,' he told her. 'Until a man chooses to free you, you're locked in.' He put the key back in the leather casket and closed the lid.

It wasn't until she moved towards the box that Melinda realised that she now had some sort of teaser tightly secured inside her cunt, a Moroccan variation of Burmese bells, and every move she made, however small, made her quiver with barely suppressed delight. It was totally unexpected. She turned a startled face to Khalil.

He grinned. 'What were you expecting?'

'I don't know. Not this. I suppose I thought it was some kind of up-market chastity belt.'

'Much more fun than that,' he assured her. 'Those are designed to prevent intercourse. This enhances it. Traditionally, you wore it under your kaftan while you modestly served your husband and his friends with their meal. With every move, your desire for sex would increase, even to the point of orgasm. He'd know that. He'd recognise the signs – and he'd know that the one thing you wouldn't dare do would be to be seen to reach a climax in front of other men. That knowledge would be enough to give him an erection and you'd both know that, as soon as you were alone together, he'd take you – quite possibly without bothering to remove the belt first.'

Melinda's mischievous smile suggested that the picture Khalil had just painted was an alluring one. 'Sounds interesting,' she said.

'Some women are said to see them as unnecessary torture. I don't think you would.' He sat down on the edge of the bed. 'Let's find out, shall we? Walk over to the door. No, not as if you were going to play hockey. Swing your hips – and don't hurry.'

She did as she was told, tinglingly aware of the desire swelling up inside her with every step.

'Come back,' he went on. When she reached the place where her nightgown still lay on the floor, he told her to stop and turn round so that her back was towards him. 'Now bend down and pick it up. No, not like that. Bend your knees.'

The excitement inside her was almost unbearable and Melinda thought – and hoped – he was going to take her from behind, but he made no move.

'Bring it to me.'

Melinda did as she was told and was rewarded with a sharp slap on her backside as she bent over to lay the nightgown on the bed. The sting made her jerk upright and the gold dangling between her legs gave a sudden unexpected nudge to her hardening clit. She knew she was coming. Knew, too, that there was nothing she could do to stop it. She moved as if to lie on the bed to enjoy it to the full.

'Stay where you are,' Khalil ordered harshly. 'Don't lie. Don't sit. Come where you are. I want to watch you get it like that.'

It didn't occur to her to disobey him. She didn't want to. There was a decided kick in having to do what she was told without a finger being laid upon her, much as she might have enjoyed the finger.

Her hips wriggled with pleasure and that wriggle gave the teaser the last jolt it needed against the heated walls of her moist sex as another of the links rubbed on her clit. She came with a little moan of ecstasy, her eyes closed, oblivious to everything except the orgasmic spasms racking a body that could neither lie nor sit and had no support from strong arms or a man's hard body.

Her eyes opened only when, as the spasms diminished, Khalil's firm hands were round her waist, sliding under the chains so that they tightened still further to nudge the 'fobs' inside her.

He held her close, caressing her whole body and teasing the lips of her cunt so that she expected him to fuck her very soon, to demonstrate that old traditions die hard – in the case of Khalil's cock, very hard indeed.

But he didn't. She could feel his cock pressing against her through the soft fabric of his suit. She knew he wanted to take her but supremely adept a stud that he was, he was also a consummate master of the art of leading a woman to the brink of bliss and leaving her there, frustrated. That way she would come on her own again while he stood there and be instantly ready to let him satisfy himself inside her when he chose to later on.

Even thinking about his penetration was enough and he lay her gently on the bed to enjoy again the sight of her body contorting to a climax against the teasers inside her.

When her body had calmed down, he threw her the nightgown. The touch of its soft satin was almost as arousing as a man's fingers would have been, perhaps because Melinda knew that as she put it on, the teaser would begin working in her again.

'Put it on,' he told her. 'I'm going now – and I'm taking the key with me.'

'But you can't!' Melinda protested. 'Leave it with Latifa.'

'And have you coax her into setting you free? No chance. The belt and its attachments are pure gold, you can bathe with it on and perform your natural functions and neither it nor you will come to any harm. But you'll keep it on. You'll eat in it, sleep in it, dress in it.

211

By tomorrow morning you'll be ready for almost anything – and after spending two and a half days watching other men take their pleasure in you, I'm going to take my own. Somehow I don't think you're going to grudge me my reward. Sweet dreams, Miss Carr.' And before she could think of a suitable retort, he was gone, taking the box with the little gold key with him, leaving Melinda with the prospect of the delicious agony of a night of sexual arousal without a man in sight to bring her off. She wasn't sure whether she was looking forward to it or not.

Chapter Eleven
Tuesday

Melinda awoke early, her body in a turmoil of plain, old-fashioned sexual lust. Every unconscious move she had made in the night, from a minor adjustment to her position to turning over, had immediately woken her up as the teaser inside her moved and rubbed against one part of her pussy or another. She had lost count of the number of times she'd climaxed and each climax had left her on the verge of the next. They all lacked the added thrill of a real, hot, swollen prick pumping into her and Melinda was honest enough to acknowledge that it wouldn't have mattered much whose it was, just so long as he was good at using it. Several of the men that weekend would have served the purpose admirably. She wanted an impatient cock inside her, and the orgasm that would bring would be something special, of that she was sure. So vivid was her image of this particular delight that she writhed between the sheets and was at once in the throes of yet another teaser-induced climax.

When the maid entered, she found her mistress, her eyes closed, bringing herself to the point of release once again. Latifa smiled and glided quietly into the bathroom before winding up the shutters to bathe Melinda's still-contorting body in the sunlight that streamed through.

'Benani's here,' the maid told her when Melinda's eyes opened as her climax subsided. 'He's waiting downstairs until you're ready. He thinks perhaps you'll want him to come up.'

'When I've had a bath and breakfast,' Melinda conceded. What she really wanted to say was an emphatic 'Yes!' and not to wait until she'd eaten, but she wasn't letting him suspect that.

That bath was like no other. Neither the teaser itself nor the heavy belt to which it was attached prevented her being thoroughly washed but the contraption didn't stop its erotic work, either. It continued as she ate her croissants and leant forward to pick up her coffee cup. Every time she did something as simple as reach for the butter, she felt it move and tease her just that little bit more. She hoped Khalil wouldn't be long in coming – in both senses of the word.

Latifa had slipped her into a simple cotton negligée after her bath but now Melinda had finished her breakfast, the maid took the garment off so that Melinda stood quite naked except for the massive belt.

'It's too warm a day for clothes,' the maid said, glancing at the sunshine outside. 'Besides, Benani will appreciate the contrast between cool, smooth skin and ornately worked gold; between the simplicity of nakedness and the unashamed luxury of the belt.' With these words, she lay the robe neatly across a chair and took the breakfast tray out with her, gently closing the door behind her.

Melinda paced impatiently up and down the room. It was warm but there was enough of a breeze coming through the open window to tighten her nipples. She knew Khalil had only to see them so ready and he would have an erection – and right now she wanted him inside her soon and fast.

She turned as the door opened. He stood there, his admiring gaze taking in every seductive curve of her body, some of them emphasised by the chains holding the teaser in place.

He stood in front of her and kissed her, slowly and hard so that she instinctively opened her mouth to accept the thrust of his tongue. She parted her legs in silent invitation. Her body cried out 'Take me!' but Khalil wasn't to be hurried. He knew how desperate she was; he knew that every time she moved she increased that desperation – but not yet. He'd take her in his own time. Today was going to be his reward for the work he'd put in setting up the weekend's highly successful contest, and for having been obliged to watch without participating. Today his own pleasure would come before Melinda's and part of that pleasure lay in watching her wrestle with the sexual frustration she was enduring.

'Undress me,' he ordered and then, as she fumbled in her eagerness to strip him naked, he added, 'No. Slowly. Take your time. I want to savour every slow moment because I know that every time your body moves, you want it more.'

She did as she was told. Taking it slowly went against what every nerve in her body wanted to do and it was torture to obey him in this, but she knew that if she didn't, he was perfectly capable of walking out of the door, taking the little gold key with him. The sexual torture that would leave her with was far worse than an extension of her present frustration. By the time Khalil's athletic body stood naked before her, his cock fully erect and straining to get into her, Melinda was frantic with unsatisfied lust.

But Khalil had no intention of satisfying her just yet. His hands ran down her body, smoothing, caressing,

215

playing with her breasts before descending to her pussy where the blonde curls were growing once more, until his fingers could tease the front of her heavily swollen cunt on the outside, in much the same way that the fobs were teasing her inside.

'For God's sake go in,' she cried out. 'Take me, possess me before I go crazy. You know I'm dying for it. You must know it's been torture since you locked me in.'

He said nothing but, with one hand under her shoulders and the other between her legs, he lifted her on to the bed. She could feel his cock testing her moist entrance before it plunged in over the rim into her tight and throbbing cunt, already hot with a night of half-satisfied desire.

Melinda's cry of delight as he entered told him he had gauged her frustration with devastating accuracy. At last! she wanted to cry out as she thrust her hips up to meet him, to feel him tight within her. With every thrust he made, the teaser enhanced the sensation she felt. It enhanced his pleasure, too, and Khalil was in no hurry to come while he could enjoy such a multiplicity of sensations. Now he knew at first-hand why rich men who could afford such luxuries went to such great lengths to have them made, and why poorer men who could only admire the few examples in museums, did so with an envy that fired their imaginations and their lust.

Melinda's state of readiness was so high that it was only seconds after his entry that she reached her first orgasm. The feel of the powerful ram inside her combined with the incitement of the teaser was so exhilarating that she knew it would be the first of many, that she could come and come until Khalil could service her no more and would be forced to withdraw from exhaustion.

It looked as if that exhaustion would be a long time

coming. He was a master of changing their positions without pulling his cock out of her. Now he pushed her legs down and spread his own over them so that hers were held tightly in place, the restriction on her movements and the tightening of her muscles around his cock adding to the golden tantalus rubbing against the whole of her pussy. She came again almost as soon as his prick resumed its steady, compulsive thrust.

This time, to Melinda's regret, it wasn't long before he climaxed as well. She lay there, feeling his come seeping out between her tightly held legs and praying that he'd stay inside her. She always enjoyed the feel of a man hardening inside her but this time it would goad the teaser into action again with no effort from her.

She didn't have long to wait and as Khalil hardened, he could feel her shudder of delight. But today was his. He would do what he liked and she'd submit to it. He waited until his erection was at its height – and withdrew with a suddenness that made her gasp with disappointment.

Knowing perfectly well what effect his action had had on her appetite for more, he turned her roughly over on to her stomach, forced her legs apart and then, as she waited eagerly for his re-entry from behind and wondered if this time he'd take her in her cunt or her arse, he surprised her again by slapping her hard across the chained cheeks of her buttocks.

The sting of his repeated slaps hurt and, as she writhed to get away from them, the fobs renewed their insistent stimulation. The combination lashed her into a readiness that forced her to raise her backside as high as she could to make his access easier. She splayed her legs. She knew that open view of her moist and swollen pussy would provoke most men into taking her straight away. She knew his prick was ready. Surely he couldn't keep it – and her – waiting much longer?

She soon found out. Suddenly he rammed himself

back inside her, and this time there was no relief. He fucked her with such force that the influence of the teaser was virtually undetectable. He intended to hurt her and he succeeded. Melinda had no complaints. After a night of half-satisfied torture and this morning's succession of small orgasms, what she wanted now was exactly what she was getting: to be fucked hard and painfully, to be taken, possessed, dominated by a man who, at least for the time being, sought nothing but his own release by turning her into a toy, an object to be enjoyed however he felt fit. Some women would have seen it as degradation. Right now he was satisfying Melinda's deepest, most primitive desires and she revelled in the feeling of total submission to the gratification of his lust to own a woman's body.

When he came again, hard and thrusting this time, there was no answering orgasm from Melinda. This no longer mattered to her. All that mattered was that he had taken her with all the primitive power at his disposal, had used her and that she had satisfied him. When she felt him pull out of her, slowly this time, she knew he had had exactly what he wanted and when he gently kissed each sore cheek of her soundly thrashed buttocks, she smiled into the duvet beneath her.

'Stay there,' Khalil told her. Melinda had no wish to do anything else and, with her eyes closed, she felt rather than heard him leave the bed.

When he came back he stood over her and she felt him touching the heavy belt. She heard the click of the key in the lock and felt his fingers unfastening the chains from the back of the belt. The clasp was unfastened and the heavy metal fell away so that only the front panels still touched her skin as she lay there. The clasp and the chains might have been undone but the teasers themselves were still inside her. She felt them at each small change of the belt and its chains. She was tired and she'd been fucked to satisfaction but that slight movement told her it wouldn't take much to rouse her again.

'Turn on your side,' Khalil said.

She did as she was told and felt the Moroccan gently pull the teasers out of her. As they touched the walls of her cunt, they flicked her heightened sensitivity back into partial arousal. The belt had been the source of hours of titillating torture and masturbation and Melinda had sometimes longed for its removal but now she felt it withdrawn, the feeling uppermost in her mind was regret.

She stayed on her side, the better to remember that last, tantalising withdrawal and heard Khalil running water in the basin of the bathroom. She supposed he must be washing the belt and if she'd thought of anything beyond that, it would have been a mild surprise that he hadn't left it to the maid to do.

She didn't realise he'd returned until he lay on the bed behind her, one leg over hers so that they were intertwined. His cock, semi-erect now, rested against her pussy to remind her there was more to come, a reminder underlined by his careless fingers absent-mindedly playing with her, enjoying her unconscious response to his touch that bode well for the next time he shagged her.

'What do you think of your museum piece?' he murmured in her ear.

Melinda smiled the quiet smile of satisfaction. 'Different,' she said. 'Agonisingly different but definitely arousing.'

'And to be taken with it in?'

Melinda shivered with remembered pleasure. 'It takes the ecstasy of being fucked to new heights.'

He chuckled. 'Doesn't it just!' There was silence for a few minutes while Khalil nibbled her ear so that she almost forgot that his fingers were working to bring her to the point that she would beg him to take her again from this new angle. When he spoke, his tone was thoughtful. 'Many men would give much to be able to experience the pleasures of the belt. Particularly those who were here this weekend. I imagine the gift wasn't entirely altruistic.'

'What are you saying?' Melinda asked cautiously. She thought she knew but she'd rather hear it spelt out.

'Your guests enjoyed themselves. Many of them were of the opinion that you'd be ready and willing to start all over again after a good night's rest – and they were quite right, weren't they? If we hadn't had an agreement, and if they hadn't had livings to earn, I think they'd have voted to extend the session still further.' He paused. Melinda felt his finger probing inside her. She moved on it. 'How would you feel about coming back to Tangier?' Khalil went on.

'For a repeat performance, you mean?'

'Something like that. Not quite the same, of course – that would be tedious – and certainly not too soon. It pays not to be too easily available. But something that included using the belt. Your estate would benefit enormously from . . . let's say, from an auction of the use of the key. On a one-to-one basis, I think.'

Melinda smiled. Now there was a really sexy idea, she thought. 'Let's just say I wouldn't entirely rule it out,' she said.

She couldn't see Khalil's answering smile of satisfaction and, in any case, her attention was diverted by the feel of his cock seeking out the threshold to her sex and then forcing its way inside, her delighted gasp telling him he had her.

The contrast with what had gone before couldn't have been greater. This time his possession of her was more like making love than merely shagging. It was as if, having seized his own gratification after days of having to watch other men take theirs on the same woman, he could now relax enough to make sure

Melinda enjoyed it as much as he, as if he doubted her enjoyment of what he'd done before.

Her pleasure was simpler, less complicated, without the teaser inside her and all the more profound for that. His penetration was deep but his fingers continued to play with her, first round her cunt and then working their way inside to discover that spot which was so receptive to a skilled touch. His success galvanised her whole body into a contortion that might well have dislodged his quickening cock had he not been prepared for it and held her tightly to him.

Melinda was already halfway to a climax when he turned her fully on to her front to increase the power of his throbbing dick. She felt the rhythmic shudders of response mounting fast as her orgasm reached its peak and pushed her butt against him, the better to relieve herself and to feel him emptying inside her. Khalil seized her hips and held them tight against him, possessing her with as much domination as he had ever done when the belt was in place.

As their lust began to subside, Melinda murmured, 'You know what I want you to do. You know how much I like it. Stay there again. We both know you can do it.'

He withdrew nonetheless, kissing her shoulder as he did so. 'I know, but you need a rest.'

'I don't think so,' Melinda objected. 'Besides, what I'd really like is for you to spend the night again.'

'And so I shall – but not here. It's time you went back to your flat, Miss Carr.' He pulled her to her feet and turned her to face the bathroom. 'Get bathed and Latifa will bring you some lunch. Then I'll take you back to the city. Go on.' And he slapped her still tingling buttocks to encourage her to do as she was told.

Laughing, Melinda obeyed.

* * *

It was late afternoon when Khalil drove her back to the city. She sat beside him, the leather box held securely on her lap, and studied his handsome profile. She was beginning to realise how sorry she was going to be to return to the humdrum world of her ordinary life. She'd certainly be back. She rather thought she wouldn't have gone home at all if it hadn't been for Khalil's common-sensical remark about not being too easily available. Besides, a self-imposed celibacy in England would greatly enhance her enjoyment of her next visit here. Meanwhile, she had tonight to look forward to.

As if he read her mind, Khalil's hand left the steering wheel and strayed purposefully to her thigh, feeling her sex through the restraint of her panties. Melinda was delighted to part her legs for him and to make sure the box was no impediment to his hand. He smiled at the road ahead as she did so and immediately, frustratingly, his hand returned to the steering wheel.

The bastard, Melinda thought without animosity. He's just teasing. Two can play at that game.

She waited until they reached a complicated junction that needed his full attention and at the precise moment she judged sex to be furthest from his mind, she put her hand on his knee and ran it quickly up his leg to his groin until it rested on the bulge in his crotch. She smiled as he hardened at the unexpected touch. Serves you right, she thought, but when she started to unzip his flies, he firmly removed her hand and placed it back on her own lap.

'Not while I'm driving,' he said, not looking at her. 'Not in the city, at any rate.'

'Then let's have a drive in the country,' she suggested.

He laughed but the suggestion clearly surprised him. 'Would you do that?'

It was Melinda's turn to be surprised. 'Why not?' she

222

replied, glancing sideways at him. 'We could get each other so fired up on the drive that we'd be desperate for the first bit of long grass or maybe we'd just pull over into a lay-by and have it off then and there.'

'And risk being seen?'

'That's half the fun.'

'Mm,' he said thoughtfully, 'but what if you *are* seen?'

Melinda shrugged. 'Embarrassment all round, I suppose.'

'But not jail?'

'Good lord, no!'

'Then that's where our cultures differ,' he commented. 'Oh, it's done, especially in a car and usually only with a woman who's a common whore, but it's a risk and buying off a policeman is expensive and carries its own risk. Not all policemen play ball.'

'You must visit me in England,' Melinda said demurely, but his only answer was a non-committal laugh.

The apartment, luxurious and comfortable as it was, seemed positively Spartan after the sybaritic indulgence of the villa. It was certainly a return to earth. On the other hand it would at least make her return to her flat in London less of a jolt. Melinda sighed. 'I'll be sorry to go back to the real world,' she told her agent. 'I can't remember when I've enjoyed a holiday more. I'm resigning myself to the next few days being something of an anticlimax.'

'Different, certainly; less . . . strenuous, perhaps, but I hope not an anticlimax,' he replied, bending down to kiss her firmly on the mouth, his arms round her holding her close.

Melinda put her arms round his neck as his tongue sought hers and her fingers played with his hair, his ears, his nape while one of his hands held her firmly against his erect prick. His hand pressing her backside towards him lay so that his fingers reached down her cleft to rest against her sex. The barrier of her clothes inhibited the sensuality of skin on skin but just thinking about taking them off was a spur to desire.

A hand slipped beneath the crisp white cotton of her shirt and unfastened her bra. It brushed the sensitive nerves of her spine so that as the garment loosened and the hand moved to fondle her breast, she felt her nipples rise with excitement.

'Undo your shirt,' he told her. He watched her breasts emerge, swollen and hard and ready for his mouth. It wasted no time. It descended on them, licking, teasing, sucking, biting, fully aware of the effect it was having as she leant back against his supporting arm, her eyes closed in rapture.

'Your tits are luscious,' he told her. 'Get rid of your shirt and bra. They're in the way.'

Melinda obeyed, thrillingly conscious of his mouth pulling at her naked nipple like some impatient child. She was conscious, too, that he had made no attempt to remove her thong and she was disappointed. Teasing had its place – my God, how it had its place, she thought, remembering the belt now locked away in its box on the table – but right now she wanted more than teasing. Or rather, she corrected herself, she wanted to know the teasing was leading on to something more.

Perhaps to make her point, she fumbled with his trousers. Khalil made no objection. He's taken the point, she decided, remembering how firmly he had removed her hand when they were in the car, but when his prick sprang free, his reaction wasn't entirely what she'd expected.

'Take off that thong,' he commanded, knowing she couldn't wait to do so, but when she had tossed it aside and fully expected him to enter her, she found herself instead forced to her knees before him. 'Lick it,' he ordered.

She did as she was told, wishing as she did so that there was a second man behind her to take her while her tongue played with Khalil's cock. She flicked over its swollen head and lingered along the slit that brought so much of her pleasure, but she'd rather that slit was inside her cunt, not her mouth.

As if he sensed this, one of Khalil's hands twisted her hair into a rope to force her head further on to his cock to suck and lick it into even stronger life. Now she couldn't get away from him even if she wanted to, even if she was choking on the force of the cock against her throat.

Suddenly he drew back and hauled her to her feet by her hair. Before she could open her mouth in protest, he had impaled her on the ramrod she'd been lubricating.

He went in so suddenly that its very force was enough to make her tremble with the excitement of lust and, as her orgasm grew, she twisted her legs around him to deepen his penetration and to give her climaxing body something firm to move against.

She came quickly, with great, shoving thrusts that brought the Moroccan to his climax just as hers had reached its peak. As she felt the rhythmic discharge inside her it was enough to bring her to another unexpected climax. He must be empty, she thought, but still he plunged into her, screwing as he did so until she climaxed for the third time in quick succession.

He let her down gently, his cock still inside her, and kissed her lips as her feet touched the floor. 'Bed, I think, don't you?' he said and Melinda felt his soft, moist withdrawal with a mixture of regret and anticipation.

Khalil guided her to the bedroom, one hand tantalisingly on her buttocks so that she flexed against it as she walked, hoping his fingers would descend that little bit further and rekindle her lust to have him once again.

He turned the coverlet back and began unfastening his shirt. 'Get in,' he said.

Melinda snuggled obediently between the sheets, watching him take off the rest of his clothes and admiring his body again. It wasn't just well honed, she thought. It was well hung, too, and she smiled quietly as she held out her hand to him and he climbed in beside her.

'A penny for them,' he said.

Melinda chuckled. 'It was private. Flattering, but private.' And she turned in the embrace of his arms, her face upturned to receive a kiss.

Now his kisses and the intimate touch of his fingers surprised her by their gentleness. It was like the gentle foreplay of a new lover in expectation of his first entry, rather than that of a man who had already taken her several times in different ways and had watched what other men had enjoyed doing to her. It was quite a change and Melinda enjoyed it, responding with fluttering fingers of her own.

When his penetration came, it was as gentle as that last time in the villa and Melinda suspected that if she hadn't formed a pretty shrewd idea of Khalil's skill as a lover and the nature of his commitment to her, she might have fallen into the trap of thinking he was in love with her. It would be very easy to delude herself that she was in love with him when he indulged her in this tenderly insistent kind of love-making. Fortunately she knew herself well enough to enjoy it for what it was. If she hadn't known herself that well when she set out for Tangier, the last ten days would have taught her that it was sex plain and simple – or even ornate and complex – with skilled men that she really craved. Besides, she reminded herself, never once since they met had Khalil called her anything other than 'Miss Carr'. If she ever felt her common sense slipping, she'd be well advised to remember that. So she responded in kind to her agent's love-making. It probably wouldn't be long before he changed the mood.

They climaxed together and lay in each other's arms, warm and fulfilled until urgent desire swept over them again.

In this warm and cosy intimacy, Khalil fondled her breasts and nuzzled her ears, while Melinda caressed his spine and his tightly muscular buttocks, happy to feel him pressed close to her.

'Will you be back?' he asked softly.

'I should think so,' she replied. 'Maybe I'd enjoy taking the path you suggested earlier.' She sensed rather than saw his answering smile and knew she'd given the reply he wanted to hear.

'I think you would,' he agreed. 'That needn't be the end of it.'

'What do you mean?'

'You've the talent and skill to provide what a lot of men want – and not only talent and skill, but an appetite for it and a taste for variety. You needn't regard the villa here as the only fitting location, any more than you need be limited to the guests you've been entertaining this weekend.'

Melinda lay very still in his arms, digesting the implications which went beyond his earlier suggestion. She wasn't sure she liked them, and told him so.

He chuckled in the darkness. 'Wouldn't it be truer to say you don't think you *ought* to like the implications, but that if you can put political correctness aside, the idea has definite attractions?'

Melinda was honest enough to acknowledge, albeit ruefully, that he had shrewdly assessed what made her tick a lot more accurately than she liked.

'There's a difference between liking the idea and being willing to put it into practice,' she pointed out. 'In the villa, the house is mine, so undesirables can be ejected and I've always known your protection is close

227

at hand. I wouldn't have those safeguards elsewhere, would I?'

'At the level we're talking about there'd be contracts to safeguard you and I'd certainly be there as well.'

'So you're talking about elsewhere in Morocco?'

'Not at all. The world is an oyster for a woman of your talents – and very fine pearls indeed can be extracted from oysters. Believe me, I'm more than capable of taking care of your interests on a world-wide basis. I can arrange it in Britain if you want me to.'

Melinda shook her head. 'I don't think so. Not yet awhile, anyway. If what you have in mind becomes what I think you hope for, it would be as well if Britain remained the one place where I wasn't known.'

'You inherited your great-aunt's common sense as well as everything else,' he commented. 'Very wise. Of course, the late Miss Carr did have British admirers who visited her elsewhere, but it wasn't in their interests, either, to pursue the acquaintance on their home territory. Discretion is a two-way affair.'

Melinda kissed him. She wondered what had started Great-Aunt Laura off on her road to Black Sheepdom and whether Khalil knew. Asking him could wait, though. Right now she had other priorities for which his cooperation was even more essential. She slid her hand between their bodies, seeking his cock and, find-ing it was still a barely strengthened willy, made to lower her head beneath the duvet so that her tongue could lick and tease it back into exciting life, but Khalil stopped her. His strong hands raised her head so that he could kiss her again.

'Not now,' he whispered. 'It's time you went to sleep. Your holiday's still got a few days to go.'

Chapter Twelve
Wednesday

Melinda was the first to wake and she studied the sleeping figure beside her with a speculative smile. She'd been the first to wake last time he slept with her, too. On that occasion she'd turned it to advantage by taking the initiative and waking him up by playing with him. She knew he'd enjoyed it. She'd so often stated her preference for being dominated that he hadn't expected her to make the first move. The question now was whether to do it again. She wanted to because she was awake and lying beside a naked, sexy man and that made her horny. The sooner she was taken, the better.

Definitely taken, she decided. It contrasted satisfyingly with the cosy warmth of last night. That had been more like seduction – and it could all too easily slip into becoming a habit. That would be dire indeed. If she made the first move now, she'd risk establishing another habit. No, it would be better to put up with a bit more delay – after all, just lying there thinking about it made her horny. She closed her eyes, the better to contemplate what Khalil's first move might be when he woke up.

She turned on to her side, almost on to her stomach so that her back was towards her sleeping partner, one leg pointing down, the other spread-eagled across the bed so that the upper half of her body was on its side while below the waist she was on her front.

That was when she realised Khalil hadn't been asleep at all. No sooner had she settled into a position which felt both comfortable and abandoned than she was aware he had turned towards her. Already she could feel the stiffness of his prick between her legs as if she were riding on it. Then his hands were on her buttocks, holding them close to him before one of them slid down to stir her rapidly rising desire to be fucked. The way she was sprawled across the bed invited violation and right now violation was what she wanted. Would he simply take her from behind? Or tie her first? That would be an interesting start to the day.

But Khalil had other ideas. He knew just how ready she was and knew, too, that gentle seduction wasn't what she was after. His probing finger was soon inside her, teasing, seeking her clit, building her lust to be taken.

Then Melinda realised that his stiff cock was gently but determinedly pressing its way up her backside, penetrating her tight anus as if it were a virgin's cunt. He pressed forward a bit and then back, forward a bit further and then back. It was a very different sensation and Melinda wasn't sure whether she liked it or not. She suspected she'd have vetoed it if it had been suggested first, but she hadn't been given the choice. She leant towards it, not quite enjoying both the tightness and the pain it caused yet not wanting it to stop.

Khalil worked on her with all the care of a considerate man introducing a virgin to the delights of the marriage bed. When he judged he was far enough in for his first time, he slipped a finger into her cunt so that both of them could be stimulated by the same finger.

Melinda knew she would soon come to this added sensation. She wanted it but she feared the pain of his thrusting, remembering the earlier experience. Khalil, however, had no intention of alienating her from an entry that many men would contribute generously to use, not necessarily as gently as he, so he withdrew. It could be developed later.

'That's enough for now,' he told her. 'Enough of that, at any rate. You'd never had it like that before this visit, had you?'

Melinda shook her head, unsure whether to be grateful for his restraint or sorry not to have taken it to its conclusion.

'And your reaction? Did you like it?'

'I'm not sure,' she replied doubtfully. 'Yes, I suppose I did – or I would if it got less painful. Does it?'

He chuckled. 'So they say. It just isn't something I want to take too far, too soon. We can work at it.' He hesitated as if unsure whether to add his corollary. 'It's never a bad idea to extend the range of your talents,' he said at last.

'You mean other men are going to want it like that,' Melinda said bluntly.

'As many as will want to experience the teaser,' he said. 'And now, because I've no wish to take you frustrated to breakfast, I'm going to have a quick shower. By the time I return, you'll have had time to decide how you most want it for what I'm afraid will have to be our last fuck for this visit.'

Melinda gave him a startled glance. 'But I thought we'd be able to continue till it was time for me to go home,' she protested, disappointed.

He shrugged. 'I'd hoped so, too, but something's cropped up. If I can get back to you before it's time to go to the airport, I shall. No promises, though.' He smiled. 'So make it good,' he said and disappeared into the bathroom.

Despite her disappointment, Melinda felt like a small girl who'd been handed a huge box of candies, each of them different but with permission only to eat one. Well, she amended, maybe two if she played her cards right. Just thinking about it, imagining the possibilities, and knowing she had only to ask – that was a great turn-on.

'Well?' Khalil asked, standing above her, the erect scimitar of his cock ready to impale her in any way she asked. 'Tied or free? Front entry or back? Fast or slow? Or will it be more exciting if I take away the choice and fuck you as it most appeals to me?'

He was right, she thought. Why hadn't that occurred to her? Anything he wanted – but she didn't want it rushed. If this was her last opportunity for sex during this exhilarating holiday, she was determined it should last as long as possible. The thought of two days of enforced celibacy in Tangier was a depressing one. Before she'd come here, it wouldn't have mattered – sex would have been just a very welcome bonus. Now it was a lot more significant. It was something she'd associate with Tangier for ever more and she didn't want it to stop prematurely.

'You choose,' she said. 'Just take it slowly. I want to enjoy it to the hilt.'

'My thoughts exactly,' he said. He parted her legs wide and thrust his prick with careful accuracy and no foreplay at all straight into her hot and waiting cunt, letting its impulsion pause briefly at her gasp of delight at his sudden entry.

The pause was brief and then he began the rhythmic thrusting. His increasing force and speed gave Melinda the pleasure of knowing orgasm wasn't far off. But Khalil wasn't planning a straightforward route to that goal. When he judged her to be well on the way, he brought her legs down alongside his own. It increased the sensual intensity of the shag.

Melinda could feel her orgasm mounting. The sensations he was inducing were almost unbearable in their power, but he hadn't finished raising the temperature yet.

His straddled legs pushed hers together between them so that his cock was gripped along its entire length. They could both feel every inch of its progress in and out, back and forth, steadily, relentlessly bringing her on, riding her to a climax made all the more exhilarating because, held like this, she couldn't have escaped it even if she'd wanted to.

Melinda trembled as her excitement rose. She gripped his cock within her as if that would delay the exquisite moment of completion and thereby add fuel to the fires of her ecstasy.

She came first, with an explosion that enveloped her whole being, made more intense by the enforced rigidity of her body. She expected his climax to follow hard on the heels of her own but Khalil chose to delay it, knowing full well that she was more than capable of coming again.

He widened his legs so that hers automatically relinquished some of the closeness which was rewarding her so deliciously. Now he raised himself and Melinda felt his cock pulling back along the warm moistness of her cunt until it had almost left. Almost – but not quite. Just as she was preparing herself for the disappointment of his withdrawal, he plunged it, slurping, back into her, enjoying her cry of delight before once again drawing it almost completely out of her again.

She'd experienced this tantalising technique before and she was beginning to think there was nothing quite like it. The conflict of semi-withdrawal, hiatus and then smooth, moist penetration to the hilt was one which brought her to a climax quickly. This time she came on a semi-withdrawal and her hips thrust up to feel more of him inside her. When that slick, rhythmic penetration repeated itself this time, it plunged so far inside her and with so much force that it felt as if her ecstatic cunt had no end. She orgasmed with shuddering joy.

Now there could be no semi-withdrawal because Khalil's own coming demanded he force himself as hard into her as he could and he did so with such vigour that Melinda cried out with mingled pain and pleasure. This is what I want, she thought. This is what it's about.

As Khalil's climax subsided, he made no attempt to withdraw, nor did he raise his body from hers. He was too heavy for comfort but Melinda wasn't about to complain. While he was on top of her and inside her, there was every chance he hadn't finished. She smiled at him. Her reward came when he fondled her breast.

'I think you enjoyed that.'

'Mmm,' she agreed, and thought she felt him stir within her – not much, but enough to build her expectations.

'Have you thought about some of my suggestions?' he asked, a finger playing with a honey-blonde tendril of hair.

'Which suggestions in particular?' she asked. She knew perfectly well but repeating them, talking about them, might be just the thing to turn him on again.

'About returning to Tangier for – oh, a repeat with variations, I suppose we could call it. To auction off use of the belt; to introduce you to some variations you might enjoy; to teach you some techniques that will enable you to give even greater pleasure to your temporary masters – and to ensure you die an even richer old lady than your great-aunt.'

Melinda chuckled. She liked the idea but she had reservations. 'If I said I didn't like the idea, you

234

wouldn't believe me because you know perfectly well how much I've enjoyed this visit,' she said. 'But what you propose is little short of prostitution and I don't think I can live with that. I know it isn't entirely logical but there seems to be a difference between doing it for fun and doing it for profit.'

He stroked her cheek; his smile was sympathetic, conspiratorial. 'Why should men who can well afford to pay for such extreme pleasure be allowed to have it for nothing? You'll be an accomplished and sought-after courtesan, not a prostitute, a common whore. You won't be doing it as an economic necessity – even without your inheritance, you can't have been a pauper – and you won't be doing something you dislike. No one will be forcing you into it and you won't have to take any man who wants it and can pay. That would be prostitution. This won't.'

Melinda knew perfectly well that his argument was as full of ethical flaws as it could possibly be, but what he was offering her was what she wanted to hear. There was just one thing he hadn't mentioned.

'And if I agree and all this wealth comes in, I take it you'll want your cut?'

He seemed surprised that she needed to ask. 'Of course. I'm a businessman. I have a living to earn. Our company did well enough looking after your great-aunt's Moroccan affairs and we deserved to. We dealt straight with her and she knew she could depend on us. We're excellent agents; we served her well and I would hope to do as well for you. You already trust me, I think.'

'Yes, I do.' She smiled. 'I think we have a deal.'

'Good,' he said, kissing her briefly and immediately withdrawing to her barely concealed disappointment. He stood up. 'I must shower and get back to my office. You'll see me again on Saturday morning, early. I'll take you to the airport.'

235

'Not until then?'

'Just two and a half days to fill,' he said, looking at his watch. 'And who knows? You may bump into an acquaintance or two between now and then.' He looked at her naked body. 'Perhaps you should sit on the balcony in the sun for a while,' he suggested. 'People in England will think it very odd if you don't return with a suntan.'

Melinda lay where she was, listening to the sound of water and wondering – against any real hope – whether he would return for one last shag before leaving for work. She wasn't altogether surprised that he didn't, but she was disappointed that he so clearly considered his goodbyes to have been said: he left the apartment without a further word, just a friendly goodbye wave as he passed the bedroom on his way out.

She dressed with care. She was on her own for the next couple of days and her experience of walking around Tangier without an escort had not only been very limited but on one occasion potentially very nasty. Definitely not jeans, she decided: too tight and too casual. The grey outfit always looked good: sufficiently elegant to shout 'unapproachable' to a certain undesirable element – provided they didn't see it as a challenge. She glanced at her discretely small gold watch. God, was that the time? No wonder she was famished. She'd give Oslo a try. It was a *salon de thé* with a restaurant upstairs and it had always looked inviting.

She crossed the road outside the apartment block and walked briskly to the restaurant about half a mile away. She was totally unaware that the holiday's exhausting and exhilarating experiences had given her whole demeanour a sexual confidence it had lacked before. It demonstrated itself in the very manner of her walk and attracted admiring glances which Melinda attributed to the fact that this particular outfit became her better than most.

She lingered over lunch – there was, after all, nothing to make haste for – and another glance at her watch told her that the shops would begin to open again in half an hour or so. Retail therapy was always a good way to fill time.

She strolled along the main boulevard towards the medina, enjoying the occasional glimpse of the sea at the bottom of the many little streets leading to the promenade. She thought wistfully that it would be rather nice to walk barefoot in the sand, but she wasn't trying that again without an escort. Khalil perhaps. She smiled to herself. No. Walking barefoot in the sand was hardly Khalil's scene.

She paused by the cannons on the terrace that over-looked both harbour and bay and decided that, for her money, it must be one of the most beautiful views in the Mediterranean. Then, her eyes satisfied, she plunged downhill into the busy street leading down to the Gran Socco and the even narrower and more bus-tling ones of the medina itself. Last time she was here, she'd bumped into Clive, which had spoilt the whole expedition. Let's just hope he's taken the hint and gone home, she thought. I want to do some shopping – at the very least, some serious window-shopping.

The goldsmith's soukh was her first port of call. A few days ago she'd have been looking to buy; now she was just comparing their goods with the gold jewellery her visitors had given her. The better shops carried comparable pieces. The majority didn't.

She enjoyed browsing among beaded and gold-embroidered kaftans in their jewel colours. It was a pity there were so few opportunities to wear such delights. There were plenty of parties to go to in London but in one of these she'd be seen either as off-puttingly ethnic or touristy tacky. All the same, she bought one in a

237

gorgeous shade of sapphire-blue – a blindingly obvious choice with her colouring, but who cared? Maybe someone would throw an *Arabian Nights* party this Christmas.

A small note of unease was struck by one shopkeeper. 'Keep your handbag fastened,' he told her. 'You're too careless with it. It's already attracted attention.'

'What do you mean?' Melinda asked. 'Who?' She could see no one.

He shrugged in the characteristically Moroccan fashion. 'A small group of boys followed you in. Or tried to. My staff spotted them and sent them packing, but you need to be on your guard.'

'Will they have gone looking for someone else or will they be waiting for me to come out again?' she asked.

He shrugged again. 'Who can say? But take care, madame.'

Melinda glanced around as she left the shop but detected nothing untoward. She'd intended to go up through the medina to take a look at the rest of that museum Khalil had shown her but she soon realised the bustling concentration of shops was beginning to thin out, replaced by narrow, windowless streets. Here only heavy wooden doors indicated the presence of dwellings and the handful of small shops clearly didn't rate tourists among their customers. She hurried her pace. It would be reassuring to see the pairs of armed policemen that safeguarded tourists in the part she'd just left. Perhaps it would be better to turn back and leave the museum to another day, perhaps even to hire herself one of the official guides.

Retracing her steps was no problem – at first. It was when the road forked that what had seemed a simple plan became complicated. She had no recollection whatever of having passed the junction, though she must have done so. She reminded herself that all roads downhill led back towards the harbour and hoped the fork she opted for was the right one.

It wasn't, and she could hear footsteps behind her now. Just one pair, she guessed, but she dared not turn back and take the other fork because to do so would take her to whoever was so determinedly following her.

Instead, she took the first little side street she came to and quickly discovered to her dismay that it was a dead end with just three firmly closed front doors at right angles to each other at the very end. Now she would have to go back.

She turned. A tall figure stood silhouetted at the entrance, waiting for her. Melinda's stomach turned in a brief moment of fear until it registered that the black, featureless figure ahead was wearing a very official-looking cap. Police? Army? Did it matter? Either way he'd speak enough French to understand she wanted to be guided safely out.

The tall figure stepped aside as she drew level and inclined his head in courteous greeting. 'Miss Carr, I think,' he said in the accent of fluent Quai d'Orsay French.

Melinda recognised Larbi immediately. Her relief was coupled with surprise that so senior an officer should be on foot and in such an insalubrious neighbourhood. 'M'sieur Larbi!' she exclaimed. 'I couldn't wish for a better person to bump into. I've got myself just a tiny bit lost.'

'Just a tiny bit,' he agreed without smiling. 'You should take more care. I gather you were warned.'

Melinda was taken aback. How could he know that? 'That was about my handbag,' she said defensively. 'I took a wrong turning somewhere back there. This place is very confusing. All the streets look the same.'

He smiled tightly. 'Not really, but you had been followed. Two of my men saw the boys when the

239

shopkeeper sent them packing and made sure they left the medina altogether. Your tail after that was of a more official nature. I wouldn't like to think anything might happen to put you off returning to Tangier.'

Melinda chuckled. 'With you to keep an eye on me, I've nothing to fear.'

Larbi's smiled was a bit more relaxed. 'My car isn't far. Why don't I take you somewhere a little more fitting and we'll have some mint tea?'

Melinda jumped at the invitation. She couldn't help wondering just what would constitute 'somewhere a little more fitting' but when the proposition came from Larbi, she was prepared to wait and see.

The respectability of Vienna wasn't quite what she'd expected, given the nature of their acquaintance so far, and she had a shrewd suspicion that Larbi had taken that into account.

'Are you allowed to do this in uniform?' she asked him as he ordered mint tea and a selection of pastries. She'd seen policemen on duty being brought a tray of tea from an adjacent *salon* but she'd never seen a uniform inside one.

'At my rank, yes,' he told her, 'and particularly when my guest is the late Miss Carr's great-niece and heiress.'

'Ah,' Melinda said. 'The late Miss Carr. What can you tell me about her?'

He shrugged. 'I never knew her. Not personally. I understand she was very beautiful in her youth and very charming, too. They say she never lost the charm and was able to sustain the illusion of great beauty, certainly until she left Tangier – and by that time she was a very old lady.'

'I don't think she ever lost, either,' Melinda said thoughtfully. 'I only met her once but she had a sort of faded beauty even then and oodles of charm, though I never had the least suspicion how it might have been used in her younger days.'

240

'The generally held opinion is that you could almost be a reincarnation of her, both to look at and in inclinations,' he told her.

Melinda found herself blushing and lowered her eyes, an instinctive gesture that did her no harm in Larbi's eyes. 'That seems to be Benani's opinion, too,' she said.

'Shrewd man, Benani,' Larbi commented. 'I gather he's had to leave you to your own devices for a couple of days?'

Melinda studied him speculatively. 'Is there much you don't know about what goes on?' she asked.

'Not in this city. It's my job and it's one I'm very good at. Do you want to spend the time entirely on your own? It would be understandable if you did, given your exertions at the villa, but I'm not convinced it's what you'd necessarily choose.'

'No, it's not,' Melinda agreed. Her mind was already jumping ahead, hoping he meant what she thought he meant. Larbi had been good. On his own, without an audience, he'd be better. Already she could feel the thrill of anticipation.

'Then this is a good time to see you safely back to your apartment,' he said, getting to his feet.

The unmarked car double-parked – with particular impunity, Melinda guessed – outside the block of flats and Larbi escorted her in. She couldn't help feeling a bit disappointed: if the car was waiting for him, he couldn't be planning to stay for long. A quick shag, maybe? Well, that could be fun and she wasn't about to turn it down, she decided as she turned the key in the door.

His hand guided her into the room. It lay chivalrously on her waist, automatically slipping down over her buttocks as she stepped ahead of him. He nodded towards the window and when Melinda turned from having lowered the shutters against the rapid onset of a Tangerine night, his cap and jacket had been neatly folded over the small dining table and he stepped into the *salon*, his hands outstretched to take hers and pull her to him.

Melinda glowed at the urgency of his embrace and the dexterity of the fingers that unbuttoned her blouse and freed her breast from the restriction of her bra. It stood forth, the darkening nipple proud and ready for the intense joy of being suckled. She felt her heartbeat quicken as he sunk his mouth, his white teeth, over that sensitive, swollen nub, biting, pulling it into him so that as his teeth bit and pulled, his tongue licked and caressed the hardening aureolae around it.

Melinda felt the sensual surge of lust sweep over her body and down to her loins. She pressed her eager pussy against the erection she could feel under his uniform, silently imploring him to take her now, without delay.

But Larbi had other ideas – and was very well aware of the advantages of leaving a hungry woman with nothing more than a tasty appetiser.

'Not now,' he told her. 'It would have to be too hurried and my taste is for more than that. You'll dine with me tomorrow?'

'Tomorrow!' Melinda exclaimed, aghast at the prospect of so long a delay and quite unable to disguise her dismay.

Larbi laughed. 'I'm afraid so. I'll make it worth the wait, I promise, and I'll be in no great hurry to finish. A car will come for you at eight. I'll be in uniform, by the way. Appearances can matter and it's better if it looks like business. Do you mind?'

Melinda shook her head. 'Only the delay,' she told him. 'Uniforms are very sexy.'

Chapter Thirteen
Thursday and Friday

Melinda looked anxiously at the clock. Khalil had always been punctual and she supposed a policeman would be, too, but one could never be entirely sure. Punctuality wasn't a noted Mediterranean characteristic, after all.

She paced restlessly up and down. This is ridiculous, she thought. I'm behaving like some teenager on a first date, wondering if she's being stood up. Only, unlike some teenager, I'm not under any romantic illusions about what's in store, so why should it matter?

She looked at her watch again. A whole minute had passed since her last check. She sighed with impatience. She knew why it mattered. In little more than twenty-four hours, she would be heading for Tangier airport and London – and once she was back in London, she would be back in the mundane world of bronzes, auctions and earning a living. She no longer needed to go out and earn a living but one needed something to do to pass the time. Earning a living was a better way than most but this time it meant that the excitement of sexual experiment would be over and done with for a while – and she didn't really want it to stop until it absolutely had to. Besides, she had an idea that Larbi had something in mind. She couldn't help wondering what. She hoped he didn't stand her up.

The intercom rang. She picked up the handset and a voice, in careful French, told her that her car had arrived. 'I'm on my way,' she said, checking herself in the mirror. She smoothed the midnight-blue dress down over her knickerless hips, threw a light cashmere shawl over her shoulders in a way that looked deceptively casual, and headed for the lift.

The immaculately uniformed young policeman opened the car door for her, barely able to conceal his curiosity. She guessed that her name and Great-Aunt Laura's reputation had preceded her and smiled her thanks.

They drew up at the same hotel to which Khalil had taken her and this time two traditionally dressed doormen sprang to admit her so that she was saved the extreme labour of opening the door for herself. Twice as many as Khalil had warranted, she noted with a smile of satisfaction. Larbi must be important.

He was waiting for her among the softly lit palms of the courtyard garden and no sooner had she greeted him and sat down than a waiter appeared from nowhere to take her order from her host. She looked around her. The Spaniards would have called it a patio, she thought, but the word had been too badly debased in England to be used for something as lovely as this. If anything evoked Tangier, it was the understated beauty of this little oasis – which she'd barely noticed on her previous visit.

'You filled your day satisfactorily, I hope?' Larbi asked, but Melinda didn't fall into the trap of imagining he had the slightest interest in how she had filled the long, dragging hours until his car arrived. She looked surprised.

'Time always flies towards the end of a holiday,' she

replied. 'So much to do, so many small presents to buy.'

'Shall we go in?' As he guided her through the doors into Korsan, she knew his hand had discovered that nothing lay between her skin and her dress. Knowing that sent a small quiver of excitement down her spine.

The meal was as excellent as its predecessor but her host hadn't the slightest intention of taking surreptitious advantage of the opportunities her clothing offered. Apart from his hand just happening to brush along her thigh on one occasion, Melinda might as well have been wearing those awful gym knickers with pockets that one saw in books about the history of underwear.

Back at the flats, he dismissed his car and driver and took the key from her to open the outside doors and operate the lift. It was he who let them both into the apartment before flooding the place with light. 'Very nice,' he said approvingly. 'Very nice indeed.'

'Wouldn't you prefer the softer wall-lights?' Melinda suggested, her fingers on the switch.

'Certainly not. I want to miss nothing.' He tossed his cap on to the table as he spoke and ran his hands firmly down her body. 'Nothing at all,' he added. 'Take it off.'

Melinda did as she was told and took her time over it. He wasn't missing much, she thought, conscious that every move she made, every inch of flesh she revealed, was drunk in by those hungry eyes. Somehow she didn't think soft seduction was what he had in mind and if the erection she could see inside his trousers was anything to go by, she wouldn't have long to wait. She remembered that he was a big man, certainly big enough to be very, very painful.

His hands, themselves trembling with excitement, ran over her naked body. Suddenly, without a hint of warning, he caught her wrists and pulled them behind her. Something snapped round them and she cast a startled look over her shoulder. She hadn't bargained for handcuffs.

For the first time this evening she felt nervous. Khalil wasn't here. She was on her own. What if Larbi wasn't as trustworthy as she'd thought? He caught the frisson of fear and smiled, knowing it would heighten the pleasure for both of them. He could dispel it with a word but he wasn't going to. Not just yet, anyway. He wanted her on the tenterhooks of fear.

He pulled her into the bedroom and here, too, he turned on every light he could find. Then, with the speed and expertise of long practice, he unlocked one wrist and almost before she realised she had a chance to escape, he brought the cuffs round the bed's tester-pole and snapped it back round her wrist. She could move up and down. She could move from side to side. That was all. She could watch him undress.

Fear is not normally a pleasant sensation but Melinda knew how much excitement this man could give her and fear gave the prospect an extra dimension that made her hotter for it than she ever recalled feeling before. This was the man who knew that fear turned her on and now he was using it to his own advantage. She hoped to their mutual advantage.

He stood before her, naked, muscled and huge and then, without preamble, rammed his massive cock so hard inside her that she screamed as it forced its way in, her juices not yet sufficient to smooth its passage. It hurt, but she made no attempt to pull back from the violation. She gave herself up to the enjoyment of every painful sensation, leaning against the tester for support as he thrust, plunged, screwed himself inside her until her cries became as much of pleasure as of pain and diminished to moans of satisfaction as her juices did their work.

Her climax came suddenly, an explosion of sexual relief that was followed almost immediately by another and another, in a rapid succession that surprised even her. Larbi still hadn't come.

He must have had the keys handy because the hand-cuffs were released after her third climax without his needing to withdraw. Now he held her close to him before forcing her backwards on to the bed. Her legs hung over the end, forcing her sex wide open to increase the power of his penetration. God! she thought, much harder and it'll come out of my mouth! Which was so exciting a prospect that she climaxed again with increased force and knew that he had come, too, as she felt his spasms of release inside her and his come seeped out again round her legs.

As soon as he had his relief, he withdrew with as little preamble as his original entry and sank to his knees between her legs, pushing them still wider apart as he did so, the better to reach the most intimate parts of her cunt. Melinda guessed that the close scrutiny of her sex that he was making would be all he'd need to harden him again. That couldn't happen soon enough to please her. She closed her eyes and enjoyed to the full his questing, exploring fingers and tongue – especially his tongue – as they played with every bit of her cunt they could reach.

Sometimes it was nothing more than a superficial dusting of tongue-tip fluttering across her swollen, pulsing outer lips; sometimes a finger rammed inside her, feeling for every ridge, awakening every nerve within. Often it was his agile tongue that slid inside, licking, tantalising her hardening nub and then, at the very moment the tongue brought her to a sudden exhilarating climax, his teeth closed on those outer lips so that pain mingled with ecstasy and Melinda's body was torn between the need for more of the one and less of the other.

Larbi was unmoved by her dilemma. He would leave bruising on her cunt and that suited him fine: as long as the bruises were there, any man would know she'd been taken before with that intense degree of intimacy. Not until he was satisfied she'd been adequately branded did he release his hold and Melinda, her eyes open now, saw she'd been right: his cock was erect and ready to subjugate her again. With a hand between her legs, he shoved her towards the bedhead until she was fully on the bed.

'Over,' he said. No sooner had she turned on to her belly than she felt his fingers widening the access to her sex, pulling the bruised skin to the sides so that his massive truncheon could enter easily to ram its way relentlessly through her body until it could ram no further.

The steady pressure of such a thick cock, well lubricated as it was now, stimulated her with a surprising subtlety as it forced its way past every nerve-ending that lurked at the surface of each hot, moist inch of flesh within. Now he was thrusting again with ever-increasing force until he knew her orgasm was rising fast. Still inside her, he rolled her on to her side so that they lay like spoons in a drawer, still thrashing against each other. Melinda had barely had time to get used to the change before he rolled on to his back, holding her firmly on to him so that there was no risk of him slipping out.

He ran a finger down her spine and between the cheeks of her buttocks. Only the fact that she was forced to sit so closely on to him prevented it pushing into her arse. 'How supple are you, mademoiselle?'

'How supple do I need to be?' Melinda replied with a little shiver of excitement.

By way of an answer, he lowered his legs but his hands tightened their grip on her hips. 'Turn around,' he ordered. 'No, not just your head. Turn your whole body round on the pivot of my cock until you're facing me – but don't let me slip out. If you do, you'll be punished.' He laughed as if he knew exactly what was going through her mind. 'Oh, yes, Miss Carr, you'd enjoy the punishment, but I promise you, you'll enjoy the pivoting far more.'

Since it was something she'd never done, never even imagined, Melinda was quite prepared to believe it was something she'd enjoy. It was going to be fun trying, she thought, especially since she'd also enjoy the consequences if she failed. It wasn't easy. Raising her legs high enough to clear his body nearly brought her off him and they both sighed with satisfaction as she descended fully on to his impaling prick.

Larbi held her firmly down as he lunged upwards to reassert his dominance over her. Her body was forced backwards against his knees, creating an angle of penetration that was deeper and more painful than any that had gone before.

Wasn't this position the one that, according to what she'd read, was supposed to give the woman absolute control over her partner? Not when the partner was Larbi, it didn't. The policeman wasn't giving control to anyone but himself. Guessing what he was after, Melinda screwed herself down on him, enduring the pain and discomfort because she guessed that, taken like this, it would be his climax that would incite her own.

It did, and as his uncontrolled relief surged into her, her own ecstatic climax took over. She thrust down on him again and again until, as she felt her orgasm wane, she also felt him begin to harden again.

This is how I like it! she thought, exultant. His legs lowered and parted, hinting to hers to come together within them. He moved more slowly, almost sensitively, now and their combined tautness accentuated the sensations as she reversed their roles and it was she who came and went, rose and fell, on his cock, moist and exciting.

I don't care if this never comes to an end, Melinda

thought, and she gasped with delighted surprise as he turned them both over again so that he was on top once more, still inside her and still with her legs tightly holding his cock in place.

Her orgasm resumed its steady, relentless rise. She could feel the muscles in her cunt clutching at the invader that was bringing her, shuddering with tension, to a climax of a power she suspected – hoped – might be the greatest yet. As the climax exploded inside her, she cried out with sheer, undiluted joy. Never, ever, in her entire life had she been fucked quite like this. She opened her eyes and looked straight into Larbi's answering smile.

'I think you found it good,' he said softly.

'Perfect,' she whispered, guessing he must soon withdraw and hoping it wouldn't be too sudden.

'Now we sleep,' he went on, drawing the duvet up over them. 'Or would you rather I left you to sleep alone?'

Her smile was tired but satisfied. 'I'd rather you stayed.'

'You realise that, if I do, I may wake you up again before morning?'

Her smile deepened. 'I'll be disappointed if you don't,' she said.

He laughed softly and gently withdrew, easing the sense of loss with a caressing kiss on the wetness of her cunt. It made the withdrawal almost worthwhile, she decided.

It was the slap that woke her up. Hard and stinging on her buttock and followed immediately by another and another as Larbi beat a tattoo on her backside. She tried to turn over to avoid the rain of blows and discovered that he was sitting on her ankles and turning was impossible.

'Stop it!' she cried. 'For God's sake, stop it!'

Very much to her surprise, he stopped immediately and laughed. 'It certainly woke you up,' he said.

'Of course it bloody well did,' she retorted in English. If he didn't understand the words, he'll understand the tone, she thought.

But he did understand the words. He laughed again. 'Turn over,' he said in English, raising himself to make obedience possible. He didn't have to ask twice.

He sat astride her and took her breasts in his hands. He rested his rapidly awakening cock between them to be fully stirred as he stroked and massaged them into a hard arousal that reflected his own. Melinda opened her legs so that her own hot and urgent swelling could be relieved.

'For God's sake, Larbi,' she breathed, 'I'm hot for it. I want it inside me. I've had a night's sleep and now I'm hungry for it. Fill my belly, Larbi. Fuck me hard.'

He wasted no time in accepting the invitation and plunged into the hot, wet welcome that greeted his penetration.

Oh, boy! Melinda thought as she felt that thick, probing dick force its way into her. This is some man. If ever a man knew what domination is, it must be this one. This is a man to belong to, to be used by for his full gratification because that way she'd not just be satisfied but maybe even satiated – and that hadn't been achieved even during the sexual assaults she'd enjoyed on this short holiday. This was her last opportunity on this visit to even partially satisfy the lust for sex the visit had revealed, and she was going to enjoy it.

She dug her fingers into his shoulders to hold him tighter, ran them down his sides to hold his taut buttocks closer and was rewarded with deeper, more intensive thrusts, thrusts that also demonstrated his immense self-control as he brought her to orgasm after orgasm, each intoxicating explosion inside her fuelled by the glowing embers of the last.

Only then did he allow himself to come and the control he had exercised up to now had its inevitable consequence in the force with which his come was pumped into the body waiting so eagerly for it.

Melinda felt it, hot and wet, and then, as his prick emptied and shrank and no longer filled her willing cunt, she felt the trickle as it seeped out. He really was some man, she thought, and turned her head to kiss him as he lay, semi-inert and very heavy on top of her.

He raised his head and smiled. 'You enjoy?'

'I don't think you need to ask,' she replied. 'I thought Khalil was good, but you . . .'

He chuckled. 'In you I rather think I've met my match. I look forward to your next visit.' His glance strayed across the room to where the antique tooled-leather box sat on the dressing table. 'That's what I want to experience next,' he said. 'I had hoped it might be on the agenda this time.'

Melinda smiled demurely. 'Benani has all that in hand,' she said. 'After all, it would never do to put all the goods in the window first time round, would it?'

He laughed and went into the bathroom. Melinda didn't waste time wondering whether he wanted company there. She knew instinctively that this was it for this visit, at least as far as Larbi was concerned and, since Khalil had made his own position clear, who did that leave? No one. She certainly wasn't going out to see what she could pick up or in the hope she'd bump into another of her guests. She had a feeling Khalil would disapprove if she did, simply on the grounds that it was bad business. She recalled wistfully that there had been another man that weekend who had been particularly gifted. He might even prove to be better than Larbi if she ever got the chance to put him to the test. She hadn't known his name but she didn't doubt he'd be as interested in the belt auction as Larbi.

At that moment, the policeman came back into the bedroom, bathed – even shaven, she noticed – and uniformed, every inch the senior police officer with nothing on his mind but work. He bent over and kissed her lightly.

'*Bon voyage*, mademoiselle,' he said. 'I look forward to our next meeting.'

Chapter Fourteen

Saturday

Melinda had barely returned from breakfast before Khalil arrived to drive her to the airport, as disconcertingly punctual as ever.

'You had a good two days?' he asked, and Melinda wasn't sure whether there was irony in his tone.

'Yes thank you,' she said. 'I seem to have acquired all the souvenirs I'll need.' She chuckled. 'Mostly edible,' she added, nodding towards two boxes of petits fours that she knew would be appreciated by her colleagues at Delamere's. There was no need to tell him about Larbi's visit, she decided, though it wouldn't surprise her to discover that he knew all about it. There wasn't much Khalil Benani missed when it impinged on his business affairs, and what was it he had said about Tangier? That it functioned like a huge village where everyone knew everything about everyone else.

'Have you packed that belt?' he asked.

She nodded. 'In my hand-luggage. I'm not risking it in the hold. I've the certificate of age in my handbag. That should see me OK through British Customs. I just hope the Moroccan ones won't be difficult.'

He accompanied her into the lift and, once it started

on its descent, slipped her keys into his pocket. 'I assume you'll leave these with me?' he enquired.

'How else can the property be properly looked after?' she asked, surprised.

'Quite. One is never entirely sure, however. Not where a woman is concerned, anyway.'

A blue-overalled porter was summoned to take her luggage into the concourse and Melinda couldn't help thinking how different it all looked from Heathrow: just one shop selling papers, magazines and last-minute knick-knacks and far more officials than travellers.

Khalil spoke to the man checking travellers in for the Heathrow flight. Melinda caught the name 'Carr' and a glimpse of a high-denomination note changing hands; she was conscious, too, of the man's surreptitiously curious glance at her.

'I've secured you an upgrade,' Khalil told her. 'In future, travel here first class. There will be a future, I take it?'

Melinda grinned. 'I think you can bet on it,' she told him.

The grin was returned. 'Good,' he said. 'A friend seems to have come to see you off,' he went on. Melinda turned to see Larbi approaching.

The policeman shook hands with Khalil and smiled at Melinda. 'I thought I'd say goodbye and wish you a safe journey,' he said. 'Also make sure you have no problems with over-zealous officials.'

'Thank you,' Melinda replied politely. And to make damned sure I get on the plane, she added to herself. She glanced at the two men and wondered just how much Khalil knew of what had transpired since he had last left her at the flat. Watching them together, she had a hunch, a gut feeling, that Larbi wouldn't have been in a position to bump into her if there hadn't been some sort of collusion between them.

The number of passengers grew and Melinda noticed

that, when Customs started to check baggage, hers was the only one to be waved through without examination. The same thing happened at passport control and again at hand-baggage examination. Larbi's escort clearly had its effect on lower-ranking officials. He accompanied her into the departure lounge and brought her some coffee.

'I'll make sure your case is safely stowed,' he told her. 'I'll come to wish you *au revoir* when they're ready to embark. Will you be all right on your own until then?'

Melinda assured him she would and privately decided her hunch that he was going to make sure she left the country was right on target.

'What have you been up to? Or do you just make friends in high places?' asked a familiar and unwelcome voice.

Melinda looked up from her coffee and saw Clive standing there. 'I thought you'd gone back days ago,' she said, annoyed to find he was still here.

'Obviously not.' His tone was sarcastic. 'That was an interesting escort you arrived with. In trouble with the police, are we?' He sounded as if he hoped he was right.

'Your other guess was better,' she told him acidly. 'Friends in high places – and they don't seem to come much higher than him. Not,' she added witheringly, 'that it's any of your business.' She hadn't wanted to see Clive again and it was depressing to have to fly home with him and field the inevitable questions he'd bombard her with. She couldn't help wondering just why he was still here but she wasn't about to ask because, if she showed an interest in his movements or motives, he'd misinterpret it as an interest in him. As it turned out, she didn't have to ask.

'I stayed in Tangier so that I was on hand if you got into any difficulties,' he said, determined to be seen to

256

have the welfare of a woman – especially a rich one who just happened to be quite a looker – at heart.

Melinda made no attempt to disguise her lack of interest or her amusement. 'With friends of that rank, you think you'd be any use? Take the hint, Clive. I just don't want to know.'

He was undeterred. She had money, after all, and it wasn't as if he was a stranger. 'I'm sure I can arrange a change of seat so we can travel back together. It'll be nice for you to have a friend to talk to.'

'I've upgraded,' she snapped.

Daunted by a quick mental calculation of the actual cash in his pocket, Clive nevertheless smiled. There was always plastic. He wasn't sure how that would work in the present situation but he'd been in Morocco long enough to guess it wasn't impossible. 'Don't worry. A big enough consideration will do it,' he assured her.

She chose to drink her coffee rather than reply, judging that an exhibition of total lack of interest one way or the other would be more effective than a protest. She became extremely interested in what was going on on the empty runway outside and decided privately that Larbi's supervision had definite advantages – and she was going to use them.

When the policeman returned, she explained her predicament. 'He's a nuisance,' she said. 'I don't want him sitting anywhere near me.'

Larbi smiled and nodded. 'Don't worry. Instructions will be given.' He preceded the passengers through the departure gate and Melinda saw him chatting to the steward at the top of the steps.

She didn't have Clive's company on the flight home and she was decidedly relieved to observe that he was detained by Customs when they got back to Heathrow. Knowing him as she did, it was hard to imagine what on earth they expected to find, and she couldn't help wondering whether Larbi's influence went further than

Morocco ... Surely not? All the same, it made you think.

Her flat was definitely an anticlimax, she thought as she opened the front door. It was a nice enough flat by most standards. Very nice indeed, actually, but it had suddenly been rendered mundane. Up-market but mundane. It would take a bit of getting used to, coming back down to earth like this.

Melinda threw her case on the bed and unzipped it to unpack. Then she changed her mind and undid her hand-luggage instead. She put the petits fours carefully in the fridge and then drew out the old tooled-leather box.

She placed it on the dressing table and opened it. The soft gold glowed on its dark-green bed. I must get a safe, or put it in the bank, or something, she thought, lifting the belt out and holding it up in front of the glass.

On an impulse she removed her jacket and her jeans and then, after a brief hesitation, her panties. Then she freed the little teasers from the hooks that secured their ends when they weren't in use and put the belt round her waist. She wondered how easy it would be to get the teasers inside her and secure the chains as Khalil had done so expertly.

It was easier than she'd thought but she didn't dare lock them in: it probably wouldn't be difficult to do but she had a nasty feeling that when she wanted to release them, sod's law would come into operation and she wasn't taking the risk.

As she moved over to the looking-glass, the teaser had its inevitable effect. Wow! she thought, letting herself luxuriate in the feelings it provoked.

She smiled at her reflection. I know what I'll do, she thought suddenly and crossed over to the wardrobe, every small movement deliciously tantalising her inner sex. She found one of the expensively discrete and well-cut trousersuits she wore for work and put it on. She turned in front of the full-length mirror and smiled at her reflection.

Quite the little puritan, she thought. Dark suit, modest neckline, tightly secured hair. Very prim and proper. And then she moved. The fobs of the gold teaser inside her jostled each other, touched, left, touched again the erotic heart of her clit, the sensitive walls of her cunt. She shivered with pleasure. The reality was so much better than the recollection. Much more of this and I'll come, she thought gleefully – and I can enjoy it to my heart's content.

She chuckled. I could even wear it to work. Look at me! Who'd guess what was going on underneath? And what if I climaxed at an auction? On the podium? In front of all those po-faced collectors? It would certainly add spice! I wonder what they'd make of it.

It was a thought to conjure with, she decided with a speculative smile.

BLACK LACE NEW BOOKS

Published in February

STELLA DOES HOLLYWOOD
Stella Black
£6.99

Stella Black has a 1969 Pontiac Firebird, a leopardskin bra and a lot of attitude. Partying her way around Hollywood she is discovered by a billionaire entertainment mogul who wastes no time in turning Stella into America's most famous porn star. But the dark forces of American fundamentalism are growing. The moral right-wing are outraged and they're out to destroy Stella any which way they can.

How will she escape their punishing clutches?

A sexy saga of guns, girls and grit!

ISBN 0 352 33588 2

UP TO NO GOOD
Karen S. Smith
£6.99

Emma is resigned to the fact that her cousin's wedding will be a dull affair, but when she meets leather-clad biker, Kit, it's lust at first sight and Emma ends up behaving even more scandalously than usual. They don't get the chance to say goodbye, though, and she thinks she'll never see her mystery lover again. Fate intervenes, however, and they are reunited at yet another wedding. And so begins a year of outrageous sex, wild behaviour and lots of getting up to no good!

**Like *Four Weddings and a Funeral* with explicit sex and
without the funeral!**

ISBN 0 352 33589 0

DARKER THAN LOVE
Kristina Lloyd
£6.99

It's 1875 and the morals of Queen Victoria have no hold over London's debauched elite. Young and naïve Clarissa is eager to meet Lord Marldon, the man to whom she is promised. She knows he is handsome, dark and sophisticated. He is, in fact, louche, depraved and consumed by a passion for cruel sexual excesses!

This tale of dark, Gothic debauchery is a Black Lace special reprint.

ISBN 0 352 33279 4

Published in March

SIN.NET
Helena Ravenscroft
£6.99

Carrie's life changes when she discovers the steamy world of adult internet chat rooms. Naturally shy Carrie assumes the identity of the sexually confident Dominique, and she's soon having a series of X-rated on-line liaisons. Suddenly she's having more fun than ever before. Is it submission or strength she wants in a lover? And can she blend all the qualities of Dominique into her own personality?

ISBN 0 352 33598 X

TWO WEEKS IN TANGIER
Annabel Lee
£6.99

When Melinda Carr inherits property from her Great-Aunt Laura there are some surprises in store for her. Her new business affairs manager, the enigmatic Khalil, is very keen to bring out her wanton side and test her voracious sexual appetite to the limit. She's soon transformed into the creature of pleasure she's always wanted to be. But what will her strait-laced boyfriend do when he finds Melinda is following in the footsteps of her scandalous great aunt?

ISBN 0 352 33599 8

THE TRANSFORMATION
Natasha Rostova
£6.99

Three friends, three lives, one location: San Francisco. This upbeat story of complex relationships is a dazzling fun-packed story of three women at the sexual crossroads in their lives. Exploring their sensual selves in that most liberal of American cities they discover things about themselves – and their friends – they never knew existed.

This is a Black Lace special reprint.

ISBN 0 352 33311 1

To be published in April

HOTBED
Portia Da Costa
£6.99

Disaffected journalist Natalie is on the trail of an exposé. Her quest for a juicy story leads her to discover that her staid academic hometown has become a hotbed of sleaze and hidden perversity. Quickly drawn in, Natalie soon falls under the spell of Stella Fontayne – a glittering drag queen at the centre of an erotic underworld. Her sister and rival Patti is in on the action, too, and nobody is quite who or what they seem in this world where transgressing sexual boundaries is the norm.

ISBN 0 352 33614 5

WICKED WORDS 4
Ed. Kerri Sharp
£6.99

Black Lace short story collections are a showcase of the finest contemporary women's erotica anywhere in the world. With contributions from the UK, USA and Australia, the settings and stories are deliciously daring. Fresh, cheeky and upbeat, only the most arousing fiction makes it into a *Wicked Words* anthology.

ISBN 0 352 33603 X

THE CAPTIVATION
Natasha Rostova
£6.99

In 1917, war-torn Russia is on the brink of the Revolution and Princess Katya Leskovna and her relatives are forced to flee their palace. Katya ends up in the encampment of a rebel Cossack army. The men haven't seen a woman for weeks and sexual tensions are running high.
This is a Black Lace special reprint full of danger, sexual tension and men in uniform!

ISBN 0 352 33234 4

If you would like a complete list of plot summaries of Black Lace titles, or would like to receive information on other publications available, please send a stamped addressed envelope to:

Black Lace, Thames Wharf Studios,
Rainville Road, London W6 9HA

BLACK LACE BOOKLIST

Information is correct at time of printing. To check availability go to www.blacklace-books.co.uk

All books are priced £5.99 unless another price is given.

Black Lace books with a contemporary setting

DARK OBSESSION £7.99	Fredrica Alleyn ISBN 0 352 33281 6	☐
THE TOP OF HER GAME	Emma Holly ISBN 0 352 33337 5	☐
LIKE MOTHER, LIKE DAUGHTER	Georgina Brown ISBN 0 352 33422 3	☐
THE TIES THAT BIND	Tesni Morgan ISBN 0 352 33438 X	☐
IN THE FLESH	Emma Holly ISBN 0 352 33498 3	☐
SHAMELESS	Stella Black ISBN 0 352 33485 1	☐
TONGUE IN CHEEK	Tabitha Flyte ISBN 0 352 33484 3	☐
FIRE AND ICE	Laura Hamilton ISBN 0 352 33486 X	☐
SAUCE FOR THE GOOSE	Mary Rose Maxwell ISBN 0 352 33492 4	☐
INTENSE BLUE	Lyn Wood ISBN 0 352 33496 7	☐
THE NAKED TRUTH	Natasha Rostova ISBN 0 352 33497 5	☐
A SPORTING CHANCE	Susie Raymond ISBN 0 352 33501 7	☐
TAKING LIBERTIES	Susie Raymond ISBN 0 352 33357 X	☐
A SCANDALOUS AFFAIR	Holly Graham ISBN 0 352 33523 8	☐
THE NAKED FLAME	Crystalle Valentino ISBN 0 352 33528 9	☐

Black Lace anthologies

SUGAR AND SPICE £7.99	Various ISBN 0 352 33227 1	☐
CRUEL ENCHANTMENT Erotic Fairy Stories	Janine Ashbless ISBN 0 352 33483 5	☐
MORE WICKED WORDS	Various ISBN 0 352 33487 8	☐
WICKED WORDS 3	Various ISBN 0 352 33522 X	☐

Black Lace non-fiction

THE BLACK LACE BOOK OF
    WOMEN'S SEXUAL
    FANTASIES
	Ed. Kerri Sharp
	ISBN 0 352 33346 4
		☐

------ ✂ --------------------

Please send me the books I have ticked above.

Name ....

Address ....

....

....

.... Post Code ....

Send to: **Cash Sales, Black Lace Books, Thames Wharf Studios, Rainville Road, London W6 9HA.**

US customers: for prices and details of how to order books for delivery by mail, call 1-800-805-1083.

Please enclose a cheque or postal order, made payable to **Virgin Publishing Ltd**, to the value of the books you have ordered plus postage and packing costs as follows:
   UK and BFPO – £1.00 for the first book, 50p for each subsequent book.
   Overseas (including Republic of Ireland) – £2.00 for the first book, £1.00 for each subsequent book.

If you would prefer to pay by VISA, ACCESS/MASTER-CARD, DINERS CLUB, AMEX or SWITCH, please write your card number and expiry date here:

....

Please allow up to 28 days for delivery.

Signature ....

------ ✂ --------------------